Cast of (

Theocritus Lucius Westborough. A ... made a name for himself solving impossible crimes.

Etienne LeDoux. An elderly Frenchman, the founder of a world-famous perfumery in California's beautiful Valle de Flores.

Jacynth LeDoux. His lovely 19-year-old granddaughter, who's wise beyond her years.

Derek Esterling. His brilliant chief chemist, who's engaged to Jacynth.

Paul Michael Chamaron. Owner of an ad agency who handles the advertising for LeDoux Perfumes.

Kay Chamaron. His clever, attractive wife, a package designer.

Stuart Grayne. An advertising copywriter who has a history with Derek. His courtly South Carolina ways make him irrestible to women.

Sam Preston. The affable sales manager for LeDoux Perfumes.

Beatrice Morton. LeDoux's secretary of seven years, a quiet, intelligent, somewhat plain young woman.

Aaron Xenophon Todd. A real estate magnate who is a shareholder in and the treasurer of LeDoux Perfumes. He's also a hard man to please.

Margaret LeDoux. Etienne's widowed daughter, mother to Jacynth.

Lung Fu. The Chinese cook, a genius at what he does.

Manuel. The Filipino houseboy, a university graduate.

Bernard Kelton. Derek's assistant, conveniently absent for the duration.

Captain Sydney Howe. A reasonably competent sheriff's deputy.

Steve Rawson. The chief deputy sheriff, an overbearing, bullying blowhard.

Plus assorted law enforcement officials and medical personnel.

In the Theocritus Lucius Westborough canon:

The Fifth Tumbler, 1936
The Death Angel, 1936
Blind Drifts, 1937
The Purple Parrot, 1937
The Man from Tibet, 1938
The Whispering Ear, 1938
Murder Gone Minoan, 1939
(English title: *Clue to the Labyrinth*)
Dragon's Cave, 1940
Poison Jasmine, 1940
Green Shiver, 1941

Poison Jasmine

by Clyde B. Clason

Introduction by Tom & Enid Schantz

Rue Morgue Press
Boulder / Lyons

Poison Jasmine

978-1-60187-028-5
was first published in 1940.

New material in this edition
Copyright © 2008 by
The Rue Morgue Press
87 Lone Tree Lane
Lyons CO 80540
www.ruemorguepress.com
800-699-6214

Restoration work on the original
dust jacket art by
Mark Terry of
Facsimile Dustjackets
www.facsimiledustjackets.com

Printed by
Johnson Printing
Boulder, Colorado

About the author
Revised introduction with new material

CLYDE B. CLASON'S career as a mystery writer took up only five of his 84 years (1903-1987), but in the short span between 1936 and 1941 he produced ten long and very complicated detective novels, all published by the prestigious Doubleday, Doran Crime Club, featuring the elderly historian Professor Theocritus Lucius Westborough. "I started writing detective fiction because a bad cold kept me home from the office," Clason wrote in 1962 to Swedish mystery critic Jan Broberg. That book was *The Fifth Tumbler,* published in 1936, and it featured people who lived in adjacent rooms along a corridor in a large Chicago hotel. To finish the book, Clason took a crash course in locks and hotel management. Such research was the hallmark of his books, including 1938's *The Man from Tibet* for which Clason read more than one hundred books on Tibet before setting pen to paper.

"To me the most important part of a book was its setting," Clason wrote. "Plot is, of course, a vital necessity to any detective story, but I always considered it as subordinate to characters and background. Once I had a group of characters put together that I could really believe in as human beings, plot seemed to work itself out rather well and without too much effort." Clason was being perhaps a bit too modest, as many critics have suggested that he ranks with John Dickson Carr and Clayton Rawson as one of the most ingenious practitioners of the locked room or impossible crime mystery.

Of his ten books, Clason considered his last five books to be far superior to the first five, primarily because he wrote those when he was working full time as a writer. After he finished his third book, *The Purple Parrot,* "I was a worn-out wreck," he admitted, having had to write evenings and weekends. His next two books, *Blind Drifts* and *The Man from Tibet,* were written on a less demanding schedule, having talked his employer (he was an advertising copywriter in Chicago) into letting him work part time. "Then I moved to California where I was able to devote my full time to writing. This increased leisure showed up in smoother, more polished writing and in more subtle nuances of characterization. I think *Murder Gone Minoan* is my best book for two reasons: first, its climax surprised even me and, secondly, I fell in love with my heroine in her white bathing suit. As second and third choices, I would unhesitantly pick *Green Shiver* and *Poison Jasmine*. These three I enjoyed writing beyond all other books." Most critics, however, would put *The Man from Tibet* among his top five.

Although Theocritus Lucius Westborough was the detective in all of his novels, he started out as just one of several characters living along that hotel corridor in *The Fifth Tumbler*. "He seemed to have more personality than the others, however, and it wasn't long before this elderly scholar (characterized by one reviewer as 'a mild little man who meddled in murder') was running the show." Clason reasoned that a detective and an historian functioned in similar ways. "A detective gathers facts—so does an historian. A detective endeavors to arrange such facts into a semblance of logical continuity—likewise an historian. A detective discards, or should discard, the nonessentials in order that the residuum may stand in its true significance with the stark reality of a monolith. And should not a disciple of Klio (the muse of history, also spelled Clio) follow the same procedure?"

In addition to writing detective fiction, Clason was a big fan of the genre, calling Dorothy L. Sayers his favorite followed by Rex Stout and Ellery Queen in that order. Clason himself published no crime fiction after 1941, explaining that his style of mystery had gone out of favor. "I can attribute that to many things, including the supplanting of the puzzle-type mystery that I liked by the so-called hardboiled school running toward sex and sadism. Now television is fast creating a new generation of illiterates in this unhappy nation. If this blight ever wears off, and I have hopes that it may, then the good old-fashioned detective story, possessing logic and literary quality, may reappear again. Certainly there has been nothing that has been able to take its place as entertainment."

Like Sayers, Clason said he turned to religion in his old age, publishing *I am Lucifer* (1960), the confessions of the devil as told to the author, and *This Rock Exists* (1962) in which he explores his own odd notions about religion. He also wrote one science fiction novel, *The Ark of Venus* (1955), and several nonfiction works dealing with astronomy as well as *The Delights of the Slide Rule* (1964), his last published book-length work.

For more information on Clason see Tom and Enid Schantz' introduction to *Green Shiver*.

Tom & Enid Schantz
September 2008
Lyons, Colorado

Acknowledgment: The editors are indebted to Jan Broberg for sharing his correspondence with Clason.

PROLOGUE

Gray beards of moss swayed from the live oaks. White Cherokee roses clambered up the tree trunks, and clusters of wild jessamine flaunted golden cups. The taller of the two young men who met in the clearing set down the black leather case he had been carrying. He shifted the mahogany box from under his arm to a stump.

"Is the site satisfactory, Mr. Esterling?"

Esterling nodded dumb acquiescence. Stu called him that! Stu, who had been his best friend for fifteen years, ever since they were tiny shavers! But they had stopped being friends two days ago. He must remember that. Stu intended to kill him.

Pictures were flashing across his mind like images projected on a screen. Impersonal scenes, mostly. The new bridge's mammoth cantilever span. Stevedores loading cotton into the hold of a tramp steamer. A black woman on an upturned tangerine box puffing a clay pipe. A wrinkled shrimp vender pushing his green cart. Wild ducks winging in hundreds from the marshes. The chimney stacks of the plant in which the senior Esterling, alien born like his son, was an executive. Calhoun in the square, frowning …

With his outer eyes he saw that Stu had unfastened the lid of the dark red box. In a nest of faded purple velvet the two long dueling pistols lay like half-coiled snakes.

"Choose yo' weapon," Stu commanded sternly.

The pistols looked exactly the same to the eye, felt exactly the same to the touch. Each was a foot long. Each had a huge octagonal barrel, age tarnished, and a mahogany stock with knurled grip. They were very old: older than any living man, family heirlooms handed down from Stu's great-great-grandfather.

Esterling lifted a pistol from the lining. It was astonishingly heavy. His hand was trembling, and he endeavored to steady the wavering weapon. "I can't let him see that I'm afraid." But Stu had seen, and his lips twisted into a cynical half-smile.

"I take it that you know how to load, Mr. Esterling?"

"Your grandpa showed us once. Don't you remember?"

Stu said frigidly, "Do me the kindness of not referring to a member of my family. You will have to load yo' own pistol."

Seconds usually loaded the pistols, Esterling recalled, but they had no seconds. Duels being illegal, seconds could be held equally guilty with principals if – would the charge be homicide? Or would the crime be called by a shorter and uglier name?

With frozen courtesy Stu extended the pear-shaped brass flask. Inverting it, Esterling pressed the knob at the base of the neck. The charge trickled into the spoutlike cap. He twisted the cap from the flask and dumped the coarse, shiny grains into the capacious barrel. Did gunpowder deteriorate with age? he wondered. Probably. But this had been well protected in its moistureproof container. He returned the flask.

Wadding was in one of the lidded compartments. The thick disks were to be tamped over the charge, not too lightly, with one of the knob-headed ramrods. He dropped in the bullet, tamping down another wad to hold the leaden marble securely in its place. Did that complete the operation? No, the percussion cap.

The raised letters on the lid of the cap box said, "Eleybro, London." There weren't many caps left, Esterling saw as he opened the round metal box. All of the tiny brass shells together wouldn't cover an area equal to a man's thumbnail. But only one was needed to convert the pistol from a harmless antique into a dealer of death.

Suddenly he knew he couldn't go through with it.

"Let's call it off," he begged. "Or fight it out with our fists. You can beat the tar out of me, I reckon."

Stu's rugged face remained glacially aloof. "Kindly address no mo' remarks to me, Mr. Esterling." He adjusted the wee ridged cylinder over the nipple in the breech of his pistol. On a branch of wild azalea a mockingbird was trilling a blithe melody.

"It isn't even a duel! No seconds. No one to give the signal."

Stu answered coldly, "The signal has been arranged," and opened the black leather case of his portable phonograph. A record was in place upon the turntable.

"Are you familiar, Mr. Esterling, with the 'Minute Waltz' of Frederic Chopin?" The other shook his head. "Then neither of us has the advantage of knowin' when the music will stop." Stu's drawling voice was preternaturally calm. "We stand back to back. When the music begins each advances ten paces, turns and faces the other. We fire when the music ends." Laying his loaded pistol on the stump, he began to turn the crank.

Stu's back was toward him; Stu's attention occupied. Esterling's thin deft fingers performed in an instant the thing he had planned to do. Stu straightened up from the phonograph. They stood rigidly, backs not quite touching, each holding in the right hand his cumbersome pistol. The needle, scratching across the outer edge of the disk, seemed long in reaching the recording. Suddenly, however, the strong fingers of a pianist launched into a madcap rigadoon.

They began their measured advance, both counting aloud. "One, two, three, four, five, six, seven, eight, nine, ten." Wheeling, Esterling raised the pistol from his side. The music sparkled, scintillated like motes whirling in the sunlight. He tried to sight along the barrel. The heavy weapon was almost impossible to hold steady. Its trigger would be stiff, difficult to pull. The myriad scents of spring drifted to his nostrils. He distinguished at once the mild, sweet odor of jessamine from the other fragrances of azaleas and roses. His sense of smell was unusually keen – a gift which should have been worth something to a chemist. But he would never be a chemist now. …

The music had altered. It had ceased to tinkle and was slow, deep, dreamy, as a waltz should be. His finger tightened on the trigger. Considerable muscular force must be exerted to fire; the sudden jerk might spoil one's aim. Perhaps Stu – better not think of it. Better not think of Stu, standing with the stony calm of a Grecian statue.

If he must think, even in the moment or two of life that remained to him, let it be about something impersonal. Esterling raised his eyes to the oak leaves, to the yellow bells dangling from the oak's gnarled branches. That, for instance. Jessamine or, as some called it, jasmine. The scientific name was *gelsemium sempervirens*. (He was oddly pleased at remembering that.) The blossoms were so abundantly fragrant that a single spray would perfume a large room. … God, he would never smell the soft, delicate odor again. He would never smell anything.

He would never see anything: the blazing colors of azaleas, cypress trees, the spire of St. Philip's, the sea view from the Battery, ships moving leisurely into harbor. He would never hear a sound again: St. Michael's mellow chimes, the throaty cries of Gullah hucksters, the lap of waves against the shore, a girl's careless laughter. He knew now what death was. Death was mere oblivion. Death was simply – nothing! The thought was unbearable.

He flung his pistol to the ground and dashed for the shelter of the surrounding trees. He dodged in and out among the live oaks. Even if Stu would shoot a disarmed adversary no bullet could follow his twisting, weaving path.

But contempt could follow faster than a man could run, scornful laughter borne on the wings of sound. Esterling sobbed, racing toward the boat he had moored to a post rotting in the grasses of the river. He had lost something that was more precious than life, that he could never regain. He knew it now.

PART ONE
BIRTH OF A PERFUME

Derek was holding the tiny bottle between his thumb and forefinger. "An extract of yellow jasmine or *gelsemium sempervirens*." The little dab of reddish-brown beard caused him to look severely professional. "The well-known climbing vine of the South." He poured a few drops onto the glass top of Gran'-père's desk, and the office was permeated by the most heavenly fragrance.

Could a scent be both bland and sparkling? Jacynth wondered. If it could be, this new one was. Bland as milk and yet as sparkling as champagne. Her small nose wrinkled appraisingly. It was like no other floral odor. ... Yes, perhaps, it held a slight hint of gardenia. It did have the smooth velvet of a good gardenia, but softer somehow, a shade more delicate. Nineteen-year-old Jacynth knew a great deal about perfumes. Naturally, since she was a LeDoux.

This one she pronounced truly exquisite. It was – her mind groped for comparisons – the very essence of spring. Not a California spring, which, when you came right down to it, didn't differ much from any other season, but that glorious early spring of the Old South where Derek had lived so many years. He had captured its intangible sweetness in his glass bottle – a kind of miracle!

For a miracle worker, however, Derek was surprisingly matter of fact.

"You can tell from this alcoholic solution of the absolute that the blossoms are deliciously fragrant. I'm sorry to say, however, it isn't practicable to cultivate them for perfumery."

His tones were crisp and efficient. Derek had two voices, Jacynth had recently discovered: one for business and the other for moonlight. It was the business voice he was using now.

"We did raise a few vines in the greenhouse for experimental purposes, but the plant isn't at all hardy north of the cotton belt, and the flowers bloom only a few weeks in the early spring. However" – Derek performed a conjurer's trick, producing two bottles in his hand where there had been only one before – "I have succeeded in producing a synthetic imitation of the aromatic principle. As to how satisfactory an imitation, I am content to let you judge." His eyes turned from Gran'-père, sweeping clockwise past Miss Morton, Mr. Chamaron; past the davenport which held Jacynth, Mr. Preston and Mrs. Chamaron; past Mr. Grayne, completing the circle at Mr. Todd, whose wrinkled face retained its usual crabbed expression.

"I am going to pass these two unlabeled bottles around the room." Derek held them up as he spoke, so that everyone could see they were exactly the same size and shape and that both were filled to the same point with a colorless liquid. "If anyone is able to tell me which is the natural floral perfume and which is the synthetic, will he or she please speak?"

Derek was just about all that a girl could ask for in a man, Jacynth reflected. He was handsome, tall, graceful; his manners were irreproachable, and his dancing was poetry. Moreover, he was a genius. Gran'-père himself had said so. It had always thrilled her to see Derek, in a long rubber apron, among the hundreds of bottles and flasks and things that were the properties of the magician's cave where he wrought his miracles. Genius! She whispered the word proudly under her breath.

Mr. Todd scowled and passed the bottles on. Mr. Grayne didn't know which was which, nor Mrs. Chamaron, nor Mr. Preston, though he should have known, considering his position. It was Jacynth's turn.

One of the fragrances was a little more delicate, a trifle less harsh, she believed. That would be the natural; the synthetics, even the best ones, were never quite so good as the perfumes extracted from actual flowers. The difference was so slight, however, it seemed scarcely worth mentioning. Mr. Chamaron couldn't distinguish it at all nor could Miss Morton, Gran'-père's secretary.

Gran'-père of course knew immediately, but that wasn't any reflection on Derek's accomplishment. Gran'-père's long aristocratic nose was one of the most remarkable noses in the world. No expert taster could perform more astounding feats with wines than Etienne LeDoux could with perfumes. He could sniff a single drop of unknown composition for a little while and then recite all the different ingredients it contained, almost the exact proportions in which they were blended.

But no one else could tell the difference between the natural and the artificial scents (Jacynth had decided by now that she really couldn't), and so Derek was vindicated as a worker of miracles. The second achievement was even more wonderful than the first. To think of producing a flower's delicate fragrance by mixing a few drops of this and a few drops of that in test tubes! It was, she pondered, rather like being God. She wondered that Derek wasn't tremendously puffed up, but he didn't seem to be at all. He was just nicely, quietly modest. She was suddenly aware of Mr. Grayne's intent gaze.

Their eyes met momentarily. His were a deep gray, she noted before he turned away, abashed at having been caught in the act of staring. His tanned face was rather interesting. Not handsome, exactly – he wasn't nearly as handsome as Derek – but strong and rugged. From his profile she saw that he had a Roman nose, an aggressive chin and wavy black hair, which descended a little bit below the temples like incipient sideburns. He would be the kind of man, she mused, who boxed and rode and sailed a boat, doing all of them better than average. She felt that she'd like to know him better, but it would be a marvel if she ever saw him again. Mr. Grayne, she knew, worked for Mr. Chamaron in Los Angeles; he probably wouldn't be back to Valle de Flores. He and she were just ships which passed in the night – one of Mother's favorite sayings.

Gran'-père rose to his feet, courtly and distinguished. "LeDoux Perfumes, Incorporated, and its president are greatly indebted to our Mr. Esterling." Gran'-père had the true grand manner; it was ingrained in every word, every gesture. "I hope he won't mind if I say our *brilliant* Mr. Esterling, for he has certainly demonstrated his brilliance. New notes in perfumery are rarely found nowadays."

Derek deserved that tribute! Jacynth clapped her hands spontaneously, and everyone else joined in the applause. Or nearly everyone. Mr. Preston even cried, "Speech, speech!" which was quite silly. Derek had just made a speech and a nice one, too. Fingering his white mustache, Gran'-père waited for the noise to subside.

"The art of perfumery is much like the art of music. The twelve keys of a piano octave suffice for many melodies, and the conventional odors, blended in different proportions, can produce many, many different scents. But a new note whets the jaded taste like the clarion call of a trumpet in a forest of violins." Gran'-père's black eyes sparkled audaciously. "Unto us a new note is born, sired by Mr. Esterling and mothered by science. The infant's birth must be appropriately heralded." He glanced toward Mr. Chamaron. "A beautiful set of swaddling clothes must be designed." His eyes rested momentarily on Mrs. Chamaron. "But first let us have the christening. Most important, is it not? Sam, do you have a name to suggest?"

Mr. Preston stood up, wiping his bald spot. "I don't know much about making your new notes, Mr. Chairman, but I can give you the selling angle. I've been in the game for a long time now, and I've learned a new trick or two, in spite of what they say about old dogs." He paused for a laugh, which didn't materialize.

"What are our biggest selling brands?" Mr. Preston asked rhetorically. "*Clair de Lune*, Love-in-a-Mist, Moonlight-on-the-Grove and *Violux*. Who buys them? Women." Mr. Preston could always be counted upon to supply the obvious. "Old women? No. Middle-aged women? No. Market researches definitely establish that perfume sales reach their peak among women of the ages of nineteen, twenty, twenty-one and twenty-two. Young girls! Just about the age of your own granddaughter, Mr. Chairman. So to know the kind of appeal we should make to interest our market, we ought to ask what interests

Miss Jacynth most." He chuckled roguishly. "My guess is it's a certain young man not a million miles away from here."

Though Jacynth tried to look as if she hadn't heard, her face burned furiously. Several people were laughing. Mr. Grayne wasn't among their number, she was grateful to see. Not that it made any real difference, of course. Derek's brown eyes flashed a message of sympathy. "Our time is rather limited, Sam," Gran'-père stated warningly.

"Young girls like romance," Mr. Preston continued, not a whit discomfited. "Not the old-fashioned kind of moonlight-and-roses stuff, uhnnuh! We're living in a modern age. Girls are a bit naughty now, or like to think that they are, which comes to practically the same thing as far as we're concerned. The naughtier a thing sounds, the more it appeals to them." He smirked, displaying his gold-crowned tooth. "Look at the popularity of Indiscreet and My Sin. Swell names, aren't they? Plenty of the good old oomph! When a competitor gets a hold of a good thing it never hurts to take a leaf out of his book. So let's call the new number Scandal, which packs the same kind of wallop."

Mr. Preston sat down, looking highly pleased with himself. "Miss Morton," Gran'-père asked, "do you agree with our sales manager?"

"Yes and no." Miss Morton's sweet, plain face looked a little flustered. She was staring downward at the carpet, no way at all to make a speech. Jacynth was sorry for her. She had always liked Gran'-père's secretary, who was quiet but worth cultivating. "I don't think my opinion's worth very much, Mr. Chairman," Miss Morton mumbled, almost inaudibly.

Gran'-père was very tactful. "There is nobody in this office who knows more about the perfume business. Please give us your ideas, Beatrice."

Thus encouraged, Miss Morton took a deep breath. "There's a lot of truth in what Mr. Preston says, but the – well, naughtiness, sounds more attractive in French. Don't you think so?"

Mr. Preston guffawed loudly; Mr. Chamaron smiled knowingly; Mr. Grayne and Mrs. Chamaron exchanged confidential glances, and Mr. Todd appeared to be shocked. Miss Morton's cheeks became a fiery red. She certainly had not intended to be facetious, Jacynth knew. "What French name would you suggest?" inquired Gran'-père.

"*Affaire de Coeur*," Miss Morton gulped. "Or something of the kind."

"Excellent!" Gran'-père turned to Mr. Chamaron, his advertising agent. "Paul Michael, your face tells me you have a great deal to say."

Mr. Chamaron nearly always did. He inflated his chest like a pouter pigeon as he stood up.

"Words have power," Mr. Chamaron proclaimed in an artificially deep voice. "They have power because of their associations. For instance, when I say 'cloud' does anyone think of the dictionary definition: 'A visible mass of fog or haze suspended at a height in the air'? Not in the least. Some of you think of black, angry, threatening storm clouds, along with thunder and lightning and a deluge. Others may think of fleecy white clouds drifting in a stately manner across a deep blue sky. Or purple clouds at sunset. Or pink clouds at dawn. The single word 'cloud' means all those and many more. Associations." Mr. Chamaron spoke with suave ease, as if he had said all this many times previously.

"Some words have few associations. Some words have many. Some words have a great deal more than others. Some words have so many that we might almost think of them as magic words. Or call them magic keys. That is what they really are, the magic keys which unlock the doors to consumer consciousness. I am going to tell you what some of these mystic words are."

Mr. Chamaron certainly could hold his audience. Jacynth didn't quite know what he meant, but when he talked she forgot about his pouter-pigeon chest and his little sorrel mustache and his stout waistline. So had everyone else, apparently.

"One such word," Mr. Chamaron continued, "is 'gold.' The word 'gold' stands for wealth, riches, power, all the luxuries of life. It means those things not just to you or to you or to me, but to everyone. That's why 'gold' is a magic word. Another word, maybe even more potent, is 'star.' " Mr. Chamaron's voice throbbed like a cello. "Is there a man so lacking in soul that he does not experience a thrill in looking into the twinkling heavens? A few, perhaps, but not very many. The word 'star' is the symbol of spiritual aspirations, just as the word 'gold' is the symbol of material aspirations. Mr. Chairman, I suggest combining these two powerful ingredients into a single word, blending them just as your scents are blended in Mr. Esterling's laboratory. My name for your new product is Goldenstar."

Mr. Chamaron took his seat on the note of climax, leaving everyone profoundly impressed. Everyone, that is, but Mrs. Chamaron, who looked as if she had heard it all before.

"Thank you, Paul Michael," Gran'-père said courteously. "Mr. Grayne."

Since Mr. Grayne worked for Mr. Chamaron, Jacynth rather expected him to praise Goldenstar as a matter of course, but, surprisingly, he did not.

"Mr. Chairman, the yellow jessamine is the state flower of South Carolina." (He pronounced it something like "Ca'olinah.") "Down there we call it the Ca'olinah Jessamine. I like that right well myself. In fact, I can't think of any bettah name."

After Mr. Grayne had sat down, his words lingered softly behind him. In some strange manner the four simple sentences made Mr. Chamaron's rhetoric seem pompous and overdone. Jacynth wondered if Mr. Chamaron liked that. His plump countenance displayed no trace of resentment, but Derek's face was as black as one of Mr. Chamaron's clouds. Perhaps Derek was vexed because Gran'-père hadn't asked for his opinion. If so, one could scarcely blame him, she meditated.

"Mrs. Chamaron."

Mrs. Chamaron wasn't just Mr. Chamaron's wife, but a person of importance on her own account. She designed packages; did it very well and made a great deal of money out of it. Her dress looked like it belonged to a woman who had been successful. It was a long-sleeved black silk jersey, and with it she wore a cleverly draped black-and-white turban. But it wasn't only her clothes. Kay Chamaron's tawny hair held golden highlights, and her eyes were a deep, rich blue, and her cool voice sounded like music. Jacynth, who admired Mrs. Chamaron very much, thought she was entirely too good for Mr. Chamaron, who was nice but nothing out of the ordinary.

"*Chacun à son goût,*" Mrs. Chamaron murmured, smoothing her dress with a slender white hand. "Mr. Chairman, while Mr. Grayne was talking, I couldn't help thinking how everyone loves the culture and the charm of the Old South. We would be making an extremely serious mistake to overlook that element in our marketing program, don't you think? I've just had some flashes for a container that I believe would have interesting possibilities. We might make it in the form of a girl, a Southern girl of the period just before the Civil War. She would have wide hoop skirts, of course, and her head could be the stopper of the bottle. That would be awfully attractive on milady's dressing table, don't you think? But we would have to have a name to fit the container. Carolina Jessamine might do, but I think an even better name would be Southern Belle. Belle fits in beautifully with a bell-shaped skirt, don't you believe?"

Gran'-père's face beamed approbation as he asked her to go ahead with the design for the container.

Jacynth's own suggestion was *Valle de Flores*. That was the name the first bearded conquistador had given to their beautiful valley, and that was the name the valley and its biggest town retained today. Valley of Flowers. It sounded even nicer translated into the stately Spanish. Jacynth had always thought that *Valle de Flores* would be the loveliest imaginable name for a perfume, but nobody else seemed to think so. Not even Derek.

Yes, Gran'-père had nodded to him at last.

"I am probably prejudiced," he exclaimed, jumping to his feet, "I'll admit cheerfully. To me the most charming name in the world is" – he made a dramatic pause – "Jacynth."

That was sweet of Derek, but it was horribly embarrassing. Gran'-père remarked, so impersonally, it was impossible to tell whether he approved or not, "My granddaughter's Christian name suggests a jasmine-hyacinth blend. But the formula doesn't contain any hyacinth, and *gelsemium sempervirens* isn't a true jasmine. Do you think the name conforms to our standards of truthful advertising, Paul Michael?"

Mr. Chamaron, smiling uncomfortably, remained diplomatically silent.

"We haven't yet asked for your opinion, Mr. Todd."

"What do I know about it?" Mr. Todd snarled. He wasn't a pleasant person. He was frightfully old – even older than Gran'-père – and he wore a black thing around his neck that you had to talk to. When you spoke to him he made you repeat everything you said at least once, sometimes two or three times. He did that just to be disagreeable, Jacynth believed. She wondered why her courteous grandfather tolerated such a rude friend. Gran'-père overlooked Mr. Todd's rudeness this time, just as he always did.

"We now have seven names to consider. Scandal, *Affaire de Coeur*, Goldenstar, Carolina Jessamine, Southern Belle, *Valle de Flores* and Jacynth. That should serve for a while." He glanced at his watch. "Let us defer our discussion until after luncheon. The savor of food does not improve with neglect."

While he was talking, he unlocked the little cabinet by his desk and brought out a bottle and a spoon. Gran'-père took a bitter tonic before every meal to stimulate his appetite. Being French by birth, Gran'-père fully appreciated the value of appetite.

Lunch was to be at the house, across the highway from the low, rambling factory building and part way up a hill. The two ranges of hills were like a pair of wrinkled lips on either side of the long wide valley. The sheltered flat land was said to have the most equable climate for flowers in the entire state of California.

The valley was beautiful. Jacynth believed that it was the most beautiful spot in the entire world. Gran'-père cultivated mostly roses and jasmine, but their neighbors, who raised flowers for the seeds and bulbs, grew practically everything: sweet peas and stocks and bluebells and ageratum and penstemons and dianthus and carnations and watsonias and fuchsias and delphinium and larkspur, to say nothing of dahlias and gladioli. There wasn't a month in the year when flowers weren't in bloom. Sometimes the entire valley was like a gorgeous oriental carpet of blue and orchid and magenta and white and pink and every other shade one could possibly think of. Valle de Flores had been well named.

The party divided into twos and threes on their way to the house, and Jacynth, for some reason, found herself walking with Mr. Grayne. He wasn't very easy to talk to.

She asked him if he were from the South, and he said that he was. She asked what state, and he said South Carolina. She said Derek had lived in South Carolina, a long time as a boy, and he said nothing at all. So she asked if he had been born in Charleston, and he said he had. She said Derek had lived in Charleston, too, and he said, rather distantly, that many people did live there. Jacynth changed the subject. She asked if he didn't think the valley was beautiful. He answered, looking directly into her face, "The most beautiful thing I have evah seen."

He had nice thick black eyebrows that matched his black hair. But one simply couldn't talk to a man who answered in such short sentences and acted as if he were bored to death at everything you said. Just as she had decided that, he smiled and said, "Tell me about yourself, Miss Jacynth."

She liked the way he said Miss Jacynth instead of Miss LeDoux. That was Southern, wasn't it? Anyway, it broke the ice between them, and she told him about St. Bridget's and the sisters and about Gran'-père and about her father who had died before she had even been born. Mr. Grayne turned out to be a good listener, even if he wasn't much of a conversationalist.

Mother was at the house, worried at having to entertain so many people. She needn't have worried, poor thing. Manuel always served beautifully, and Lung Fu cooked like an angel. Not only Chinese cooking (which would have been rather monotonous), but any kind of cooking. The Chinese, Gran'-père had always claimed, were the only race in the world besides the French who were civilized enough to understand the art of cookery.

Gran'-père had ordered the lunch himself: hot consommé, sole baked in white wine with a sauce of shrimp and mushrooms, potatoes julienne, a plain lettuce salad with a simple oil and tarragon-vinegar dressing and a dessert of whole raspberries beaten up in cream. There weren't any cocktails. Cocktails numbed the palate, Gran'-père claimed.

There was wine, however, a vintage white Graves, neither particularly sweet nor particularly dry, but gloriously in between. As soon as it had been served Gran'-père stood up, glass in hand, to propose a toast.

"Shall we drink to Mr. Esterling's yellow jasmine?"

"Yellow jasmine," everyone echoed, standing up, too.

But Gran'-père suddenly set down his wineglass, almost untouched, and pressed his forehead between his hands as if it pained him. His eyes were blinking in a funny way; he just couldn't seem to hold the lids open. He tried to smile. "Please excuse me," he apologized in a queer choked sort of voice. "A bad attack of indigestion."

Jacynth was thoroughly frightened.

PART TWO
YOU HAVE CAUGHT
MURDERERS BEFORE

The inn was a sprawling structure of peaked gables and green shutters, as thickly vine covered as any aged manor house. Quitting the bus which had met his train at the station, Westborough sauntered into the cool interior.

The room clerk handed him a pen and a card. He wrote, "T. L. West, Chicago," and returned the pasteboard, feeling a little foolish as any man must when necessity compels him to masquerade under an alias. The clerk nodded recognition of the name.

"I believe we have some mail for you, Mr. West."

The "mail" consisted of a single letter. It had been posted locally, and the address was handwritten: "T. L. West, Watsonia Inn, Valle de Flores, California. Hold until arrival." Westborough twirled the envelope between thumb and forefinger. The flap bore a return card in small blue capitals: "LEDOUX PERFUMES, INCORPORATED, P.O. BOX 341, VALLE DE FLORES, CALIFORNIA."

"Will you pardon me?" he apologized, tearing the flap open. The message, handwritten like the address, was annoyingly brief.

"I thank you for your kindness a thousand times. If it pleases you I will come to your room at seven-thirty o'clock on Monday morning. L."

"Dear me," Westborough commented, cramming the letter into his pocket before he followed the bellboy upstairs.

He liked the quiet, leisurely atmosphere of the inn, and he was delighted with the cream-colored wallpaper and gay curtains of the room which had been assigned to him. The walnut furniture was a trifle old fashioned in design, but Westborough found it pleasing. Like Mr. Hardcastle, he loved everything that was old: old friends, old times, old manners, old books and old wine. …

The quotation could not be completed; there was no old wife. Nearly half a century ago, when men lived in a different civilization, under a different code, fate had decided the matter, and so Westborough's modest, retiring life had been devoted to scholarship. His works on Trajan and Heliogabalus had enjoyed a measure of success, and he was now engaged on a third, *Julian the Pagan*, in which he sought to throw new light on the strange career of the most maligned character of Roman antiquity. The task, however, was being undertaken under circumstances of curious difficulty. Westborough could not keep himself from involvement in murder mysteries.

Only four short months ago his quiet life had been shattered by halberd and dagger and poison. A year ago it had been the affair of the Cretan snake goddess, before that a naked novelist, and before that a Tibetan lama's stolen manuscript. Still other cases had preceded these four. Westborough did not particularly seek murders, but murders, it seemed, sought him with persistent and alarming regularity. As witness, the airmail letter now reposing in his coat pocket.

When the bellboy had left him to solitude he compared it closely with the missive he had just received, his mild blue eyes peering intently through his gold-rimmed bifocals. Westborough was a small man, not over five feet six inches in stature, frailly built. His face, broad and high in the forehead, narrowed to a small pointed chin; his hair was sparse and silvery. He looked far from imposing, but a number of persons had found him a formidable antagonist. He had made heroic efforts to keep his avocation of criminology a secret, but truth is very nearly as pervasive as cosmic rays. As again witness, the airmail letter.

He was about to peruse it once more when an advertising folder on the writing desk captured his eyes: "Historic Valle de Flores and its world-famous inn welcome you." Westborough knew only of Valle de Flores that the little city was situated a hundred and fifty miles north of Los Angeles on the coastal route to San Francisco. He was anxious to learn more. His active, inquiring mind fastened upon very nearly every piece of stray information that floated within its range.

The folder told him that the valley had been discovered and named by Don Gaspar de Portola, governor of the Californias, in 1769 during the first expedition to discover the port of Monterey. (Portola had stood on the shores of Monterey Bay without recognizing it, Westborough recalled from the storehouse of his memory.) "The valley is approximately thirty miles long, varying in width from one to ten miles, and its western end opens directly on to the Pacific Ocean," Westborough read. "Climatic conditions are surpassed nowhere in the state of California." (He wondered what the Los Angeles Chamber of Commerce would say.) "The valley is a noted agricultural region. It is famous for its cattle, its vegetables, but most of all for its flowers. Thousands of tourists come annually to view its scenic splendors when the fields of the great flower-seed farms blaze in gorgeous color." Westborough skimmed rapidly through the text until he encountered the name LeDoux.

"The jasmine farms of southern France are duplicated in the fields of Etienne LeDoux, 'maker of sweet smells,' whose scent factory is the only one in the United States able to compete successfully with the great industries of Grasse. As popular with the ladies as imported perfumes are *Clair de Lune*,

Love-in-a-Mist, Moonlight-on-the-Grove and other California-made fragrances. With true French courtesy, Mr. LeDoux welcomes the visitor to view his modern plant, ten miles west of Valle de Flores, but an integral part of the community. And when you have seen how perfumes are manufactured, drive further, a bare mile or mile and a half along a quiet country road to the sparkling blue waters of our own Pacific, whose tempering influence keeps the nights of Valle de Flores so cool that blankets are always necessary. It was here, among the giant sand dunes, that the motion-picture epic, *Beau Peste*, was filmed."

Westborough decided that he had read far enough. He made mental note of the facts just gleaned from the folder, and reread his airmail letter.

The entire message was handwritten. It had been penned by a man in a hurry, Westborough had already decided from the large bold strokes which formed the letters.

Mr. Theocritus Lucius Westborough,
Hotel Equable,
Chicago, Ill.

Dear and Esteemed Sir:

Your fame (I do not refer to your notable biographies of Roman emperors) has penetrated even to this remote wilderness. I hesitate to intrude my own problem into your personal life, but the matter is of urgent importance to me and to those dearest to me. To speak of money to a man like yourself is folly, but rest assured that we shall not quarrel over your terms. Shall I continue?

Briefly, I want you to be my house guest for the week beginning Monday, July 3, when I am entertaining rather a large party. The nature of your mission I would rather explain to you in person, but I give you my word, *foi de gentilhomme*, that it is nothing which in any way you will find discreditable. You have caught murderers before, Monsieur Westborough.

I beg and pray that you will accept. My cook is good, and I have an excellent cellar. I believe that you will enjoy your visit, as I know I shall enjoy entertaining you. Do I convince? If so, please relieve my anxiety by dispatching to me the following wire:

AM INTERESTED IN FINANCIAL PROPOSITION YOU HAVE OUTLINED.

T. L. WEST

That name is not your own, but it is necessary that you take precautions. Others besides myself may be aware of your enviable reputation.

We must have a lengthy interview in private, a matter by no means simple to arrange. I suggest, therefore, that upon arrival at Valle de Flores, which must be no later than Sunday, you go directly to the Watsonia Inn, where you will find your room comfortable and the cuisine beyond reproach. Sign the register as T. L. West, the name you will assume during your visit. Once more may I stress the urgency of taking precautions. Your true name and the nature of your errand will be known only to myself.

I shall arrange to get in touch with you shortly after your arrival at the inn. Please accept the enclosed for traveling expenses.

Gratefully and hopefully,
ETIENNE LEDOUX

The "enclosed" had been a check amply sufficient for railroad fare. Regretfully locking the unfinished manuscript of *Julian the Pagan* in his safe-deposit vault, Westborough had answered the siren call.

He did not think that he would be sorry. An unsolved mystery offered pleasing divertissement for a mind a little wearied of the tribulations of Flavius Claudius Julianus. Moreover, the personality of the writer of this epistle was in itself intriguing. "My cook is good, and I have an excellent cellar." "You will find your room comfortable and the cuisine beyond reproach." Minor touches, but significant. They indicated a man of the world, a *bon vivant* and, above all, a courteous gentleman. Westborough put away his two letters and stepped into the bathroom. Refreshed by a bath and clean linen, he descended to make trial of the vaunted cuisine.

The dining room was an indoor flower garden. Westborough caught his breath. Great fan-shaped sprays of watsonias curtained the windows. Bowls stood on each table bearing still other of the gladiolus-like blossoms: orange, scarlet, cardinal, rose, pale pink and pure white. If this were a sample of what the valley could do, decidedly the beautiful Spanish name was well merited.

He saw that every table was already taken. An elderly waitress inquired if he minded sharing a table with another gentleman. No, he did not mind in the least, he returned meekly, provided that the other gentleman was also willing. The other gentleman, a diner on milk toast and tea, grunted but did not actively object. Westborough seated himself and ordered the table d'hôte. "The watsonia, I believe, is a South African member of the iris family," he tentatively offered as a conversational tidbit.

His neighbor of the toast and tea mumbled an unintelligible reply. "The flowers are very beautiful, are they not?" the little man persisted. The question wasn't answered. "If I had only two loaves of bread I would sell one and buy a hyacinth," the historian continued meditatively.

"The more fool you," snapped the man across the table.

He was about Westborough's age, possibly a few years older. He wore horn-rimmed spectacles, and his thick gray brows joined to form a bushy V just above the root of his square-tipped nose.

Westborough said mildly, "I was quoting a Chinese saying."

"The only thing Chinese I like is tea."

Westborough smiled, relieved to discover a common interest. "If I am not mistaken the discovery of the beverage is ascribed by Chinese tradition to the Emperor Shên-nung in the third millennium before Christ."

His neighbor lifted the V of his eyebrows. "Do you know anything else?" he demanded tartly.

"A little," Westborough owned.

"Do you know the difference between green and black tea?"

"The leaves for green tea are withered and fired immediately; the leaves for black tea are fermented before firing."

"Humph! How's oolong tea prepared?"

"The leaves are partially fermented before firing."

"What's hyson?"

"A Chinese term referring to leaf size."

"What kind of tea is raised in Darjeeling?"

"A fragrant, full-bodied leaf, gratifying to the palates of such tea connoisseurs as yourself."

"Humph, you do know a few things," the other acknowledged gruffly. "Tea is my hobby. I've drunk it every way it's served. With milk like the English. With lemon as you probably take it. With a spiced candy like the Russians. Pulverized and whipped in hot water the Japanese way. Cinnamon flavored or scented with jasmine as the Chinese like it. But I tell you" – his voice rose to a shrill note of complaint – "never in my life have I tasted such slop as this!"

"Rather a strong protest," Westborough observed. "May I inquire why you find the present beverage so distasteful?"

"Sewn up in a little bag," the other returned furiously. He beckoned to the waitress. "Take this mess back to the kitchen. If no one here understands how to make tea I'll have to tell you. Take a clean teapot and pour boiling water over the leaves. That's simple enough, isn't it? Water over the leaves. Do you think you can remember it?"

The waitress glowered silently, whisking pot and cup away. Westborough tried his fruit cocktail and found it excellent. "Are you a tea taster, Mr.—"

"Todd. Aaron Todd. No, I'm in the real-estate business." Todd chuckled mordantly. "Not much money in that lately." He studied Westborough's face with a pair of piercing gimlet eyes and said accusingly, "You've never been in business. Professional man?"

"In a way." Westborough was about to explain further when he remembered Etienne LeDoux's letter. "Pray allow me to introduce myself. My name is West."

"West!" Aaron Todd appeared astonished. "Not T. L. West?"

"Guilty," the historian replied, managing to conceal his own surprise.

"How well do you know LeDoux?"

"Not very well," Westborough said truthfully.

"And yet you're willing to entrust your savings to him. Your hard-earned savings!" Todd added portentously, "But for the lucky accident of meeting me, Mr. West, you would almost certainly have been swindled."

The waitress grumpily deposited a fresh pot of tea, and exchanged Westborough's empty cocktail cup for a plate of cream soup. She departed, scowling. The historian was not inclined to blame her for the lack of radiation of sweetness and light.

"How should I have been swindled?" he asked.

"By buying LeDoux Perfumes stock, of course," Todd returned crustily.

Westborough checked his denial. "It is not then a desirable investment?"

Todd snorted. "Don't dignify an outright swindle."

"But surely Mr. LeDoux is a man of honor," Westborough protested.

"LeDoux is a spellbinder, a hypnotist. He will make you believe anything he wants you to believe. Do you see me, Mr. West?"

"Yes," Westborough replied, looking across the table. "Indeed, I do."

"You see a man who has been swindled."

"Dear me."

"Thousands of dollars."

"But surely you hold some security."

"A few pieces of paper purporting to be stock. LeDoux Perfumes, Incorporated, is not operating at a profit. What's more it never did operate at a profit. What's more it never will operate at a profit. What's more it wouldn't operate at all, if LeDoux wasn't able to find a few easy marks like ourselves. I take it, Mr. West, that you do not want to lose your savings?"

"Indeed, I do not," Westborough declared.

"Then have nothing to do with yellow jasmine."

"What is yellow jasmine?" Westborough asked.

Todd's keen little eyes stared shrewdly. "You mean to say you traveled all the way here from Chicago without even knowing the perfume you were going to help market?"

"Mr. LeDoux called it by another name," Westborough improvised on the spur of the moment. "Something like jasmine but not the same thing."

"Gelsemium?" Todd asked.

Westborough nodded immediately. The noun sounded familiar, but for the moment it meant nothing. Gelsemium was Latin in form, but not true Latin, he recognized, merely a Latinized word. *Gelsemino?* Yes, to be sure, the

Italian for jasmine, but he was traveling in a circle. No, he was not. *Gelsemium sempervirens*, of course.

"The Carolina yellow jessamine," he said aloud. Slowly the wariness faded from Todd's sharp pinched face.

"That was one of the names mentioned at the recent conference," he admitted.

The waitress brought a steak as thick as a layer cake; for the next few minutes Westborough's attention was fully occupied. Todd drank the last of his tea and rose to his feet.

"We'll be seeing something of each other during the next few days, I 'spect. Don't allow LeDoux to make a fool of you."

"I shall not," Westborough answered. "Good night, Mr. Todd."

When the little historian had finished his meal he sauntered into the lounge. Flowers and an enormous hearth rendered the huge beamed room attractive. On both sides of the hearth were bookcases. He looked for and found the Encyclopedia Britannica.

After reading and rereading the article headed "Gelsemium" he went thoughtfully to his room. The Britannica had opened an amazing topic for speculation.

II

Etienne LeDoux smiled with Gallic charm. "You are wondering what manner of man is this LeDoux who writes the strange letter, *hein?*" He bolted the bedroom door, adding in a low voice, "We can talk here undisturbed."

The perfumer, an older man than Westborough had expected, carried himself with soldierly erectness. It was evident that he had not shirked his military training; the Frenchman's slight limp might well have been a *souvenir de guerre*, the historian mused. LeDoux's hair and mustache were silvery gray; so also was his beard, a dignified imperial such as the third Napoleon had favored.

"I trust, Mr. West, you do not object to my calling you by the false name? If we accustom ourselves to its use beforehand, slips of the tongue are less likely."

"True," Westborough acknowledged. "I do not in the least object."

"You are wondering why I have sent for you, *n'est-ce pas?*" LeDoux frowned downward at his white shoes. "A little over two weeks ago, on Thursday, the fifteenth of June, an attempt was made to poison me. I swallowed the poison, *mon Dieu!*"

Westborough gasped. "I am glad to see that you recovered," he rejoined finally.

"Yes, I live to tell the tale. But it was a very near thing. I tasted nothing, such was the deadly art with which it had been given to me. Nor do I know – you may surmise from the fact that you are here – the identity of the poisoner. *C'est le diable!"*

"Do you suspect a certain person?" Westborough asked.

"Eight persons had the opportunity, but I suspect none of them. *Grand Dieu*, none can be suspected!"

"Perhaps if you related the circumstances," Westborough hazarded, finding the enigma puzzling.

"But of course. We were in my private office at the factory, discussing the marketing of a new perfume originated by my chief chemist, Derek Esterling. Mr. Esterling is engaged to my granddaughter, Jacynth, but the fact can have no possible bearing."

LeDoux's waxen-white face conveyed the impression that he was not entirely sure of this. Not nearly so sure, at least, as he would have liked to have been.

"Were your granddaughter and Mr. Esterling both present?" the historian inquired aloud.

"Yes, both of them."

"And the remaining six?"

"My sales manager, Sam Preston. He has been with me for five years and has made a good record. Miss Morton, who has been my secretary for seven years. Chamaron, my advertising agent, an old and valued friend. Mrs. Chamaron, who has designed several packages for LeDoux products. A Mr. Stuart Grayne, an employee of Chamaron's agency, whom I met for the first time that morning. You see the situation is impossible!"

"And you believe that the poison was administered by one of those in your office?" Westborough questioned.

"I am sure of it," LeDoux returned, but he did not explain why.

Westborough counted on his fingers. "You have named only seven," he objected. "You told me eight people had the opportunity."

"A thousand pardons! I overlooked Aaron Todd."

"Dear me!" Westborough explained. "I am acquainted with that gentleman. I dined with him last night."

LeDoux's mouth dropped ruefully. "But how unfortunate! More than unfortunate, disastrous! I dare not introduce you as Mr. Westborough."

"Mr. Todd knows me only as Mr. West," Westborough elucidated. "I met him for the first time last night."

LeDoux broke into a dry chuckle. "I am relieved," he confessed.

"Mr. Todd is an interesting character. I believe he mentioned that he was in the real-estate business."

"He buys cheaply and he sells dearly. Sometimes he deals in other things than real estate. But that does not matter, Mr. West, I assure you."

"May I ask his connection with your company?"

"He is treasurer and a heavy stockholder. The largest individual stock-holder next to myself."

Westborough decided against mentioning Todd's warning. "May I ask another question, Mr. LeDoux? Why were you so particular concerning the exact wording of the telegram you requested me to send?"

LeDoux shrugged his shoulders. "It is necessary to explain your presence, *mon ami*. What more natural than to cast you in the role of a distant capitalist? I trust you do not mind my showing your wire to Mr. Todd? He is sharp as a needle, that one. Without such tangible evidence as a telegram I could not hope to allay his suspicions."

Westborough sensed that his future host was not being entirely frank. There was a deeper game between Todd and LeDoux than either of those gentlemen was willing to reveal.

"I am sorry that I interrupted your narrative, Mr. LeDoux. Pray continue."

"Actually there is very little to tell. Miss Morton made a stenographic record of the business proceedings, in case they are of any interest to you. At noon I suggested that we adjourn to my house where luncheon had been ordered for ten."

"Ten?" Westborough repeated.

"My daughter-in-law joined us. But that meal has no bearing. I was poisoned at the office, not at the house. The poison was in my stomachic – a tincture of gentian with bitter orange peel and cardamom."

"The virtues of gentian were mentioned by Pliny, if I remember correctly."

"Your erudition is surprising. Since I take a teaspoonful of the tincture shortly before every meal I keep a bottle in my office. In a locked cabinet, I might add, though that fact also has little bearing. Shall I relate my actions in detail?"

"Please do."

"I unlocked the cabinet – the only key is on the ring in my pocket – removed the bottle and a spoon. I measured out a teaspoonful and poured it into a tumbler with a little water from a pitcher. The tumbler and the pitcher were standing on a tray on top of the cabinet. My secretary had put fresh water in the pitcher early in the morning and had washed the tumbler at the same time. The tumbler, I may say, is made of a deep indigo-blue glass, and it is difficult to see its bottom."

"Is the pitcher of the same color glass, also?"

"Yes."

"Pray continue."

"I swallowed my medicine – fortunately not to the dregs. I tasted only the usual bitter taste, I may mention. At the beginning of luncheon I was seized by a sudden violent attack. The symptoms were peculiar. I had difficulty in keeping my eyes open, for one thing."

"Ah!" Westborough exclaimed. "And did you also experience double vision?"

"*Comment diable!*" LeDoux exclaimed. "Are you clairvoyant?"

Westborough smiled. "Far from it. May I ask the grounds on which you base your belief that the poison had been placed in the tumbler or pitcher?"

"Not belief," LeDoux corrected. "Knowledge. In the tumbler, by the way; the pitcher was innocent."

Westborough waited expectantly.

"That sudden, strange attack could not come without a reason, I knew," LeDoux explained. "But there was no use in alarming my friends and family needlessly; I pretended that it was merely an attack of indigestion. Assisted by Mr. Preston and Mr. Chamaron, I went upstairs to bed. Though very weak, I did not lose consciousness. A doctor was summoned, *naturellement*, but while I was waiting for him I talked to my secretary in private. Alarm was written all over her face. Beatrice is devoted to me. I told her nothing, but I asked her to do a great deal. I asked her to fill three small bottles with the liquid in the tumbler (if any remained), with the water in the pitcher and with the unadulterated gentian tincture. These to be labeled A, B and C, respectively, and carried at once to Los Angeles for chemical analysis. You will realize, I think, why I did not desire to employ the facilities of my own excellent laboratory. Miss Morton returned to my office immediately; fortunately, no one had been there in my absence, and the evidence was intact. She drove at once to Los Angeles in her own car."

"A long drive," Westborough commented.

"To her, nothing. Her mother and brother are in that city, and she makes the jaunt almost every other weekend. Miss Morton took the three bottles to the chemical analyst I had mentioned; his report was mailed to me in three days' time. *Voilà!*"

LeDoux reached into his coat pocket. "Allow me to read what this eminent authority says of the matter. 'Bottle B: contains water with slight mineral impurities …' That is nothing, that one. 'Bottle C: ten per cent of gentian with orange and cardamom, in forty-five per cent alcohol. Bottle A: the above gentian tincture with a content of the toxic alkaloids gelseminine and gelsemine.' These, *mon ami*, are constituents of gelsemium."

"A preparation made from the roots and rhizomes of the Carolina yellow jessamine," Westborough contributed.

III

"It would appear that you know everything," LeDoux declared, astounded.

"Very little," Westborough returned modestly. He would have liked to add that his knowledge of gelsemium was limited to the article in the Britannica. But to mention that, he would have to say why he had looked up the topic of gelsemium, which would lead again to Mr. Todd, a bypath he preferred not to reenter at present. "Does anyone else, Mr. LeDoux, know that you were poisoned?"

"Only the poisoner."

"Not the doctor who attended you?"

"I do not think so. He acted very puzzled."

"He gave you the right treatment, however, it would seem."

"I am here," LeDoux answered dryly.

"Your secretary must have her suspicions?"

"Her suspicions, perhaps, but she can know nothing definite. She has had no opportunity to read the analyst's report."

"Your secretary may be eliminated from the crime on logical grounds," Westborough cogitated. "She had an unparalleled opportunity to destroy the evidence, but did not do so. The poisoner would have acted very differently under the same circumstances. Do you not agree?"

"Yes, the point is well taken." The perfumer paused indecisively. "The next time I may not be so fortunate. For myself, I do not care. I am old; I have lived my span; my time will come within a few years under any circumstances. But I do not wish to die and leave unprotected *ma petite-fille*, Jacynth."

"You anticipate danger to her also?"

"I do not know what to anticipate. I did not believe that I had an enemy in the world. Yet I have. A cowardly, treacherous enemy. *Mon Dieu*, I shall go mad!"

"Logic admits three possibilities," Westborough stated reflectively. "The toxic substance – it would be a liquid, would it not? – was placed in the tumbler before you took your seats. It was placed there while you were seated or, thirdly, after you had adjourned the formal meeting and before you took your stomachic."

"Not the last," LeDoux objected. "I was mixing the bitters before anyone left his or her seat."

"Could the poison have been dropped into the glass before the meeting was called to order?"

"It is possible. There was a little confusion at that time, I remember."

"Are you able to name any person who could not have placed the poison then?"

"Sam Preston was late. He didn't come into the office until after the others had been seated."

"The poison might also have been put into the tumbler while the meeting was in progress. For that reason it is important to know how you were seated."

"I was at my desk at the south side of the office. The cabinet was on my right. Let me see – the positions of eight persons are rather difficult to recall. There is a davenport at the north end of the office. Jacynth was there, near the door, on the west side of the room. Mrs. Chamaron was on the other end of the davenport, and Preston sat between the two ladies. Yes, that is right. So far I am sure. The remaining details, however, are hazy."

"That is only natural. May I interrupt with an irrelevant question? How old is your granddaughter?"

"Nineteen."

"That is not very old," Westborough said with a smile. "Was it not a little unusual to bring her to a business meeting?"

"Not in the least. Since she will inherit my entire interest in LeDoux Perfumes, Incorporated, I wish her to learn how the business is conducted. Jacynth has a lively, quick intelligence. Her grasp of our problems sometimes astonishes me."

"Youth is naturally tenacious of what it imbibes," Westborough murmured. "I am indebted to Quintilianus. Do you anticipate an early marriage?"

"I hope not." LeDoux's face darkened. "Jacynth is still too much of a child."

"I have interrupted your trend of thought," Westborough apologized. "We were discussing seating arrangements."

"Esterling was on my right," LeDoux owned a little reluctantly. "The cabinet was between us. Miss Morton was on my left. I can't place the others."

"There remain only three positions to be located," Westborough observed, making a rough diagram. "Mr. Chamaron, Mr. Todd and Mr. Grayne."

"Todd was next to Esterling. And Chamaron – let me see – Chamaron was on the opposite side of the room. Between Miss Morton and the door."

Westborough drew two rather approximate circles and inscribed them "Td" and "Chmn." LeDoux surveyed the diagram with interest. "Grayne sat between Todd and Mrs. Chamaron," he declared suddenly. "I recall that he whispered something to Mrs. Chamaron."

Westborough added the last notation, observing, "It would seem, sir, that only yourself and Mr. Esterling were within striking distance of the cabinet."

"It could not be he," LeDoux rejoined hoarsely. "I trust Derek implicitly. He's the most brilliant man who ever worked for me, and he is engaged to Jacynth; almost a member of my own family. I would rather believe it of anyone in the world but Derek Esterling."

Westborough folded the diagram into his coat pocket. "The trail has grown cold," he said gently. "It would have been better if you had reported your suspicions directly to the police."

But he thought he knew why Etienne LeDoux had not.

"I offer myself as a human guinea pig, m'sieur. My life is in your hands."

"But – dear me!" Westborough stammered. "I do not understand." "This week another conference will be held to discuss the marketing of our new yellow jasmine perfume. The factory is an inconveniently long distance from town. What more natural than that I should invite my business associates to be my house guests? All have accepted, everyone who was in my office on that morning. But with them will be a certain capitalist from Chicago. He has wired me his object in coming; I have exhibited his telegram freely; his presence will be accepted by my *confrères* as a matter of course." LeDoux leaned forward confidentially.

"He is desperate, this poisoner, or he would not resort to such desperate measures, *ma foi!* Having failed, he will try again at the earliest opportunity, the opportunity I have provided. The attempt on my life will be repeated, m'sieur; I have no doubts. But the amazing genius of Theocritus Lucius Westborough will nip the plot in the bud, *n'est-ce pas?*"

"But," Westborough remonstrated weakly, "I do not know that—"

He suspended the sentence abruptly as a knock sounded on the door.

IV

"Who knows of your presence at the inn?" LeDoux asked in a sibilant whisper.

"One person only."

"Todd?" LeDoux knit puzzled brows. "It is slightly – one might say peculiar. In personal financial expenditures the gentleman inclines to the parsimonious. Yet he spends the night here in preference to my house. Strange!"

"Perhaps it is not he," Westborough suggested. The knock was repeated. LeDoux threw the door open.

"Morning, gentlemen," Todd greeted them in a nondescript cackle. His sparse hair, parted just above the left ear, was slicked close to the scalp with water. "Surprised to see me?"

"You spent the night here?" LeDoux questioned.

"What do you think?" Todd retorted brusquely.

"But why, Aaron, did you not inform me of your arrival? I could have sent the car for you last night."

"Didn't want to put you to trouble," Todd mumbled. "Thought I might as well go to bed early and take the bus out to your plant this morning. Bus runs on an hourly schedule, don't it? Had your breakfast, Etienne?"

"Yes, I have."

"Well, I haven't, and I'm hungry. How about you, West? Care to eat?"

"If the delay will not cause Mr. LeDoux any inconvenience."

"No inconvenience at all," LeDoux returned. "While you two gentlemen are in the dining room I will buy my fireworks. Lung Fu would never forgive me if I returned empty handed."

Todd's face twisted into a grimace. "To really celebrate the Fourth," he said, "it takes a Frenchman and a heathen Chinese."

"The Chinese invented fireworks, I believe," Westborough observed pedantically. "At least they invented gunpowder."

"And now the Japs are making 'em pay for it." Todd chuckled unpleasantly as they descended to the ground floor.

The morning sunlight streamed through the windows of the dining room. Fresh bowls of watsonias had been placed on the tables. "Costs a fortune to eat here," Todd grumbled.

He ordered orange juice, buttered toast and tea – orange pekoe. "And none of your tea bags," he scolded. "Put the leaves in the pot and pour boiling water over them. Boiling, mind you. I don't want any more slop."

Westborough, who had grown attached to the continental form of breakfast, required only rolls and coffee. When the waitress had left, Todd said:

"I'm not going to let Frenchy LeDoux make a fool of you. Not so long as my name is Aaron Xenophon Todd."

Westborough thought that he had never known a man who looked less like an altruist than Aaron Xenophon Todd.

"You don't trust me," Todd muttered. "So I've got an ax of my own to grind, have I? Well, what is it? Answer me that, West."

The man was old and ugly. His forehead sloped backward in a series of horizontal corrugations. Folds of withered skin hung about his neck; his withered eyelids slightly resembled a lizard's scales. But there was force to him, power.

"Are you married, Mr. Todd?"

"Think I'm a fool?" Todd snapped.

Westborough smiled. The fractious reply had given him his cue.

"No, I do not. I think you are what might be called a sharp customer." He saw by the glint in Todd's hard little eyes that the doubtful compliment did not displease him. "One would have to rise at a very early hour in the morning to get ahead of you. Is that not so?"

Todd chuckled. "Been rising early all my life."

"Exactly. Yet Etienne LeDoux, a blender of perfumes, swindles you of a large sum of money with ridiculous ease. You will pardon me if I do not believe it."

"Eh?" Todd exclaimed. "What say?"

"I said that I did not believe it."

Todd indicated the black disk which hung about his throat. "Don't hear very well," he explained. "Believe what?"

The man's hearing had been perfect up to this point, Westborough was sure.

"Believe that Mr. LeDoux swindled you," the historian said in a normal tone of voice.

"He did," Todd maintained. "Stock's not worth the paper it's printed on. Look before you leap, West. Better be safe than sorry."

"A stitch in time is worth nine," Westborough added. "Yes, to be sure. But the fox said the grapes were sour."

"What say?" Todd asked, conveniently deaf again.

"Something about a fox."

"Ox?"

"No, fox."

"Haven't seen one for a long time," Todd observed. "Not many foxes around these parts."

"Except two-legged ones," Westborough qualified. "How is your tea, may I ask?"

"Eh?"

"Tea," Westborough enunciated distinctly.

"Oh, tea. It's drinkable."

LeDoux found them finishing their breakfast in frigid silence. "I have taken the liberty of having your luggage transferred to my car," he explained. "We can leave immediately. Your bills have been paid. Not a word. You are my guests."

"A fool and his money," Todd muttered as they walked outside.

LeDoux piloted his big sedan through broad avenues lined with drooping pepper trees into the open country. The valley, level as a table top, was bounded on north and south by low ranges of hills. The entire terrain seemed to be one vast flower garden. They passed a field of golden marigolds and rose-pink scabiosas, another of zinnias, a third gaudy with multicolored snapdragons. All of these, LeDoux explained, were grown commercially for the seeds.

"When one flower dies another takes its place, but flowers there are always. We are fortunate, we who live here."

"You are indeed," Westborough concurred. "I have seen only one spot in the world to equal this; to wit, the hills of the Var."

"Ah, the Var!" LeDoux sighed. "You awaken old memories. I was born in Grasse. The family of LeDoux have been scent makers for many generations."

"May I ask—" Westborough began curiously.

"Competition, hélas, forced me to sell an old established business. Rather than work for others I determined to emigrate to America. If wines can be successfully made in California – and some of the local vintages very nearly equal those of France – why not perfumes? Everything grows here, mon Dieu! Jasmine and roses, I reasoned, are no more difficult to cultivate than the grape."

"Not so difficult," Westborough opined.

"No, not so difficult. But no sooner had I proved the possibility of success than there came the war. *Mais que voulez-vous?* I returned to fight for France, as all of her sons must. I had a wife, however, my good Cecile, who nursed our infant business with diligence and competence. She is dead, *hélas!* Her ashes repose next to those of our only son, my unhappy Raoul." Turning in at the factory gate, LeDoux parked in the large lot reserved for the cars of his employees.

Four men and three women awaited them in LeDoux's private office, where the first of the business conferences was about to take place. Experiencing the confusion which invariably results when one is introduced to a great many people in rapid succession, Westborough concentrated on the creation of a mental image for each. Long ago he had learned that when one is able to recall distinctly the physical appearance of a person, the name is apt to come to mind as a matter of course.

He began with LeDoux's granddaughter. Small and piquant, she was with her slim figure and undeveloped breasts as yet very much of a schoolgirl. Her hair was a warm, rich brown; she had gathered it into a roll at the back of a slender neck. Her upturned nose had an elfin tilt, and her gray-blue eyes were the "heavenly blue" shade of Ming porcelain. She welcomed him with charming courtesy. A most likable child, this Jacynth. (The *a* of her odd Christian name was given the long pronunciation, and the accent was placed on the first syllable.) Was the name derived from that beautiful orange gem, the jacinth? Or was it a new form of the almost obsolete Jacintha? Still pondering the question, the historian was presented to LeDoux's chief chemist.

Derek Esterling was just under six feet in height and perhaps ten years older than his youthful fiancée. A scientist, unquestionably. He had the confident mien of a young doctor. … Perhaps that was due to the little trace of chestnut beard below the sensitive mouth. He gave a slight impression of a mind tormented by inner turmoil. His face, however, was handsome; his body, strong, well knit and graceful.

Politely Westborough turned his attention to the ladies.

Beatrice Morton, a quiet young woman in a brown skirt and a tailored blouse, he would have known immediately; she was born to be a secretary as the sparks fly upward. Despite a sweet face and soft brown hair, Miss Morton could not be called pretty. Her chin was too unfortunately short, her mouth too wide, her nose too broad and with too large nostrils. But he found her *simpática* almost from the first. Her smile was friendly, her forehead broad and high, and she had intelligent hazel eyes.

Westborough, being a simple soul who preferred a country garden to a night club, liked Kay Chamaron less. She was in the early thirties, chic, smartly dressed, perhaps also beautiful. Certainly she was most attractive, if one has a fondness for tawny yellow hair and eyes of brilliant mazarine blue. Her cheekbones were the merest shade prominent; her hands were tapering white lilies tipped by gold-painted nails. When she gestured he was reminded, for some reason, of the human pattern woven by Cambodian dancing girls near the ruins of Angkor Wat.

The youngest of the three remaining males, a broad-shouldered, narrow-waisted young giant named Stuart Grayne, was unmistakably a Southerner. "I am happy to know you, suh," he acknowledged the introduction. The drawling soft voice fell pleasantly on the ears, and the big spatulate fingers pressed Westborough's frail hand with considerate gentleness. He was in his late twenties, the historian estimated, about the same age as the chemist, Esterling.

The pudgy man, whose sandy hair surrounded a shining bald spot, was Sam Preston, salesman by birth and sales manager by achievement, an excellent representative of the "good-mixer" caste which has made America what it is today. Preston was jocose and waggish in manner. He laughed heartily and often, slapped his companions gustily on the back. Of the same type, but more urbane, more sophisticated, was the advertising agent, Paul Michael Chamaron.

Chamaron, portly and prosperous in the early forties, had the face of a beaming cherub and an advertising man's ingratiating smile. His sorrel hair matched his little sorrel mustache. On one of his plump, well-manicured hands he wore an intaglio ring. His tie, an expensive silk foulard, had probably been selected by his wife. She bullied him a little, the historian speculated, deciding also that Mr. Chamaron probably took regular bedroom exercises to reduce a not ungenerous waistline.

They were all above average in intelligence, Westborough pronounced. With the single exception of Aaron Todd, they were all friendly, seemingly kindly people. Yet one, undeniably, was a potential murderer. "Which one?" Westborough sighed in dismay.

If he failed in the difficult task of untangling this Gordian knot, the life of Etienne LeDoux might well pay the forfeit – an appalling prospect!

Which one, indeed?

V

Three or four rather good etchings decorated the walls of the office, and a large photograph of Jacynth stood in an easel frame on LeDoux's rosewood desk. The little cabinet at the side of the desk was of rosewood also, fitted with brass hinges and a brass lock. Lifting the blue glass pitcher from the tray atop the cabinet, LeDoux beckoned to his granddaughter.

"Please bring fresh water, *chérie.*" He raised his voice slightly as Jacynth went out the door. "Will you kindly take the same seats you occupied at our last conference? You, Mr. West, please take the extra chair next to Mr. Chamaron."

Jacynth returned with the pitcher, which her grandfather replaced on the tray, saying, "The meeting will please come to order."

The meeting was conducted in the semi-parliamentary procedure so dearly beloved by American business. LeDoux, who presided, was addressed only by the title of "Mr. Chairman." The first item of business, of course, was the reading of the inevitable "minutes."

" 'A conference was held on the forenoon of Thursday, June fifteenth, at the office of Mr. Etienne LeDoux, president of LeDoux Perfumes, Incorporated, to discuss marketing plans for yellow jasmine perfume, a new synthetic product of the LeDoux laboratories,' " Miss Morton recited in a level voice. " 'Those present were: Mr. LeDoux, Mr. Aaron Todd, Mr. Derek Esterling, Mr. Samuel Preston and Miss Beatrice Morton of LeDoux Perfumes, Incorporated; Mr. P. M. Chamaron and Mr. Stuart Grayne of Paul Michael Chamaron, Incorporated; Mrs. Kay Chamaron and Miss Jacynth LeDoux.

" 'Mr. Esterling exhibited the new perfume and explained its nature. Mr. LeDoux requested each of those present to suggest a name. The names suggested were: Scandal, Mr. Samuel Preston; *Affaire de Coeur*, Miss Beatrice Morton; Goldenstar, Mr. P. M. Chamaron; Carolina Jessamine, Mr. Stuart Grayne; Southern Belle, Mrs. Kay Chamaron; *Valle de Flores*, Miss Jacynth LeDoux; Jacynth, Mr. Derek Esterling.

" 'Mrs. Kay Chamaron offered the further suggestion that the container be modeled in the form of a hoop-skirted girl of the Civil War period, the girl's head to be the bottle's stopper. She was asked by Mr. LeDoux to prepare sketches of this design.

" 'The meeting was adjourned for luncheon at the home of Mr. LeDoux. Owing to the sudden illness of the chairman, the discussion was not resumed.' "

Miss Morton's mellow contralto ceased abruptly. "Are there any additions or corrections?" inquired the chairman. There were neither. There never are on such occasions, Westborough mused. The human memory is easily cowed by the bully called Documentary Evidence.

"The minutes will stand as read." LeDoux rose to his feet, a courtly representative of the world's most civilized race. "The unfinished business would appear to include the selection of a name."

"Mr. Chairman." Chamaron bobbed up from his chair like a bouncing ball. "Everyone is naturally prejudiced in favor of the name he or she proposed; we can talk all day and not get anywhere. I suggest that the consumer be permitted to name the product. Let ballots be printed with the seven names listed in alphabetical order and a square opposite each name for the consumer to list her preferences. My organization is prepared to handle all the details. We would hire three or four young women, preferably college students in search of summer employment, to go from house to house in a typical perfume-conscious community, and—"

"What's he saying?" Aaron Todd inquired in a loud voice.

"A market research," Stuart Grayne whispered.

"Nonsense," Todd said bluntly. "What's a perfume-conscious community?"

"A community whose women are habituated to the use of perfume would be a perfume-conscious community," Chamaron explained, slightly nettled.

"Well, what's a community?"

"A community? Why, an aggregation of houses."

"Don't women in apartments use perfumes?" Todd demanded.

"Order, please," LeDoux expostulated, interrupting the little ripple of laughter. "The suggestion will be carefully considered, Paul Michael. Mr. West, you were not here on the previous occasion, and so can have no prejudice in favor of any name. Which one of them appealed to you the most?"

"My opinion is valueless," Westborough evaded.

"I think not," LeDoux demurred. "Your opinion rarely is valueless, Mr. West. Please tell us."

"I believe I preferred the name Southern Belle."

Westborough was rewarded by a dazzling smile from Mrs. Chamaron. He thought: "This is fantastic. It's impossible that any of these people can have murderous intentions."

"Southern Belle," LeDoux said, "is also my favorite. I am going to ask everyone present to state his or her objections. We'll begin with you, Sam."

"Okay by me, Mr. Chairman. Southern Belle ought to be a honey if we present it in a fancy packet like Mrs. Chamaron can work up. But what we really need to smooth out the bumps in the w. k. sales curve is a low-priced line. Something to sell to the ten-cent-store trade!"

LeDoux frowned. "We are not in the business of manufacturing cheap perfumes, Sam. I hope and pray we never will be. Mr. Grayne."

"I like Southern Belle right well, Mr. Chairman, but I still like Ca'olinah Jessamine. Why not use both of them, suh? Southern Belle to go in large type and underneath in small type Ca'olinah Jessamine."

"Or Carolina Yellow Jasmine," LeDoux amended. "Yes, that's a very good idea. Beatrice, please make a note of Mr. Grayne's suggestion. Derek."

"I'm a chemist, not an advertising man." There was unexpected virulence in the speaker's tone. "I've already had my say on names, I believe."

"Jacynth."

"I like Mr. Grayne's idea very much."

"Mr. Todd."

"Call it what you like."

"Beatrice."

"I think Southern Belle's just dandy."

"Paul Michael."

"You put me in a difficult position." Chamaron stretched leisurely to his feet. "Any objections I might have to the name are open to misinterpretation." He glanced humorously across at his tawny-haired wife. "In the interests of domestic tranquillity, I prefer to vote for Southern Belle. Seriously though, I do think the name has merit."

"Mrs. Chamaron."

"Paul Michael isn't afraid of me at all." Mrs. Chamaron laughed musically. "Really, he rules me with a rod of iron, as Stuart Grayne can testify. Mr. Chairman, I'm flattered to think that you approve of my name, and I've been very busy planning the nicest kind of container for you. Would you care to see some watercolor sketches?"

"I would like everyone in the room to see them."

The sketches, done with pleasing verve, depicted a demure young lady in poke bonnet and ringlets, whose flaring skirt was a trumpet-shaped yellow flower.

"The skirt was Mr. Grayne's idea," the artist explained. "The yellow jasmine is his state flower; do you all know? We can actually use yellow glass, if you like. The bottles won't be cheap, of course, but I don't believe that the cost will be at all prohibitive for a deluxe perfume. I've already secured quotations from two different factories."

"She's adorable!" Jacynth breathed. "Any girl would be crazy to have that little lady on her dressing table."

"So glad it pleases you," Mrs. Chamaron murmured sweetly.

"Good tie-in," Chamaron offered to no one in particular. "Yellow skirt, yellow jasmine."

"Humph!" Aaron Todd sniffed, perfunctorily thumbing the several sketches.

"The gal's got class," commented Sam Preston. "We can go to town on that number."

LeDoux said: "There is no question, Kay, but what you have surpassed even yourself. We'll have a talk later on about the quotations."

"Nice going, Kay," Grayne whispered. "But I knew all along they'd like it."

The discussion, turning to advertising media, speedily became technical. Westborough stifled several yawns, finding it increasingly difficult to conceal his ennui. Perhaps, in time, however, he might come to learn something of business methods, a subject on which he was lamentably ignorant.

"It's twelve-thirty now," Miss Morton finally whispered to her employer.

LeDoux said aloud, "In one minute, my friends, we will adjourn."

Unlocking the door of the cabinet, he brought out a bottle and a teaspoon. He measured a teaspoonful of liquid into the blue tumbler and added a small quantity of water.

"Bitters are excellent for the digestion," he declared, raising the tumbler to his lips. "Usually they are quite harmless. On rare occasions, however, it is not so."

He drained the glass and restored it bottom upward to the tray. For a single instant no one stirred. Then Preston jumped quickly to his feet.

"Mr. Chairman, I move we adjourn."

The motion was carried unanimously.

PART THREE
DANGER! *POISON!*

The house, halfway up a hill on a cleared level resembling an enormous step, was a big two-story residence, "American Mediterranean" in style, blue shutters and window frames contrasting with gleaming walls the color of cream cheese. From the highway, its terraced gardens appeared nearly as inaccessible as an eagle's eyrie.

A graveled drive rose steeply to garages hollowed like air-raid shelters into the hillside; from these a flight of stone stairs mounted to the court. The house was built in the form of a square-sided *U*, closed at the mouth by the wire fence which segregated it from the uncultivated brush of the hills. The stone-paved court was adorned by dagger-pointed agaves, by a covered swing and stone benches, by a table beneath a giant scarlet toadstool of an umbrella, by a small open-air swimming pool. Above, at the second-floor level, a balcony with rails and balusters of stained brown wood circuited the three inner sides of the *U*. The effect was rather like the courtyard of a Tibetan lamasery, Westborough mused.

A woman stepped into the patio to greet their large party. "Margaret, this is Mr. West," LeDoux said. "Mr. West, my daughter-in-law."

"You are welcome, sir." She was a harassed dumpling of a woman whose features were an older and coarser edition of Jacynth's. "I think that everything is ready, Father."

A white-jacketed Filipino houseboy served a truly excellent lunch. One could not guess from the menu or from the food that LeDoux's cook was Chinese. The wine was one of the great white burgundies, a Montrachet, 1926. Under its subtle influence tongues loosened, laughter became general. Westborough turned his head at a remark of Derek Esterling's. The chestnut-bearded young chemist was discussing the history of synthetic perfumes.

"Progress may be said to have grown in geometric ratio, after, however, an appallingly slow start. In 1834 Mitscherlich discovered nitrobenzene or essence of mirbane."

"What's that?" Chamaron asked.

"There's some in my lab." Esterling seemed to be a trifle annoyed by the interruption. "The first synthetic aromatic, but not identified as such until 1855. Twenty-one years and nothing accomplished, and for the next thirty years very little more. Fifty years ago the abilities of perfume chemists were

39

limited to the production of artificial oil of almonds, artificial oil of winter-green and a few fruit ethers."

Westborough found the topic of absorbing interest. "And today, Mr. Ester-ling?" he inquired. "How many perfumes may be produced artificially to-day?"

"It is necessary to draw a distinction between synthetically and artificially," Esterling contended. "All blended perfumes – whether extracted from flow-ers or not – are artificial products in a sense. The term 'synthetic' should be applied to the purely chemical products such as heliotropin, terpineol and ionone."

"I beg your pardon," Westborough apologized. "What I meant to ask was how large a proportion of perfumes can be produced synthetically today."

"Practically all of them," the chemist replied.

LeDoux inhaled deeply of the pale wine's subtle bouquet. "The sentence, Derek, should have been qualified by three additional words: *after a fash-ion.*"

"I disagree," Esterling said shortly.

"Are the natural odors considered to be superior to the artificial – I beg your pardon – synthetic odors?"

"Nature is an incomparably more delicate chemist than man," LeDoux maintained.

"Perhaps," Esterling took up the thread. "But where would the perfume industry be if it weren't for the synthetic chemist? Can you extract from the flowers, in adequate quantities for manufacture, the essential oils of helio-trope, lily of the valley, lilac, cyclamen? You know it's impossible. But all of them can be and are manufactured in the laboratory, and I could name others. Violet and jasmine—"

"Jasmine!" LeDoux broke in heatedly. "If the day ever comes when jas-mine flowers are no longer grown—"

"It will come," Esterling declared with assurance. "Synthetic jasmine oil grows better all the time. It's only a question of improved analytical tech-nique."

"I suppose that you are right." LeDoux's finely drawn face expressed in-tense gloom. "Our beautiful blossoming fields" – he waved his hands toward the open french doors – "unnecessary! Our noble art degenerated to a few stinks in a laboratory! Well, I am old, *grâce à Dieu;* my day will soon be ended."

"Gran'-père!" Jacynth called solicitously. "You mustn't talk like that. Oh, you mustn't!"

Her anxious glance banished completely one monstrous suspicion from Westborough's brain.

Immediately after the meal, while they were strolling into the living room,

LeDoux caught Westborough's arm. "Have you seen our gardens?" He propelled the guest quickly outside.

Below a broad brick promenade the gardens descended in a series of three terraces. LeDoux led the way down a flight of steps to the bottom level, some fifty feet above the highway, where a hedge of hibiscus flamed in gigantic blossoms.

"We can talk a few minutes in safety," the perfumer said.

"Didn't you take an appalling chance?" Westborough asked.

"I think not. The glass was empty; you may be sure I ascertained that. As for the pitcher – do you recall that I sent my granddaughter for fresh water?"

"Yes, but the bitters?"

"The bottle, m'sieur, was in a locked cabinet. A cabinet to which I alone possess the key. No, I took no chances. Did you know the reason for my—"

"Gasconade," Westborough suggested. "I endeavored, I hoped, to make the most of the opportunity which you so courageously provided."

"And you saw?"

"Your secretary suppress a slight shudder."

"That means nothing," LeDoux asserted confidently. "She has natural grounds for suspicion. She alone. Except, of course, one other person. You saw nothing else?"

"Nothing at all significant."

"Nor did I. Our poisoner is well able to control the facial expressions."

"It would appear so," Westborough agreed. "Dear me. Rarely have I encountered a more perplexing human problem than this one promises to be. So many suspects, so few clues, no motive of any description. I thank you for bringing so absorbing a case to my attention." He smiled gently. "But perhaps you will not thank me."

"I do not believe you will fail."

"In the bright lexicon of youth – the quotation is scarcely germane. We may, I believe, reduce the number of suspects by four. Mr. Preston may be eliminated because he did not arrive in time to put the poison into the tumbler before the meeting, and from where he sat it was not possible for him to do so afterward. Miss Morton because she had the unique opportunity to destroy all evidence of poisoning and did not do so. Mr. Grayne because he was at that time a total stranger to you and your family. And your granddaughter because – dear me! That so lovely a child could plot so foul a crime is beyond all reason. May I ask," he inquired with apparent irrelevance, "if the aromatic principle of a plant may be contained in its roots?"

"In some cases. Angelica and vertivert, for instance, and, of course, orris root."

"The classical Greeks of Elis and Corinth were renowned for unguents of orris," Westborough remarked. "I was referring specifically to the Carolina yellow jasmine."

"Esterling made no use of the root," LeDoux returned slowly. "He extracted the essential oil from the blossoms with solvents."

"Therefore, Mr. Esterling could have had no legitimate reason to purchase or prepare a tincture of gelsemium?"

"None."

"Dear me. I should like very much to look into Mr. Esterling's laboratory."

"You suspect—"

"As yet nothing," Westborough interrupted quickly. "Nor must others be given the opportunity to suspect *our* intentions. The matter should be handled in the most casual manner possible."

"Suppose I were to suggest to my guests that we precede the afternoon's business session with a tour of the plant? Culminating, of course, in the laboratory."

"A splendid idea."

"No one is working there today. Kelton, Esterling's assistant, is away on vacation. When I steer the party from the room, could you—"

"Contrive to remain behind?" Westborough finished. "Yes, that will make an excellent beginning. But let us not delude ourselves that—Dear me! Here comes your granddaughter."

Jacynth ran lightly down the stairs. "What is keeping you so long, Gran'-père? Don't you know that all of your guests are impatiently waiting?"

"Tyrant," LeDoux laughed. "I was only showing Mr. West our flowers. He says that the hibiscus are beautiful."

"I don't like them; they're almost scentless." Jacynth buried her small nose in a mammoth rose bloom as she spoke. "A flower without scent is like something made out of cloth and cardboard. Scent is the real life of a flower, don't you think?"

"I believe you are right," Westborough acknowledged. He found her charming. She displayed a deference to gray hairs surprising in an age when grace and manners seem to be headed fast for civilization's dump heap. Jacynth had been convent educated, he recalled; doubtless that accounted for her rather old-fashioned courtesy.

She slipped her hand confidingly on her grandfather's arm as they ascended the stairs. "Gran'-père, why don't Derek and Mr. Grayne like each other?"

"I haven't noticed that they don't," LeDoux answered.

"It's very plain to me. Why, they hardly ever speak to each other!"

"But, *chérie*, they are practically strangers."

"Strangers?" Jacynth echoed. "I wonder. Mr. Grayne was born in South Carolina, and Derek lived there a long, long time."

"My dear child, that is no guarantee at all that they could be previously acquainted. Presumably a great many people live in South Carolina."

"Yes," she returned, "but when two people from the same state are introduced away from home, they are usually awfully pleased to meet each other. Isn't that so, Mr. West?"

The historian agreed that it was. He also thought (though he did not voice the reflection aloud) that for nineteen years Jacynth LeDoux was rather a shrewd judge of human nature.

II

"The jasmine smell is pleasing, is it not?" LeDoux asked of the guests who strolled with him between the rows of fragrant shrubs. "But we turn in disgust from the stench of rotting fish. Why is it so?" He shrugged expressively. "The world holds not one man wise enough to say. Odor, ah, it is an indefinable! Like electricity, *hein?*"

The perfume maker owned substantial orange groves. He cultivated roses and tuberoses in quantities, but above all else he raised jasmine, the Catalonian or Spanish jasmine of the Var flower farms, the renowned *grandiflorum*. Japanese girls, wicker baskets strapped across their shoulders, were plucking with both hands at the drooping branches. The great white clusters emanated a delicate sweetness, waves of odor surging as insinuatingly against the brain as the echo of a well-loved melody.

"You will remember this day," LeDoux prophesied. "Sounds may be forgotten, pictures and color tones lost, but scents linger forever in the memory. Why, I do not know, but I assure you that it is true. A single whiff of jasmine perfume will restore the sight of these fields again."

The party had split tacitly into tiny subgroups. Grayne and Westborough, as the two strangers, had been naturally selected for the host's special care. Jacynth walked with Esterling; Preston was with Mrs. Chamaron, and Chamaron with Miss Morton. Pleading the responsibilities of a hostess, Mrs. LeDoux had asked to remain at home, and Todd had said gruffly that he preferred a nap on the davenport in LeDoux's office to the afternoon heat of the flower fields.

They returned at a leisurely pace to the factory, a rambling one-story edifice with a Spanish tile roof. A curving drive flanked by ashen-gray olive trees led to the front entrance. A neat green lawn surrounded the premises, and honeysuckle and bougainvillaea clung to the stucco walls. "You provide a most attractive place in which to work," Westborough commented.

"To create beauty, we must labor in an atmosphere of beauty, *n'est-ce pas?*" LeDoux's face held the fondness of a parent gazing on his dearest child.

They paused momentarily in the cool of the checking shed to watch the pickers' baskets being weighed. "Pounds and pounds of flowers are gathered every day!" LeDoux exclaimed. "Would you like to see what becomes of them all?"

"Very much so," Westborough replied in behalf of his companions. United once more (except for Todd), they entered a large and very well-lighted room containing many rows of long tables. At each table half-a-dozen girls were painstakingly placing the star-petaled blossoms on long glass trays coated thickly with grease.

"One cannot use force against a flower," LeDoux asserted. "To crush the bloom would yield nothing. The jasmine surrenders its scent slowly, as it dies."

"The perfume material exists in the form of a gradually decomposing glucosidal compound," Esterling enlightened them.

LeDoux added a few technical details concerning the process.

"Odor is absorbed by fat: that is the basis of the *enfleurage*, perfected by generations of French perfumers. We use a mixture of purified tallow and lard, the *corps*. Each tray or *chassis* is in a frame, as you see; when the trays are stacked one above the other they form a series of nearly airtight boxes. The labor is tedious, *mon Dieu!* We must change the flowers every twenty-four hours, and it takes about fifty days to produce the best grade of jasmine pomade. Three pounds of flowers scent but one pound of fat *corps*, and that is nothing! We must have four pounds of pomade for every gallon of alcohol used in the manufacture of jasmine extract."

"Now do you see why perfumes cost dough?" Preston demanded jocularly. "Pure floral perfumes are just about worth their weight in gold. No kidding, folks."

"For under fifty dollars a pound," Esterling broke in, "we can buy the very best synthesis of the absolute jasmine. We could make a jasmine oil ourselves for considerably less than that. Manufacturing costs could be cut enormously."

"Quality would suffer," LeDoux declared.

"Only so keen a nose as your own, sir, is able to detect the difference. In time all perfumes will be synthetics. Nothing can stop it."

The Frenchman's shoulders drooped with seeming fatigue. "Jasmine and rose," he said, as if his chief chemist had not spoken, "are the two most important floral odors in perfumery; we use them to round out almost any bouquet. Violet, *hélas*, has waned in popularity, but we still make an excellent violet blend. Come, I will show you."

A genuine violet fragrance, extracted wholly from the blossoms of *viola odorata*, is perhaps the most expensive of all perfumes, Westborough learned with interest. In the manufacture of LeDoux's *Violux* the costly pomade extract was supplemented by chemicals. The violet pomade was not essential at all, Esterling contended.

LeDoux answered sharply. Employer and employee might have posed for statues labeled Tradition and Progress, Westborough reflected. … No, he reconsidered, the difference was not quite so obvious. Esterling was the scientist, realistic and efficient; LeDoux the instinctive artist. … Jacynth took her grandfather's side in the dispute.

The understanding between the old man and the young girl was very powerful. It was Esterling who was made to appear the outsider, the intruder. But the alien was Jacynth's fiancé. … The historian realized that his mind had found a circular track and was traveling around and around in the same groove.

He knew nothing, really; nothing as yet. Fresh evidence must be collected and sifted, sifted most thoroughly before he would dare to venture an opinion, even to himself.

They had to go outdoors again to reach Esterling's laboratory, which stood apart from the main building and could be entered only by walking the length of a large greenhouse. The sun streaming through the glass panes spun an agreeable tapestry of light and shadow. Westborough sniffed the pleasant earthy freshness of green things pushing from moist soil.

"What does your garden grow?" he asked, smiling.

"Flowers for experimental purposes." Esterling had stepped naturally into the role of cicerone.

"Such flowers as the Carolina yellow jasmine?"

By way of answer, Esterling pointed to a shrub about eighteen inches high, bearing small glossy pointed leaves. "That's one of the plants. You should have seen it a few weeks ago! But the flowers vanished in a hurry."

"Did you use the root as well as the flowers in your experiments?" Westborough asked cautiously. He noted that the chemist seemed genuinely puzzled by the query.

"The root? Why, no. There isn't any odorous principle connected with that." Esterling reached into his trousers' pocket for the key to the laboratory.

"That would appear to be a very good pin-tumbler lock," Westborough said conversationally. "Might one ask what valuables are stored within?"

Esterling turned his head, his manner conveying a trace of annoyance. "You will have to ask Mr. LeDoux that question."

"All of the essential oils are stored in the basement vaults," LeDoux informed them. "And they are costly, *mon Dieu!* Some, as our friend Sam has said, are worth their weight in gold. But why do we make the delay in entering, Derek?"

Gratings of bars had been placed on the outside of all the laboratory windows, Westborough saw at once. The isolated building was very nearly burglarproof. A huge table in the center of the single big room appeared loaded to the gunwale with glass funnels, vats, flasks, retorts, test-tube holders,

Bunsen burners, a number of bottles and a huge glass condenser. Inspecting this paraphernalia of the chemist's craft, Westborough was moved to quotation:

> *"Now that I, tying thy glass mask tightly,*
> *May gaze thro' these faint smokes curling whitely,*
> *As thou pliest thy trade in this devil's-smithy –*
> *Which is the poison to poison her, prithee?"*

"Poison?" Esterling's voice seemed to hold a faintly uneasy note. "We don't deal in those here, Mr. West."

"Dear me," Westborough said mildly. "I am almost certain that I heard you mention essence of mirbane at luncheon."

"Oh, that! I'd forgotten." The chemist stared abstractedly at a folding cot standing untidily against one wall. "It's quite dead here today," he said after a few seconds. "My assistant's away on his vacation."

Esterling resented the invasion of his little kingdom, perhaps. Scrutinizing the array of cabinets, Westborough saw at a glance that all doors were closed. He tried one, found it unlocked, and, in order not to appear too inquisitive, immediately transferred his attention to the rubber aprons hanging along a wall.

"Perhaps our guests would like to see where the essential oils are stored," LeDoux suggested. Esterling moved aside the room's single small rug, disclosing a trap door. While he was unlocking it with another key, LeDoux sauntered casually toward the rubber aprons.

"Your opportunity, *mon ami*," he whispered briskly. "Be warned when you hear the words 'oil of jasmine.' "

"A most fascinating workshop," Westborough replied in ordinary conversational tones.

Esterling, lifting the trap door, had revealed a ladder staircase. "The oils have to be kept in a cool dark place," he explained. "Otherwise they will deteriorate. Our storeroom's below."

"An Aladdin's cave," LeDoux added with a chuckle. "But do not expect to smell any marvelous odors in it. The concentrated essences are terrible, *parbleu!* One would never believe that in dilute state they become delicate perfumes. You lead the way, Derek, please."

Alone in the laboratory, Westborough scuttled quickly to the nearest cabinet. The shelves were filled with so many bottles it did not seem that it would be possible for him even to read the labels in the short time at his disposal. That, however, he did not attempt. Moving the bottles gently, he commenced to search the space at the back of each shelf. The four cabinets held a great many shelves to be thus explored, but fortune took a hand in the quest. He made his discovery in the first cabinet.

The little bottle lurked unseen behind taller comrades in the middle of the third shelf. Taking care to hold it only by the rim of the neck, he drew it from its hiding place. The inscription was typewritten on the printed label of a Los Angeles wholesale druggist:

FLUIDEXTRACTUM GELSEMII
Contents: 2 Fluid Ounces
Danger! POISON! ! !

"Dear me," Westborough observed inadequately. He made a mental note of the name and address of the druggist. The find had been made just in time, it seemed, for LeDoux's voice was now ascending audibly from the basement storeroom.

"The odor is strong, narcotic. Do not smell it, I beg of you. You will not like it, and it may give you a headache. It is not good to smell the undiluted oil of jasmine."

Westborough hurriedly restored the gelsemium to the rear of the cabinet shelf.

III

Margaret LeDoux (née Margaret Hawkins) was wrinkling her forehead at the little desk in her father-in-law's study where she sometimes sat to plan the intricate business of running the household. Did she run it, or did Father LeDoux run it, or did Lung Fu? Margaret could never be quite sure.

She looked five to ten years older than her chronological age. Ugly gray streaks marred the brown of her hair. Margaret never dyed them. She didn't care that she had grown into a dumpy little frump. Life had been cruel to her, so terribly cruel that after twenty years her scarred soul still shrank from contacts with the outer world. She was ill at ease with all except three: Jacynth, Father LeDoux and, lately, Derek.

Of the three, Derek understood her the best, she often fancied. Jacynth was too young, Father LeDoux too lofty and inaccessible, but the gulf between Margaret's forty years and Derek's twenty-nine was easily bridgeable. Derek was considerate and attentive, an unfailing gentleman. Sometimes he reminded her a great deal of Raoul, though no one could ever be so gallant, so tender. Raoul! He had swept her whole being into the whirlwind of his passion before he had walked to his death with a song. ... After twenty years why must she keep eternally dwelling on that one memory?

She saw again the fog closing like a giant hand over the little cottage which had sheltered their love. She would never be able to get the sight out of her mind. Never, never. It was etched on her brain in letters of fire, that nightmare of blood and terror. She made a determined effort to concentrate all of her thoughts on Father LeDoux's guests.

She sighed. There were so many of them! Eight extra people to entertain from Monday through Friday – why, it was like managing a small hotel! She didn't mind the extra work it made her, if only the servants didn't complain.

Lung Fu probably wouldn't. He enjoyed cooking and would go to any amount of trouble to please those who were properly appreciative of his artistry. Manuel, however, might turn sullen. Secretly she was a little frightened of the Filipino houseboy, who always made her think of a slick brown monkey.

Normally Manuel was courteous, obliging, amazingly efficient. He overlooked nothing, neglected nothing and asked little in return, but Margaret could never bring herself to trust him. The California prejudice against Orientals? No, she had no prejudice at all against Lung Fu, who, behind the yellow mask of his Chinese reserve, she recognized as a lovable human being. Lung Fu she could understand, but not Manuel. The very way he stole about the house, silent as a shadow … Idly she wondered how Manuel and Lung Fu got along together.

But she had no time for considerations like these. The problem was still unsolved, the problem over which she had pored most of the afternoon. How to put eleven persons into eight bedrooms.

The luggage now stacked along the front hall mutely testified to her inefficiency in room planning. It was the luggage belonging to Sam and Beatrice and Derek, Mr. Todd and Mr. West. The Chamarons were already settled in the front bedroom next to the upstairs sitting room. They had driven in last night, with Mr. Grayne, and the problem had been vastly simpler then.

Did the Chamarons really get along as well together as they seemed to? Margaret was doubtful. Kay was too smart, too clever. A woman – at least in public – should display a degree of deference to her husband's opinions, but Kay – and Paul Michael was a fine man, too! Kay Chamaron was letting her business success go to her head, Margaret pronounced judgment. Some women weren't able to stand an uninterrupted run of being praised and flattered. Well, this wasn't settling anything.

Mr. Grayne was at present the sole occupant of the room next to the Chamarons', and the room contained twin beds. Should she put Derek in there? Why not? They were approximately the same age, both Carolinians (at least Derek had lived in South Carolina for a long time); by all known rules they should get along beautifully together. Some hostess instinct whispered to her that they wouldn't. Derek didn't like Mr. Grayne, she believed; it wouldn't be a good idea to force them to be roommates.

However, there had to be three doubling ups; mathematically, there wasn't any other solution. The Chamarons were one unit settled, but there must be two more. Why not pair Mr. West and Mr. Todd? No, old men were likely to have hidden defects, such as false teeth, which they weren't anxious to reveal to strangers. Besides, Mr. Todd was so cranky that it seemed a shame to inflict him on nice mild-mannered little Mr. West.

Rather a pity that Sam and Beatrice weren't married, Margaret reflected with one of her rare flashes of humor. Another married couple would simplify matters greatly. But Sam (no one who had known him longer than half an hour ever called him anything but Sam) had a wife visiting in Kansas City, and Beatrice probably would never marry.

Poor Beatrice! She was getting on now, close to twenty-eight. Such a nice girl deserved something better out of life, one would think, but maybe Beatrice actually liked office work. She had a very responsible position with Father LeDoux and she earned a fine salary, even if she did spend most of it in taking care of her mother and helping her brother's large family. Fred Morton's three children were like leeches draining Beatrice's purse. But Beatrice never seemed to complain. These vaporings were getting one nowhere.

Beatrice, naturally, would have to have a room to herself. Not naturally, either; she could share Jacynth's. Or Jacynth could move into her mother's room and surrender her own to Beatrice. But Jacynth liked being alone. ... Mrs. LeDoux raised discouraged eyes to the well-stocked bookcases.

Half of the titles were in French. Father LeDoux had never neglected his native tongue; and Jacynth had been bilingual, almost from her first baby words. There was very little Hawkins in Jacynth, Margaret mused, half regretfully, half proudly. She was all LeDoux, just like her father, just like – *Raoul!*

The cottage where they had spent their three days as husband and wife ... Oh, but she mustn't think of it!

She wondered (as she had wondered for twenty years) if Father LeDoux had objected to his son's hasty marriage. Raoul had never told her. When she first met Father LeDoux he had been kind. Then, as always. There was no kindness in the world like the enormous and never-failing kindness of Etienne LeDoux.

Fog closing like a clammy invisible hand above the honeymoon cottage on the bluff above the sea ... But she must try to forget. She must think only of her problem. Perhaps ...

Derek came into the study, whistling rather nervously. "Sherry is being served in the living room," he told her.

"Yes, I know," Margaret said absently. "Nobody will miss me."

"I always miss you," he countered. "You look worried, little lady. Something on your mind?"

Derek was always so thoughtful! She could take her troubles to Derek, and he wouldn't laugh as the others did sometimes, Jacynth and her grandfather.

"I'm nearly frantic," she confessed, breathing, however, more easily than she had for hours. "Everybody's luggage still in the hall! What will they think? But eleven people! And only eight bedrooms. I simply haven't been able to decide what to do."

"A tough nut, all right," Derek agreed, properly sympathetic. "Well, let's try to figure something out."

"I thought that perhaps Jacynth could move into my room," Margaret hazarded.

"I don't see why you or Jacynth or Mr. LeDoux should be put to any inconvenience," Derek returned. "Let me see, five extra bedrooms. One for the Chamarons leaves four. Four rooms for – Sam, Beatrice, Todd, West, myself, Grayne – six. Put Grayne and Sam together, and I'll bunk over at the lab."

"You can't stay there," she objected.

"Why not?" He whistled a few more bars – a sort of waltz tune that she didn't recognize. "There's a cot."

"Bedding?" she asked doubtfully. "Of course, we could—"

"Oh, the lab has everything necessary," he interrupted. "I often spend the night when I've been working late on an experiment and don't want to bother to run back to town. Call it settled, shall we? Now are you going to join us in the living room?"

"Perhaps, later. I'll have to tell Manuel where the luggage should go. Oh, dear! So many people!"

"So many people, so much trouble," Derek said gravely. "Poor little lady!"

IV

"Since Eve ate apples," Byron once observed, "much depends on dinner." This being unquestionably true, it was scarcely surprising that the talk in the living room had turned strongly upon food.

"I tell you," Preston proclaimed dogmatically, "you can't beat Frisco for restaurants. Hundreds of 'em, every single one grade A-1."

Chamaron nodded agreement. "There's one I particularly remember, a French restaurant on Pine Street. Camille's Rotisserie." He relaxed blissfully in his chair. "A filet mignon two inches thick, buried under a sauce of marrow and mushrooms. Ah, and the salad! Such dressing as only the French can mix."

"You eat too much," snarled Aaron Todd. "Digging your grave with your teeth!"

"But don't you think," Kay Chamaron sweetly interrupted the stricken silence, "that it's as pleasant a way to die as any?"

"I'm a moderate eater," Todd cackled. "Always was. I've lived eighty years, too. That's more than anyone else here can say."

"Yes, indeed," LeDoux intervened with polished ease. "Speaking of restaurants, my friends, may I mention Antoine's?"

"*Huitres en coquille à la Rockefeller!*" Westborough cried ecstatically.

"*Pompano en papillote*," LeDoux added. "And let us not forget *pommes soufflées – mon Dieu*, what savory morsels! There is no cooking in the United States to compare with that of New Orleans."

"Charleston's cooking isn't so bad," drawled Stuart Grayne. "Evah sample she-crab soup?"

"Sea crab?" Preston emended.

"*She*-crab," Grayne insisted. "And there's shrimp pie and shrimp soup and shrimp pilau – all mighty tasty. But a good pine bahk stew, that, ladies and gentlemen, is something to dream about."

"The stew is made of pine bark?" LeDoux asked curiously. "But how odd!"

"The stew is the *color* of pine bahk, sir," Grayne corrected. It's a soht of fish chowdah, made in a Dutch oven. Put a layer of fried onions at the bottom. Cover them with hot water. Add a layer of fish, a layer of sliced potatoes, another layer of onions, another layer of fish, and so on, covering them all with water. Season and let simmer, while you make a sauce of melted butter and Worcestershire and catsup and pepper and curry powdah. Then ladle the stew into the sauce and cook together till brown. You may then prepare yo'self for a feast."

"A delicious one, undoubtedly!" Westborough exclaimed. "Dear me, I am reminded of Thackeray's delightful ballad:

> *"This Bouillabaisse a noble dish is –*
> *A sort of soup, or broth, or brew,*
> *Or hotchpotch of all sorts of fishes ..."*

"Ah, the bouillabaisse!" LeDoux broke in delightedly. "Lung Fu does not do too badly with it. Perhaps—" He glanced at his watch and shook his head regretfully. "*Hélas*, there is not time tonight. But tomorrow, I promise you. Tomorrow night, *mes amis*, you shall taste a Chinese rendering of our great French dish."

Strolling in from the hall, Esterling crossed the room to speak confidentially to Chamaron.

"Would you mind stepping out on the terrace?"

"Glad to, old man." Chamaron excused himself from the company.

They descended the garden stairs to the second level. Chamaron offered his cigarette case, and they smoked for a minute or two silently. The advertising man could (and did on numerous occasions) chatter for an indefinite period about nothing whatsoever. However, he selected his tactics to accord with the psychology of his man. Esterling wasn't a prattler.

"It's about Grayne," the chemist said at length. "How does he happen to be working for you?"

"Quite a story," Chamaron answered. "He was in New York, with Rood and Krau, but they let him go when they lost the Citrus Products account. You know the Citrus Products people? I finally succeeded in selling the idea to them that their advertising ought to be handled locally. Grayne dropped me a line to say that he'd been working on Citrus Products copy for several years and that he wondered if I had anything in the offing. Krump of C.P. spoke highly in his favor, and – well, I did need a man at the time, as a matter of fact."

"Has Grayne made the grade with you, Paul Michael?"

This, Chamaron reflected, was the first time he could remember that Derek Esterling had addressed him by either of his given names.

"Oh yes, Stuart has great ability."

"Where was he before Rood and Krau?"

"Drifting around from job to job," Chamaron answered. "On the streets a good share of the time. The advertising business is tough."

"Is it now?" Esterling smiled. "That's very interesting."

"What's on your mind, Derek?" Chamaron asked.

"I dislike to remind you of the obvious," Esterling remarked, "but I'm not without a certain influence here."

"I know that," Chamaron owned, a trifle uneasy.

"I don't like your profession," Esterling said meditatively. "Nothing personal, you understand. I just don't happen to like it. You make prostitutes out of scientists, for one thing."

Chamaron was well schooled in controlling his temper. Every advertising man has to be.

"Is that why you wanted to talk to me?" he asked.

"Not exactly. Even though I don't like advertising I'll have to admit it's sometimes necessary. And I've got nothing against you personally, Paul Michael."

"Thanks," Chamaron mumbled. "I'm glad to hear it."

"You and I can be friends if you like. It's entirely up to you."

Was the fellow leading up to a request for a loan? It sounded very much like it. Well, if Esterling wanted money he should have any reasonable amount but … Chamaron ground his cigarette butt beneath his heel. He had met them before, these takers and askers of business bribes. Hell was much too good for them, in the considered opinion of Paul Michael Chamaron. What was it Esterling had just said? Advertising makes prostitutes out of scientists? By God, *he* ought to know! A supposedly reputable scientist crying that he was for sale as shamelessly as any bawd. *Prostitutes!*

"My dear fellow," Chamaron said aloud, "if it's a question of temporary financial difficulties, I shall be only too glad to—"

"What the hell do you think I am?" Esterling broke in angrily. "Some cheap chiseler? I've got a favor to ask of you, I'll admit. I want you to fire Grayne."

Chamaron was genuinely astounded. "I can't do that," he made a feeble counter. "Grayne's valuable to me."

"So is the LeDoux Perfume account. All of that" – Esterling's arm swept toward the factory grounds below them – "will be under my control someday."

"I suppose that's true," Chamaron acknowledged, not in the least happy. LeDoux Perfumes had been one of his first accounts and was now his oldest. It had been profitable to him financially, and in losing it, he would lose a prestige of even greater value than the lost commissions. Advertising agencies are sometimes (by no means always) erected upon a flimsy structure of faith, hope and charity. Remove the key card of faith, and the whole pasteboard edifice crumbles. Chamaron had seen the tragedy happen to others. He didn't intend that it should happen to him.

"What have you got against Stuart?" he sparred.

"My business." Esterling's features had hardened into a face of concrete.

"But my dear fellow! Turning a man out of a job in these times is like throwing him to the wolves. I can't do that without cause. It's – it's inhuman!"

"In this case it's justified. You can take my word for it."

"You met him for the first time about two weeks ago."

"I've known him since I was five years old. We were friends for fifteen years. Close friends."

"What happened?"

"That's between him and me," Esterling retorted sullenly.

"Why do you hate him?"

"It's not a question of hate."

"It *is* a question of hate – and malice and spite and personal vindictiveness." Chamaron, carried away by the warmth of his feelings, was speaking rather strongly. "What did Stuart do to you?"

"I found him out." Esterling plucked a long pointed leaf from an oleander. "He has personality, I'll admit. Charming with the ladies and a man's man among men. You like him. So does your wife."

"Leave my wife out of it," Chamaron ordered sharply.

"Women find him irresistible," the chemist continued pointedly. "And men

– well, I fairly worshiped him for fifteen years. Until—" He shredded his leaf. "Beneath the polished South Carolina gentleman is a primitive savage. I'm telling you the strict truth. Grayne's basic instincts are those of a murderer."

V

"I don't believe it," Kay Chamaron protested. She was creaming her face at the dressing table, while her husband, flat on his back in striped silk pajamas, forced his legs through the motions of riding a bicycle. "You can never make me believe anything like that against Stuart."

Chamaron parked the imaginary vehicle and sat on the edge of his bed. "Esterling has some kind of ax to grind, all right."

"And you're going to turn the grindstone?"

"I didn't tell him I would."

"And you didn't tell him you wouldn't." Kay removed the excess cream with a facial tissue and wheeled to face her husband. The soft rose of her negligee had transferred its glow to her naturally pale skin. "What *are* you going to do, Paul Michael?"

"Esterling can do us a lot of harm," Chamaron reminded her.

"Esterling is a snake," Kay returned peremptorily.

Chamaron found the whisky he had foresightedly packed in his bag. "Like a bedtime nip?"

"Without a chaser?" she shuddered. "Thanks, no."

"This is the kind that doesn't need a chaser." Chamaron tilted the bottle to his lips. "It's been treated so you can drink it straight. Clever idea! I wish I were handling the advertising."

"Let's stick to the point," his wife suggested.

"What is the point, Kay?" Chamaron screwed on the cap and put the bottle back.

"You know very well what I'm talking about. Stuart. It's a question of justice."

"Is that all?" he asked, watching the color surging faintly to his wife's throat.

"Paul Michael, you are perfectly impossible!"

"Look in the mirror," Chamaron directed. "Do you see that woman?"

Kay made a face at the reflection. "Ugly wench, isn't she? Cheekbones like an Indian's."

"No slander," Chamaron cautioned. "I happen to love that woman."

She patted her husband's hand, not unfondly. "Rather a nasty person, my dear."

"She merely happens to be more intelligent than her husband," Chamaron said.

"Oh no!"

"And at least ten years younger."

"Poor darling! This sudden feeling of inferiority isn't the least like you."

"Like?" he repeated questioningly. "Adjective, conjunction and verb. It's the latter that interests me. Do you like Stuart?"

"Of course."

"How much?"

"Not so well as I do you."

"That," Chamaron said solemnly, "is what I wanted to know."

"If you'd only tell me what you intend to do!"

"If I only knew!"

"I know what I'd do. I'd go straight to Mr. LeDoux."

He shook his head. "Not yet. We're not ready for a showdown."

"Aren't you and I – together – as valuable to him as Esterling?"

"My dear, the woods are full of advertising men. There are even, strange as it may seem, other package designers. But good perfume chemists don't grow on every bush." He climbed under the bedcovers. "And Esterling is engaged to LeDoux's granddaughter. We'd wreck our ship on that rock, sweetheart."

"It's a shame," Kay stormed. "Jacynth is too good for him. Why do women fall in love with the men they do?"

"Why did you fall in love with Stuart?" he demanded bluntly.

"I didn't." Kay climbed into the bed beside her husband's. "Don't you trust me at all, Paul Michael?"

Leaning across the space separating the two beds, he kissed her hair, then her cheek. "Shall I tell you a story? Once there was a little girl who lived on a farm."

"Ranch," she corrected absently.

"She wanted to see life, so she came to the big city and enrolled in an art school. Because she was a clever little girl she won a prize offered by a local manufacturer to encourage what he termed 'useful arts.' So she decided to become a package designer. Then she called at the office of an advertising man to sell him an idea her clever brain had evolved for one of his clients, and he took her to lunch."

"Many times," Kay reminisced. "Dinner, too."

"After three years of buying lunches and dinners he decided it would be cheaper to marry her."

"Hasn't it been?"

"He didn't make a very romantic husband, I'm afraid."

"He's been a satisfactory husband."

POISON JASMINE

"And then along came a tall dark man from the South, just her age."
"Stuart is three years younger."
"So for the first time," he concluded gently, "love entered her life of toil."
"It isn't true!" she protested. "I love you, Paul Michael."
Chamaron reached over to switch off the light.

VI

Westborough turned from the hall into the room which had been assigned to him. It was a pleasant room. Small blue forget-me-nots sprinkled the wallpaper; a taffeta spread covered the bed, and the furniture was comfortable. He was fortunate to have a room to himself; the house was dreadfully crowded.

He folded the coat of his linen suit neatly over a hanger in the closet. The little man was always tidy with his clothes. He was about to unknot his tie when the door opened abruptly. As softly as a shadow, LeDoux glided into the room.

Westborough said mildly, "I rather expected to see you tonight."

"It is natural that a host should be anxious concerning the comfort of his guests," LeDoux declared in a low voice. "Is everything satisfactory, m'sieur?"

"More than satisfactory."

"I did not exaggerate concerning my cook?"

"Your cook is a true artist."

LeDoux turned the key of the hall door very quietly. "Did you discover anything in Derek's laboratory?"

Westborough admitted a little reluctantly, "I am sorry to say that I did."

"Gelsemium?"

"A two-ounce bottle of the fluidextract. I estimated that about a teaspoonful had been used."

"*Belle-de-nuit!* Is that a fatal dose?"

"It might be fatal. Gelsemium is an acute poison."

LeDoux sank into a chair, his face waxen. "*Parbleu*, can there be a shadow of doubt? That knave, that scoundrel, that assassin! He shall answer for his crime tonight."

"A poisoner is the most contemptible of created beings," Westborough sympathized. "But the natural warmth of our feelings must not blind us to justice. There are others who could have done this thing besides Mr. Esterling."

"And hidden the poison in his laboratory? The laboratory to which he alone has the key?"

"He alone?" Westborough echoed. "Is that literally true?"

"Derek's assistant also has a key," LeDoux admitted. "But Kelton cannot be involved. He was not in my office that morning."

"Can you be sure of that fact?"

"*Certainement!*"

"You do not have a key yourself?" Westborough inquired. The question proved to be disgruntling, he saw. LeDoux kindled immediately.

"Is it that I am suspected of poisoning myself?"

"Dear me," Westborough answered meekly. "I merely asked if you had your own key to the laboratory. Surely that is a natural inquiry?"

"I have no key. In the whole world there are only two such keys in existence. Ask Derek if it is not so. There is no one else who could have done this frightful thing. No one but Derek."

"I am sorry that I cannot agree."

"You think he is innocent?" LeDoux demanded incredulously. "How can it be possible?"

"Some other person may be using the laboratory as a convenient cache."

"But the lock, m'sieur? One cannot escape from that."

"The lock offers difficulties, I own, but perhaps not insuperable ones. There are ways in which locks may be illegitimately opened."

LeDoux raised his fine aristocratic head. "May I ask if you have positive reason for believing Derek Esterling to be innocent?"

"One excellent reason. The trail has been too clear."

"I do not understand your logic."

"Would Esterling, for example, employ gelsemium, the one poison to be associated with his experiments with the Carolina jessamine?"

"Why not?" LeDoux demanded. "He alone would be likely to know of it."

"But one does not write one's name in the room in which one has committed a crime," the historian contended.

"Vanity might induce one to do that very thing. Vanity coupled with a warped brain."

"Esterling's brain is not warped," Westborough disputed. "He is a keenly intelligent scientist. Granted that he is morally capable of killing by poison – though I have seen nothing to warrant such an assumption – he would use arsenic, strychnine, anything which would not reflect back to him personally."

"Perhaps he could not obtain arsenic or strychnine."

"Dear me, but he could!" Westborough exclaimed. "It is not difficult. One buys in a seed store, merely by tucking it under one's arm and paying for it, a vermin killer which contains a small percentage of strychnine. A chemist of Mr. Esterling's ability would probably find the separation of toxic agent from filler an easy task, and it would be difficult, if not impossible, ever to trace the source. Arsenic is readily purchased. One walks into a pharmacy where one is not personally known; one says, 'I want an ounce or two of sodium arsenate to kill ants.' One signs a false name in the poison book. ... What procedure could be simpler? Yet with these baneful substances readily available, Mr. Esterling needs must use the one poison peculiarly qualified to direct an accusing finger in his direction. More! He afterward allows the bottle to remain in his laboratory, hidden so carelessly that a casual search brings it to light within three minutes. Worse than stupid, moronic! You will pardon me if I do not believe it of Mr. Esterling."

"What *do* you believe?" LeDoux asked.

"As yet I preserve an open mind. The bottle bore the label of a wholesale druggist in Los Angeles. The Davis Wholesale Drug Company on South Figueroa Street. Is the firm known to you?"

"But naturally. Davis is our most important Los Angeles jobber."

Westborough lifted his eyebrows. "Dear me, I had no idea. Perhaps that fact may be significant. At any rate, I have taken steps. This afternoon I wrote to a friend in Los Angeles; wrote, I might add, in your own office, under pretense of making a memorandum of the business proceedings. Your secretary was kind enough to furnish an envelope, and I inserted the letter myself in the bag of outgoing mail, as I did not wish anyone to see the address."

"Who is this mysterious friend?" the perfumer inquired.

"Captain Albert Cranston, of the Bureau of Investigation of the sheriff's department. I had the great pleasure of being associated with him a year ago in the case on Mr. Paphlagloss' island. "

"I know of your work on that case," LeDoux said. "What is it that you wrote?"

"I asked him to trace the purchase of two fluid ounces of fluidextract of gelsemium which had been bought at the Davis Company some time prior to June fifteenth, possibly by someone connected with LeDoux Perfumes, Incorporated. That is all."

"*C'est bon!*" LeDoux exclaimed. "You have done well."

"Unfortunately tomorrow is a holiday; Captain Cranston will not receive my missive until the fifth. But I stressed the need of prompt attention, and his bureau is efficient. I think we may safely count on receiving an answer by Thursday morning."

"What kind of an answer is it you expect?"

"With luck, a description of the person who bought the gelsemium. In the meantime," Westborough paused, "may I make a suggestion? Treat Mr. Esterling exactly as if nothing had occurred."

"You ask a great deal, *mon Dieu!*" LeDoux spluttered. "Though it is difficult for me to play the hypocrite, that I might do, but my little Jacynth? Must I allow the engagement to continue?"

"Dear me, how can it be broken?" Westborough asked. "You must assume that Mr. Esterling is innocent until his guilt is proved."

"I cannot do it," LeDoux demurred. "*Ce n'est pas possible!*"

"Only for a day," the historian pleaded. "If Mr. Esterling bought the poison we shall know the fact without fail. He is, fortunately, of distinctive appearance."

LeDoux touched his beard, the trim pointed beard of a Frenchman. "You mean this, m'sieur?"

"Exactly," Westborough said.

PART FOUR
VIOLETS AND BOUILLABAISSE

Stuart Grayne didn't see any reason why he shouldn't open the Fourth of July with a dip in his host's swimming pool. He sprang high into the air and doubled up into a jackknife. Hitting the water with the speed of a torpedo, he coasted just above the concrete bottom until his body's natural buoyancy impelled him to the surface. A few strokes brought him to the shallow end. He turned and swam back again, arms and legs moving effortlessly in the rhythmic precision of his crawl. After about fifteen minutes of the pleasurable exercise, he became aware that someone else had dived into the pool.

It was that nice kid, Esterling's fiancée. "Hello," he called, burying his head in the water's coolness. "Hello," she answered as he emerged for a gulp of air. Beneath a red bathing cap her small face was elfin, piquant.

They completed four or five turns, swimming silently. The kid was as much at home in the water as a playful young seal. When they were toweling, he saw that her skin had been burnished by the sun to a golden beige. She had long dark lashes, and her lips were soft and full and red. There was a tiny mole at the back of her right ear, he saw.

It seemed too nice a day to go immediately inside. They lingered by tacit consent at the edge of the pool, chatting about this and that while their bare toes dangled in the sea-green water. Presently he found that he was talking about Charleston.

Part of it was an old story to Jacynth. Derek had told her about it before, but she did not interrupt to say so. Derek had never talked as this black-haired man, whose Southern voice was as soft as the drone of bees.

As if he sensed her love for flowers, he began with the camellias, blooming the winter through in waxy rosettes of cream white, shell pink, deep rose or flamboyant crimson.

"But they die as the azaleas are born. The glory of the azaleas is the glory of a Charleston spring."

"We have azaleas here," she informed him, like a loyal Californian. "Lots of them."

He only smiled. "Not the same as these, I reckon."

He told her of bushes, twenty and twenty-five feet high, so covered by blossoms that not a branch, not a twig, not even the smallest leaf could be seen. Their colors, he said, are all colors: pink, cerise and crimson; magenta, pale orchid and royal purple, even pure white.

"There are whole islands of azaleas in Cypress Gardens. I'd like to take you there during a full moon."

She knew about Cypress Gardens. One sat in a boat which a guide paddled through the old rice plantation that had been transformed into a water garden. Derek had told her all about it.

But Derek hadn't been able to make her see the inky water, jet black and yet so miraculously clear that actual upside-down trees seemed to grow beneath its surface. Derek had told her too of Middleton and Magnolia, but this man brought them to life for her – the great plantation gardens. She wandered with him where mockingbirds sang in woods of moss-draped live oaks.

She was conscious of his body now, of his broad shoulders and well-muscled chest, of his slim waist and flat stomach. But most of all she was conscious of his magician's voice, conjuring from the very air those magnificent pictures.

"There are gardens in the city, too," he said. "Let me tell you ..."

They rang the little bell before the wrought-iron gate of a gabled Georgian house; they swept down a curved staircase from the white-columned piazza into a walled court. She could see white roses and purple wistaria and yellow jessamine as he talked ... the golden bells, so deliciously fragrant, hanging there over old brick walls.

"It's beautiful!" she exclaimed, scarcely daring to breathe lest the dream flowers vanish.

"Inside the ceilings are high, with eighteenth-century molding. A big house and big rooms! The furniture would fetch a fortune at auction, but you may be sure it never will be sold as long as its owner lives. A cut-glass chandelier is suspended in her living room; on special occasions the candles are still lighted."

"Oh!" she cried, her eyes bright. "What's the mistress like?"

He said simply, "An old lady with lace at her throat."

"How nice!"

"You'd find her so, Miss Jacynth. You and she would get along. She believes in old-fashioned things: pride and honor and decency and hospitality and kindliness – all the outmoded virtues that the world's discarded."

She noted the ardent glow suffusing his bronzed face.

"You love Charleston so," she murmured. "Even more than I love Valle de Flores."

"It's my home, honey."

She remembered that she was engaged to Derek, and that this man, Stuart Grayne, had no right to use an endearment. But "honey," she also remembered, was the common pet word of the South. Probably it had come so easily to his tongue that he wasn't even conscious of having used it.

"Why don't you go back there to live?" A little shyly she added, "Stuart."

"When you choose a path, Jacynth, you have to follow it no matter where it leads: up hill, down dale, in New York or out to California. Usually it ends in nothing – most paths seem to do that these days – but it's yours, and you have to keep on it. That's the way the world wags."

She watched him as he lay on his back, looking into the blue over the patio. Above and below the bathing trunks his tanned body was lean and muscular. She turned away to gaze into the pool.

The water, she noted, had become a tranquil emerald. A few minutes ago they had been splashing frantically; now the water was as calm as if that splashing had never been. By things like that one may know the passage of time. It was one of the funny deep thoughts which sometimes came to her.

"Cigarettes would be in my room," he fussed, fumbling through the pockets of his terrycloth robe. "Well, it'll only take a jiffy to run upstairs."

"No, please don't. Things always change somehow when a conversation's been interrupted."

He sat down at once. "For some reason that's true, honey."

Honey again! But Jacynth hated coyness.

"Life's queer," he said, regarding his toes in the pool. "Not a very original observation."

"Not very," she agreed.

"We bring our troubles on ourselves, mostly. I reckon my own tough breaks were just my sins finding me out."

She studied the slope of his forehead, the arched bridge of his nose, the set of his firm mouth. She remarked again the way in which his wavy black hair descended below the temples.

"I don't believe you have any sins, Stuart," she said.

"Oh, I'm a thoroughly bad lot," he insisted. "One of the world's worst tempers, to begin with. It's got me in a mint of trouble."

"Men are so vain! Even if they're meek as mice they like a woman to believe they've had a terrible past."

"Did you learn all about men at St. Bridget's?" he questioned. She saw how his gray eyes were laughing at her.

"Anyway, I do know about them," she maintained, a little provoked. "You, for instance! I'll bet you never did anything really wicked."

"Let's start with gambling," he suggested, still laughing.

"Everybody does that," she argued. "When everyone does a thing it can't be wicked."

"You have the makings of a fine logician about you, Jacynth."

"Do I win the bet?" she demanded.

"Not yet. I'm still wicked."

"Prove it." She was lying on her stomach, her chin resting in her palms. "Name one wicked thing."

"I was in a duel once. That ought to win for me, I reckon."

"A real duel? With swords and pistols?"

"Just pistols."

"I didn't know anybody ever fought duels these days." (But he was like his archaic Charleston; a man out of the past.) "Were you hurt?"

"Not a scratch."

"Was he? The man you fought?"

"Thank heavens, no! I could never have forgiven myself."

"Why did you fight?" she asked.

"Romantic ancestors, I reckon." His laughter held a faintly sardonic tinge. "Your grandfathers can tempt you to all kinds of foolishness. I slapped his face and called him a coward. Then he said he'd meet me."

She sat up, very prim and straight. "How old were you?"

"About as old as you are now."

"A mere boy," she declared scornfully. "Even so, you should have known better. Did you miss him?"

"I never fired."

"I'm glad you came to your senses."

"It wasn't that." His eyes had become stern and proud. "Having started the thing, I had to finish it, naturally. But he threw down his pistol and ran away."

She thought: "Suppose Stuart *had* been killed?" And she was furious with herself for thinking about it. Because she loved Derek. With all her heart, all her mind, she was in love with Derek.

"I'll have to be fair to him," Stuart's voice went on. "When I picked up his pistol I found out something. They are old, old dueling pistols, so old they have to be loaded with ball and powder. There's a little copper percussion cap which the hammer strikes; he'd thrown that cap away. He did it deliberately, I realized afterward, so his pistol would misfire."

"That was brave."

"It was, yes. But then he spoiled it."

"You can't blame him, can you, for not staying there to be killed?" Suddenly she was on her feet. "I know now! It was Derek, wasn't it? That other man?"

"No," he replied, but his face gave him away.

"It was! That's why you and Derek don't speak to each other. I know it."

He said slowly, "If I could lie worth a hoot I'd keep on telling you it wasn't. I don't know how you ever guessed, Miss Jacynth. I didn't mean for you to guess."

"You intended to kill him!"

"Reckon so. At the time."

"That's horrible! You'd shoot a man like a beast."

"It was a duel," he answered lamely.

"A duel!" she flamed. "I'd call it murder."

Turning, she ran into the house.

II

"How sweet you look!" exclaimed Kay Chamaron, who had just that moment entered Jacynth's room. "I love that little Basque blouse on you. And pink is perfect with your deep brown hair. But of course you know that. French girls are born knowing everything about clothes."

Jacynth recalled something Gran'-père had said in a rare moment of cynicism, that when people were unusually nice to you they usually wanted something.

"You look awfully well yourself," she said aloud.

It was true. Kay's dinner gown was a stunning moonstone blue, perfectly suited to her tawny hair and deep blue eyes, but, then, everything that Kay Chamaron wore magically adjusted itself to her personality.

"You flatter me!" Kay laughed, a cool bubble of laughter. "I've been trying to get you to myself all day. I've felt, Jacynth, that I'd like to know you better."

"And I'd like to be friends with you," Jacynth returned. She saw that Kay was using the new golden shade of nail polish, which toned very well with her hair. Kay opened a gold-and-enamel cigarette case.

"We really don't have a very long time before dinner, do we? I'm a nuisance, I know, barging in this way when you're trying to get ready, but I simply had to talk to you. It's frightfully important to me. Paul Michael's my husband, you see!"

"Yes," Jacynth agreed, considerably puzzled.

"He's one of the kindest men on earth. And he's known you since you were nine years old. Isn't that right?"

"I suppose so," Jacynth answered, wishing that Kay would come to the point.

"During all that time he's handled your grandfather's advertising. This account means a lot to him, Jacynth. If he were to lose it, it would almost break his heart."

"But he won't lose it!" Jacynth exclaimed. "Why, Gran'-père wouldn't have any other advertising agent."

"There are others in the business besides your grandfather," Kay declared meaningly.

"Mr. Todd? He owns stock, of course."

"Horrible old man." Kay shuddered.

"I don't like him, either," Jacynth confided. "But you don't need to worry about him. Gran'-père will never—"

"It isn't Mr. Todd."

"Mr. Preston?"

"Sam Preston and Paul Michael are the best of friends, dear. It's Mr. Esterling."

"Derek? I don't understand."

"He has greater influence over your grandfather than any other person."

"He deserves to have," Jacynth replied a trifle stiffly. "There wouldn't be any new Southern Belle perfume if it weren't for Derek."

"True, dear," Kay admitted, "but he shouldn't have anything to do with the advertising."

"He doesn't."

"He thinks he does. He's already threatened Paul Michael with the loss of your grandfather's account."

"Derek can't do that."

"Paul Michael believes he can – at least someday."

"But why?" Jacynth wondered. "I can't see why—"

"Blackmail," Kay interrupted sharply. "He has even mentioned the price."

Jacynth jumped up indignantly, the wide skirt of her pink organdy sweeping the tops of her pink sandals.

"It's true," Kay insisted. "He issued an ultimatum – that's the only word for it. Paul Michael has to discharge Stuart Grayne or take the consequences."

"Oh!" Jacynth said weakly. She sat down, feeling a little shaken inside. More than a little shaken. If it were true, Derek was contemptible. But Derek wasn't contemptible, she knew. Therefore ...

But some instinct told her it was true. That man had tried to kill Derek. That swashbuckling bully with his dueling pistols! Mr. Grayne of Charleston, taking into his own arrogant hands the powers of life and death. Derek had the best of reasons for hating him.

And for whom was Kay Chamaron pleading? Not for pompous Paul Michael, with his plump soft hands and chest like a pouter pigeon. Paul Michael could jump into the Pacific for all his charming, clever wife would care. It wasn't Paul Michael; it was Stuart Grayne. The gallant Mr. Grayne. The killer Mr. Grayne!

"Really," Jacynth answered frigidly, "I don't believe it's any of my affair."

III

Downstairs the male members of the party were enjoying vermouth and bitters in a living room vividly Chinese. Beams of black teak stretched across the ceiling; the lacquer wallpaper was dotted by coolies and mandarins, peach trees and pagodas; there was a flowery Chinese rug and a cinnabar vase and a dragon-carved teak cabinet. All of these *chinoiseries* would undoubtedly have made the room gloomy if it hadn't been for the tremendous view window.

This monstrous lattice of glass squares took up a major portion of an entire wall, overlooking not only the terraced garden but the jasmine fields across the highway below. It was growing a little too dark for jasmine fields, however, and Westborough was glad to return his attention to the conversation of Mr. Samuel Preston.

"Be better with gin," the latter confided, gulping his second vermouth with a wry face. "Between you and me, pal, the French are a backward race."

"I have never found them so," Westborough returned, thankful that his host was some distance away. "What was it you were discussing, Mr. Preston?"

Mr. Preston had been discussing a great many things:

He'd been in France once. Looked like we'd have to go again, didn't it? But he didn't think that the United States should meddle in European affairs. They hadn't paid us for the last war yet. Mr. Preston didn't think much of any European government.

But he didn't think much of the New Deal either. In fact, he thought very little of it. Individual initiative and enterprise were being destroyed, the qualities that made America great. People didn't have any self-respect any more. Look at those loafers on relief!

And look at him, Sam Preston. Perfumes! Hell of a business for a man to be in, wasn't it? There was money in it, though, and the advantage of making one's home in Valle de Flores. Preston and Mrs. Preston and young Wilbur Preston (who was working as lifeguard at a Santa Monica beach this summer) were crazy about Valle de Flores. It was never too hot and never too cold. Did Mr. West know that the temperature didn't vary more than a few degrees from winter to summer? The Chamber of Commerce had the dope. Preston was putting all his savings into real estate. Someday property here was going to be worth real dough. And then he could quit the perfume racket, which, he admitted, was sort of pansyish.

"*Autre temps, autre moeurs*," Westborough murmured. "Napoleon, if I remember rightly, was devoted to eau de cologne. And the use of fragrant oils in ancient Athens was carried to such an extreme, it is said, that Solon promulgated a sumptuary law forbidding their sale to the men. It may be argued that the classical Greeks indulged in practices which today would be called depraved. To a certain extent, that is true. *Tout comprendre, c'est tout pardonner!* But the Romans, one of the most virile races in history, were even more addicted than the Greeks to body fragrance. Slaves would carry the golden vessels of sweet-scented oils and unguents through the streets to the *thermae* where their masters bathed. The perfumers' guild is reputed to have occupied an entire street in Capua."

He saw that Preston was regarding him with considerable interest. Startled, Westborough realized that he had stepped out of character.

"Where'd you learn all that stuff, Ted?" (After some thought Westborough had decided that his first name might be temporarily altered to Theodore.)

"Dear me, I really cannot say. Odds and ends of reading, I presume."

"You could build a swell ad campaign from that angle," the sales manager mused. "Slaves carrying perfumes, dancing girls, all the Cecil B. DeMille stuff. Speaking of advertising, that wife of Paul's is a keen-looking number, huh?"

"Indeed a most attractive woman."

"But if I was Paul I'd tie a can pronto to that fellow's tail." Preston directed a waggish glance across the room toward Stuart Grayne. "Good looks, nice manners and a Southern accent are one hell of a hard combination to buck, old boy."

"Indeed? But surely you do not think—"

Preston proclaimed jocosely, "I think just what you'd think, Ted, if you knew what I know. Kay's office is in with Paul's, so she sees Stu Grayne every day, and Stu's the type women go nuts over. Even Jacynth, who hasn't been engaged more 'n a month, is beginning to fall for him."

"Surely not," Westborough protested.

"Just take a squint at Derek Esterling, pal. Ever see a sourer puss?"

"He certainly does appear to be glum. May I ask if—"

The historian stopped quickly, seeing that the ladies had just entered the room. Miss Morton walked toward them, willowy in white organdy. "May I procure you a vermouth?" he inquired.

Returning with the wine a minute or so later, he found her alone on the cushioned seat below the view window, Preston having been lured away by the superior charms of Mrs. Chamaron.

Westborough did not regret the chance for a tête-à-tête with his host's secretary; he had a question he had long wanted to ask. It would have to be led up to adroitly, he realized, and even then she might refuse to answer. However, there certainly seemed to be no harm in seizing the heaven-sent opportunity.

"Mr. Preston was just telling me about your advertising ideas, Mr. West." She sipped slowly of the dry vermouth. "I am very much interested."

"I fear," Westborough said, "that they are advertising ideas only in Mr. Preston's mind." He repeated the information he had just given to the sales manager.

"How fascinating," she commented. "Perfumery is a very old art, isn't it?"

"Extremely old. The Egyptians had an extensive knowledge of the properties of aromatic balsams some thirty-five hundred years ago. The Greeks had learned the secret of dissolving floral odors in olive oil – essentially the same process as the *enfleurage* practiced today in Mr. LeDoux's factory. The Romans perfected solid unguents and liquid perfumes, spending fabulous sums to surround themselves with sweet smells. Such luxuries as fountains of rose water were not uncommon. Heliogabalus, about whose life I have writ—"

Westborough remembered his role in time to change the sentence. "About whose life I have read with interest, is said to have bathed in a wine of roses."

"Mr. West, you surprise me. I had no idea that you were such an authority on perfumes."

"Merely a few facts gleaned from books. In comparison with such men as Mr. LeDoux and Mr. Esterling my knowledge is trifling."

"You are entirely too modest, but I will agree with you about Mr. LeDoux. He is supposed to have the best perfume nose in the United States today."

"Do you enjoy working for him?" Westborough began his campaign.

"Very much. He's been – oh, I can't tell you how kind he's been to me. A man's secretary comes to know him inside and out, all his faults, all his virtues. She may even know him better than his wife."

"And does Mr. LeDoux pass the acid test of familiarity?"

She nodded promptly. "There's nobody in the world quite like him."

"Tell me about yourself," Westborough requested. "What do you do outside of office hours?"

"Nothing very exciting. I don't want to bore you, really."

"You won't bore me," he said.

"Well, I have a room at Valle de Flores with a dear old couple who treat me just like their own daughter. I have my own car, and now and then I drive to Los Angeles to see my brother and his family. Mother lives with Fred because she likes the city, but his salary is less than my own, and he has a wife and three of the sweetest children you ever saw to support, so 'Aunt Beatrice' has to help our a bit. I don't mind doing it; really I don't. For amusements – well, I take hikes through the hills now and then. I know quite a bit about nature lore, if I do say it, and it comes in handy for my Sunday-school class. Really, it is hard to know what will interest children these days. Then I teach swimming to a class of girls, and go to the movies and read books from the lending library – it all sounds very stupid, doesn't it?"

"It sounds like a very nice life."

"The nicest part is really my work with Mr. LeDoux."

Westborough decided to risk his question. "May I ask, Miss Morton, if

Mr. LeDoux approves of his granddaughter's engagement to Mr. Esterling?"

"I really couldn't say."

"I believe you could," he differed. "A man's secretary, as you have just said, knows his foibles better than anyone else." Her raised brows were thin dark threads.

"Could you not stretch discretion just a tiny point," he pleaded. "I assure you the matter shall go no further."

She yielded unexpectedly. "I don't think Mr. LeDoux likes the idea one bit. But that's just between ourselves; you understand?"

"I understand," Westborough replied.

He wondered if he did.

IV

The dining room was gay and bright and modern, frivolous as froth or a cocktail lounge. Its pale jade walls held gilt-framed landscapes: waves breaking over a barren rock, a desert sunset flaming in the colors beloved of Vincent van Gogh. Seven rose candles flamed from the silver candelabra in the center of the long damask-covered table. They had been lighted by Mrs. LeDoux just before dinner was announced, a fact afterward to be of some importance.

Indeed, Westborough was destined to pore over every minute of that hour, treasuring each newly recalled incident – the insignificant and the bizarre alike – as a dog does a resurrected bone. But even when his memory eventually became as a polished steel mirror faithfully reflecting every smallest detail of that astounding Fourth of July evening, even then he would not know.

The odd number of their party being so awkwardly divided between the sexes, no possible permutation provided an escape from the social contretemps of seating four men together. The four were LeDoux, Westborough, Chamaron and Esterling. From there on the women were correctly alternated. Each member of the feminine quartet had attired herself in a shade oddly emblematic: Mrs. Chamaron was sophisticated in moonstone blue; Mrs. LeDoux anxious in gray, Miss Morton tranquil in white, and Jacynth youthful in pink.

A talented businesswoman, a flustered hostess, a self-effacing office worker and a *jeune fille!* Add to them a manufacturer of perfumes, a student of history, an advertising agency head, a chemist, a copy writer, a sales manager and a crabbed capitalist – strange threads which fate had chosen to weave into an even stranger tapestry.

Beaming delightedly, LeDoux lifted the lid of an enormous china tureen.

It was the promised bouillabaisse – a French dish concocted by a Chinese cook from California seafoods.

"I have tasted in the kitchen, my friends." The perfumer's beard and mustache gleamed benignly white under the mellow candle glow. "Lung Fu has made the sauce in the authentic manner of Marseilles, with white wine and olive oil and saffron from Saintonge."

> *Indeed, a rich and savoury stew 'tis,*
> *And true philosophers, methinks ...*

Westborough quoted to himself from Thackeray's ballad.

LeDoux placed a slice of toasted French bread at the bottom of each soup plate. The yellow broth soaked into the toast, while he added the solid portions of fish and shellfish: bass and halibut and salmon, lobster, clam and crab. ...

> *Green herbs, red peppers, mussels, saffron,*
> *Soles, onions, garlic, roach, and dace:*
> *All these you eat at Terré's tavern,*
> *In that one dish of Bouillabaisse.*

The last guest was scarcely served when the odor of violets drifted mysteriously into the room.

Perfumes which enchant in the boudoir are *de trop* at mealtime. Floral fragrances and food odors, despite the fondness of luxury-loving Romans for the combination, do not blend well together. Etienne LeDoux could not possibly be responsible for the gustatory outrage. A Frenchman will sooner turn to crime than spoil the taste of the food he serves. The thoughts passed in hurried review through Westborough's head as he glimpsed his host's troubled countenance.

The odor was not entirely pleasing. It was too crude, too pungent, an olfactory caricature of what the true violet scent ought to be. Instead of recalling the picture of tiny purple flowers peeking modestly from green leaves, it suggested, somehow, a bus load of factory girls on a holiday. What was the simile that LeDoux had used yesterday? "A fine perfume is a chord of scents, blended as the harmonies of music."

This, decidedly, was not a chord: it was merely a single note. Repeated over and over, it did not intrigue; it bored.

And having bored, it vanished.

As swiftly, as unaccountably as the violet odor had appeared, it was gone, fading from Westborough's nostrils like a perfumed ghost. "Dear me," he exclaimed uncomfortably. "This is rather weird."

Chamaron, looking equally shaken, observed, "I read about a Hindu yogi who knew the trick of producing smells out of the air."

"Out of the laboratory," LeDoux emended, frowning severely. He demanded of Esterling, "Do you deny that this is ionone?"

"Of course it's ionone." The chemist was immediately on the defensive. "But why should I bring ionone into your dining room, sir?"

"It's under my foot." Lanky wisps escaped from Mrs. LeDoux's rolled hair as she stooped to the floor. "A little glass bottle."

Snatching it fractiously from his daughter-in-law's hands, LeDoux strode through the french doors to the terrace. During that instant a candle went crazy.

V

The candle had gone mad. There wasn't any other term to employ. It had flared like a nova into brilliant, intense green. Gasping breathlessly, Miss Morton flicked her napkin at the chlorochrous flame. Esterling reached for a water glass; Grayne puffed out his cheeks and blew prodigiously.

The last effort was the successful one of the three. The green blaze was extinguished; in fact, so were the normal flames of two other candles. LeDoux moved toward the light switch. Chamaron, Grayne and Esterling blew simultaneously upon the four candles still burning. Eleven men and women regarded each other in a bewildered silence.

"What the devil's going on here tonight!" Preston demanded.

Returning to his chair at the head of the table, LeDoux calmly filled his soup plate from the depleted tureen. "Someone," he declared coldly, "apparently derives amusement from childish pranks, but I see no reason for interrupting our dinner. I beg of you all to eat your bouillabaisse."

"Too rich!" Todd yelped, rudely pushing the dish aside. "Tell the Chinaman to fix me some milk toast."

LeDoux rang the bell for Manuel. He said nothing, but two spots of red were glowing in his granddaughter's cheeks. She looked very lovely, Westborough mused, regarding the girl from across the table. So young and untouched!

"The bouillabaisse," the historian truthfully informed his host, "is indeed a culinary triumph."

"Delicious!" Chamaron confirmed at once. He added, selecting his words with the care of an epicure, "Savory, hot and pungent. A neat combination of flavors. The almond touch is very intriguing."

The last remark, one of those born to languish in a conversational vacuum, elicited no response; so unobtrusively did it float upon the air that only three persons could afterward recall having heard it. Yet it was, by far, the most important utterance of the meal.

LeDoux had turned from the table at that moment to give Manuel the order for Todd's milk toast. Upon such slight pivots do destiny's wheels revolve. None of the three who did hear Chamaron's comment deemed it worthy of discussion. The bouillabaisse surfeited the taste buds with its varied tangs. Who was to say from the savor alone what it did or did not contain? No one, and therein lay the tragedy.

The stew or broth or chowder, whatever one wishes to term the immortal dish, would have sufficed for a meal, but a roast followed it. With the roast went a red Rhône, and with the dessert small glasses of honey-sweet Château Yquem. Serenely contented, they trooped from the dining room to view the fireworks.

Lung Fu was grinning with delight as he placed the first rocket in a homemade trough. "More than any other race," Westborough reflected, "the Chinese are swayed by manifestations of beauty." The rocket whisked skyward in a luminous parabola and exploded into a gigantic blue-and-gold chrysanthemum. Westborough peered inside the big box containing the fireworks. The second rocket perished in a cloud of green-and-red baubles. Westborough's groping hand withdrew a small cardboard cylinder. Only Etienne LeDoux was watching. The historian found it simple to escape from the terrace. He stepped into the deserted dining room, closing the french doors quietly behind him. In a few seconds he had stripped the candelabra of its seven rose candles.

Carrying the plunder with both hands, he stepped from the dining room into the living room and from the living room into the front hall. The house remained gratifyingly empty. He ascended the stairs and followed the second-floor corridor to the back of the east wing. Since his bedroom was out of view of the terrace where the others were gathered, he ventured to turn on a floor lamp. Using the little bedside table as a workbench, he moved the lamp to direct its light on the candles and opened the smallest blade of his penknife. LeDoux found him there five minutes later.

"Ah, *mon ami*," the perfumer exclaimed, "I followed you as soon as I could. *Cette chandelle du diable* – the work of a lunatic, *hein?* One is insane, demented. Can there be other explanation?"

Westborough said, "I do not presume to know why it was done, but I do believe I have learned *how*. Another of the candles was treated in the same manner. A small blade like a reamer to carve a tiny hollow in the side. A pinch of that" – he indicated the minute heap of biscuit-tan powder which he had emptied on a sheet of white note paper. "The wax is replaced, pressed into place with the fingers, sealed with a match flame, the candle polished vigorously with a cloth – unless one looks closely, one cannot see where the incision has been made."

"But when the burning wick reaches the powder, *pouf!*"

"*Pouf*, indeed," Westborough concurred gravely. "It is interesting to note that the two candles were set to blaze at different times. My estimate is that there would have been a three or four minutes' interval between the flares had all the candles not been extinguished."

LeDoux was regarding the fine-grained tan powder. "I shall have this analyzed tomorrow."

"May I venture a prediction? I am almost certain that the substance will prove to be a mixture of potassium chlorate or perchlorate with either the nitrate, chlorate or carbonate of barium. Pyrotechnists employ such a combination to produce a green flare."

"*Bon Dieu*, but I am stupid! I bought colored fire myself only yesterday."

"I have one of your pieces here." Westborough inserted his thumbnail under the lid of a green pasteboard cylinder. He pried loose an inner partition with his penknife, disclosing a quantity of the same fine-grained, biscuit-colored powder. He placed a small pinch in a metal ash tray, turned off the floor lamp and lighted a match.

There was a puff of brilliant green, intense and momentarily blinding. "The same kind of light exactly," LeDoux declared.

"But the other was not taken from this package," Westborough informed him. "I found this one sealed tightly. It had not been previously opened."

"I bought two such green flares," the perfumer recalled. "Only two, I believe. … Yes, I am sure."

"I suggest, then, that we hasten to retrieve the second."

But when they reached the terrace it was already ablaze with green.

"*Nom d'un nom!*" LeDoux's exasperated countenance was sickly hued under the glaucous glow. "Our evidence is burning, like Scotland in the song!"

VI

A flaming arrow burst into a shower of silver tears. "Painting the night with colors more brilliant than the artist's palette," Chamaron remarked.

Finding the phrase pleasing, he repeated it; then he saw that Kay had moved from his side and was chatting animatedly with Stuart. The advertising man started toward them. "May I speak to you alone?" Esterling asked.

Chamaron nodded. Though not anxious for the interview, he could think of no way to avoid it gracefully. The chemist led the way to the walk on the east side of the house. Looking upward, Chamaron noted a light burning in one of the upper rooms. "That's strange," he observed. "I thought we were all on the terrace."

Esterling refused to be diverted. "What's your decision?"

Chamaron puffed out his cheeks. He was going to make an enemy, and the making of enemies, particularly when they were in a position to do him harm, was a luxury in which he never indulged. In this case, however, he had no alternative.

"You made some rather strong charges."

"Yes," the chemist owned.

"Are you able to prove them?"

"Of course not," Esterling exclaimed angrily. "There weren't any witnesses."

Chamaron studied the lighted window. The blind was down, but he could see the movement of a shadow across its surface. A man's shadow! Which man had left the terrace?

"Whose room is that?" he asked.

Esterling shrugged. "You forget I'm not sleeping at the house. What difference does it make, anyway?"

"I don't know that it makes any, but some rather queer things have happened here tonight. That violet smell appearing from nowhere. And then the candle."

"The violet odor," Esterling declared, "was undoubtedly caused by the usual commercial mixture of the isomeric alpha and beta ionones. I can't explain the candle. Probably both tricks were only silly practical jokes."

Chamaron absently regarded the fronds of a golden palm tree, which had just made a miraculous appearance in the southern sky.

"But who's the joker?"

"I'm not," Esterling said curtly.

"Nor I. But who is? LeDoux, no. Todd or West, absurd. Beatrice, ridiculous. Jacynth or her mother, preposterous. Stuart, I know he didn't. Kay, out of the question. So who's left?"

"Preston," Esterling replied promptly. "Sam is quite capable of that sort of stunt. Once he loaded my tobacco pouch with powder from a shotgun shell; it blew up like Vesuvius." The chemist laughed, a trifle nervously. "There's your practical joker. Now please tell me what you've decided about Grayne?"

Chamaron reached for his cigarette case. "I've decided to keep him."

Esterling stood very rigid, very quiet. "Very well," he said finally. "I'm glad to know where we stand."

"Now let me explain, old man." Chamaron discovered he was pleading to empty air. "Hell!" the advertising man said aloud, and walked back to the front terrace.

Kay was still chatting with Stuart. "He's twenty-nine; she's thirty-two," Chamaron reflected, a shade wistfully. "I'm forty-two. Three years don't amount to very much, but ten years?"

"May a mere husband have a word with his wife?" he inquired.

"Of course," she smiled. "Stuart, I see that Beatrice just dropped her hand-kerchief."

Grayne stooped, but Esterling had stooped first and recovered the hand-kerchief. The two men scowled at each other without speaking, then Grayne turned his back and walked toward the rocket trough. Todd was arguing in strident tones with Lung Fu that the angle of elevation should be altered.

"The crusty old buzzard actually sounds happy," Chamaron observed. "Let's go inside for a moment, Kay."

They stood at the entrance to the darkened living room. "Did you tell Stuart that Esterling tried to get his job?" Chamaron asked.

"No."

"Don't. Under any circumstances. Don't tell anyone. Will you promise me that?"

"I promise, Paul. But why so anxious?"

"I don't want any more trouble with Esterling than I can help. Stuart's hot tempered. A regular pepper pot."

"A gentleman of the old South." Kay laughed musically. "Do you remember that afternoon at the races? That man who had bumped into me and was so nasty about it afterward?"

"I'm not likely to forget."

"Stuart knocked him down," she recalled.

"While I," Chamaron added glumly, "stood by and did nothing."

"I'm very glad you didn't, Paul Michael. It was silly to make a fuss over anything so trifling. Besides, he was a tough-looking hombre."

"Meaning," Chamaron said, "that if I had intervened he would probably have knocked *me* down."

"I didn't mean anything of the kind."

But she did; they both knew it.

"Well," Chamaron interrupted the awkward silence, "I told our chemical friend to go to Halifax. But it may cost me the LeDoux account."

Kay patted her husband's arm. "That was sweet of you. Shall we go on outside again?"

"If you don't mind," he said, "I think I'll go up to the room and lie down for a while. I seem to have developed a headache for some reason."

"Too much wine," Kay scolded. "Tummy feel upset?"

"A little."

"Perhaps it was the bouillabaisse. Yes, I'm sure it was the bouillabaisse. When will you ever learn to go lightly on anything so rich? Darling, you know what lobster always does to you."

"Stop talking like a wife!" Chamaron rubbed his head. "All I need is to lie down a while. Maybe I'll treat myself to a bromo."

"Want me to mix it?"

"I'm quite capable of the simple task, thank you. You run out now and have fun."

He walked slowly up the stairs. His head seemed to grow steadily worse; in fact, his brain seemed ready to explode like one of the rockets they had just been watching.

He thought: "I'm going to be sick, all right. Maybe Kay was right about the bouillabaisse. It *was* too rich! Kay knows what I should and shouldn't eat. She's been a good wife to me."

He reached the head of the stairs. "But she loves Stuart," he thought. "All our lives are twisted up together like odd bits of string. And there's nothing any of us can do to straighten out the tangle. That's the hell of it!"

VII

The last rocket had gone, an evanescent spray of silver, aluminum and cyclamen, but Lung Fu and Manuel were doing very well with sparklers and flowerpots and colored flares. Just now the terrace was emanating a green glow, eerily suited to the materialization of demons.

Jacynth tucked her arm into that of her fiancé. "I'm in the mood for a walk," she told him.

They descended the stairs to the bench under the orange tree. Jacynth liked to sit here with a book on lazy summer afternoons, raising her eyes occasionally from the printed page to look across the road at the jasmine fields. Derek put his arm possessively around her.

She didn't want him to kiss her now, not until they had had their talk. Sulkily he lighted a cigarette; it made a tiny glowing hole in the dark. The colored fires, the dancing sparkles vanished suddenly from above their heads. The murmur of voices died with the fireworks, telling her that all Gran'-père's guests had gone into the house.

Silver-white, the moon broke through smoky clouds. A segment had been bitten from the side of its perfect circle. Under the moonlight, the upper half of Derek's face was that of a handsome boy, but the beard made him look older. That little dab of chestnut beard added dignity, depth, wisdom. The thought flashed absurdly across her mind that the strength of Samson had been in his hair. If Derek ever shaved his beard ...

Jacynth giggled. The thought was too silly. "I'm glad I amuse you," Derek said coldly. He was still smarting, it was apparent, over the refusal of his caresses. Abruptly merriment left her. She sat straight and unpliant on the bench beside the man she had promised to marry.

His voice deepened, lapping her with soothing tenderness. "Jacynth, sweet, darling! Why have you turned against me? What have I said to you?"

"It's what you said last night to Paul Michael."

He drew back, startled. "I know what you asked him to do," she continued accusingly. "About Stuart Grayne."

Derek averted his face. "It's nothing for you to bother about," he said after a time.

"It is, since I'm engaged to you. Why do you hate Stuart?"

"I don't hate him."

"You do," she insisted. "You're so – so vindictive. Is it still over that duel?"

His fingers shook as he crumpled his cigarette. "You learned about it from him, didn't you?"

"Yes, I did."

"It was kind of him to tell you," Derek observed sarcastically.

"Is it true?" she asked.

"True that I ran?" His voice betrayed his pain. "Yes, it's true. I didn't want to fight him. I fixed my pistol so it wouldn't fire."

"He told me that," she broke in.

"He did, did he?" Derek was furious. "I'm grateful for his magnanimity. Well, you know now."

"Yes, I know."

"And you want to say you can't marry me. Isn't that it, Jacynth?"

She thought: "Oh, Derek, poor, hurt boy! I'm years older, really. It doesn't make sense, but it's true. I know what's going on in his mind now, everything he is thinking, feeling, but he doesn't know what's going on in mine. Not the least bit."

Aloud she said: "Derek, don't be silly. It happened ten years ago."

"Nine years," he emended absently.

"Whenever it was, it doesn't make any difference to me. Wouldn't make any difference," she corrected, "if it weren't for what it's doing to you now, Derek, inside."

"Jacynth!" She read the surprise in his startled exclamation. "I always thought of you as someone very young," he whispered. "Someone to be taken care of. I didn't know that you were so grown up, so – so understanding."

"I want to understand," she answered.

"Don't you despise me?"

"Of course not."

"Even for what I said to Chamaron?"

"Oh, that!"

He said apologetically, "When you've hated a man for nine years—"

"But you mustn't," she interrupted fervidly. "Hatred is so useless, Derek. The one useless emotion."

"Wise little Jacynth! But you're right. It's worse than useless – corrosive. An acid you pour into your own brain. I can see that now."

His hands gripped her tightly, the fingers digging into the flesh of her upper arms. Hurting her, but she didn't mind. Their lips met in the darkness, drawn together by some miraculous magnet.

"I'm glad," she thought. "I'm proud I was able to help him." She rested her head in the circle of his arm. "Is it because I love him? It must be that. What else can it be?" His voice came to her faintly.

"I'll tell Chamaron that I didn't mean it. That's what you want me to do, isn't it?"

"Yes," she answered.

He rose to his feet, determined and confident. "Let's go up to the house, dear. I'll tell him now."

Inside, at one of the two bridge tables, Kay, jubilant because she and Mr. West had bid and made a small slam, said that her husband had gone to their room with a headache.

Derek slipped quietly upstairs.

VIII

Seldom had Westborough enjoyed a game more. Kay Chamaron interpreted his bids with almost psychic precision, and the cards were coming their way enough to give North and South, represented by Messrs Todd and LeDoux, a rather uncomfortable time of it. Picking up his hand, the historian now discovered that he had dealt himself the following excellent combination:

Spades: AKQ953   Diamonds: void
Hearts: KQJ76   Clubs: AK

He had just opened with a two-spade bid when Derek Esterling returned to the living room.

"Pardon me, Mrs. Chamaron. Does your husband ever take sleeping powders or tablets?"

"Sometimes." Her manner was noticeably snippy.

"Then that's why he was sleeping so soundly." Relief was evident in Esterling's voice.

"We're playing bridge, young man," Aaron Todd asserted gruffly. "Pass."

Kay Chamaron bid three hearts. LeDoux passed. Westborough, much elated, made a bid of four no trump. If his partner had the heart ace they could – was there not a phrase? – "go to town." Todd passed. "Five hearts," said Mrs. Chamaron.

She couldn't rebid the suit without the heart ace, the historian gleefully realized. "He didn't wake up when I turned on the light," Esterling continued. LeDoux passed for the second time.

"Seven hearts," Westborough proclaimed. Todd doubled. There were two passes. Though they were vulnerable, the historian recklessly redoubled.

"He was sleeping as if he'd taken some kind of soporific."

"This is a bridge game, not a health clinic," Todd informed the chemist cuttingly. LeDoux led a low diamond.

A bell rang somewhere in Westborough's brain, pealing a warning that was almost, but not quite, below the level of conscious thought.

"Did you try to waken him, Mr. Esterling?"

"Not after I found out he really was asleep. Say, pretty!" The chemist transferred his attention to the cards which Westborough was just laying down. "A blank in diamonds! There goes your ball game, gentlemen."

"Pray excuse me for a few minutes," the historian pleaded. He was probably acting the part of an officious fool, he mused on his way upstairs. If a man took a sleeping draught, that was definitely his own affair. Still …

The Chamarons occupied one of the front bedrooms, he recalled. The door wasn't locked. Opening it, he pressed the light switch. Chamaron was lying on the bed face down, fully clothed. Grasping the inert figure lightly by the shoulders, Westborough turned over the nonresisting body. Chamaron was not sleeping; it was readily apparent. His eyes were open in a strange, fixed stare. There was a peculiar almond smell on his breath.

The skin was clammy to the touch, the lips as purple as if stained by blackberries; the purple color showed also in the nails of the frenziedly clenched hands. Westborough saw that Etienne LeDoux was entering the bedroom.

"Our minds run very much in the same groove, *mon ami*. He is not dead?"

"He is not dead," Westborough repeated. "But he must have a doctor immediately."

There was an extension telephone in the little upstairs sitting room. "*Sacré!*" LeDoux ejaculated as he replaced the receiver. "The doctor is out, *la bonne me dit:* a Fourth of July excursion. Fortunately, he is expected to return at any minute; I left word. What is it that you think?"

"My medical knowledge is slight, but it would appear – dear me!"

"You suspect poison?"

The historian nodded. "The almond odor of the breath, the cyanosis of the lips and fingernails – these symptoms strongly suggest prussic acid."

"But that acts with lightninglike rapidity, *bon Dieu!*"

"Yes," Westborough acknowledged.

"What is it that one does?"

"There is very little that one can do. Do the others suspect why we are up here?"

LeDoux shook his head as they walked back into the bedroom. "They are still at the bridge," he said. "I asked Jacynth to play my hand; Esterling will take your place." Bending over the unconscious Chamaron, the perfumer pressed his nose close to the livid lips.

Suddenly he straightened up from the bed. "No, it is not the odor of bitter almonds! Similar, yes, but not the same. The odor, *mon ami*, is that of the essence of mirbane. I do not mistake a smell."

Westborough experienced an emotion of unrestricted relief. "Then there may be still time to save him. I wish, however, I knew what treatment should—"

The telephone began to ring in the adjacent sitting room. LeDoux went to answer it while Westborough removed the unconscious man's coat and shoes. The perfumer returned, excited and exultant. "Dr. Baring is on his way here now, *grâce à Dieu!*"

"You told him what we have learned?"

"*Naturellement!* He said to do nothing until he arrives."

Something stirred at the back of the historian's brain, some trivial memory striving to assert its importance. The recollection exploded as suddenly as a firecracker.

"Does nitrobenzene have an almond taste?" he asked.

"An almond odor," LeDoux corrected. "The taste is said to be hot and pungent." His lips formed a shade of a smile. "I am, however, content to accept hearsay evidence for that."

"Perhaps," Westborough hazarded, "the odor might be mistaken for the taste."

"It is possible," LeDoux acknowledged. "One says basically there are but four tastes: the sweet, the sour, the bitter and the salt. It is the odors which impart the illusion of a variety of flavors. Why does the subject so interest you at so crucial a moment?"

"I should like to question your cook about his bouillabaisse."

"You are mistaken." LeDoux's mind had leaped with French quickness to the kernel of Westborough's thought. "The dish was served at the table, and no one else is ill."

"It does seem difficult," Westborough admitted. He remembered the violet odor, the pyrotechnic candle. "Dear me! Doubtless I am wrong, but since there is nothing we can do for poor Mr. Chamaron until the arrival of the doctor. I suggest that we have a brief talk with Lung Fu. Do you mind?"

"I do not mind, but I am curious. I am sensitive to flavors. A racial quality, *n'est-ce pas?* The bouillabaisse was exactly as it should be. *Précisément!*"

"Yet Mr. Chamaron declared that he detected an almond flavoring in his portion," Westborough recalled.

"Paul Michael said that?" LeDoux lifted rather bushy brows in an expression of extreme surprise.

"Did you not hear him?"

"*Mais non!* It could not have been so. My poor friend was mistaken. I am familiar with the ingredients of that recipe, and almond extract is not among them."

"Nevertheless," Westborough insisted, "I should like very much to hear what your cook has to say."

Lung Fu, who had returned to the kitchen to toil at a great stack of dishes, received them with philosophic calm.

"I wish, Mr. Lung," Westborough began politely, "to congratulate you on the production of that delicious bouillabaisse."

"Thank you." The innate reserve of the Chinese race thawed slightly under the compliment. "So glad it pleased you, Mr. West."

"It contained a tiny bit of almond extract, did it not?"

"No almond extract." Lung Fu was economical of his words.

"Not even a soupçon?" Westborough persisted. "I am almost sure that I detected—"

The Chinese shrugged, as if the topic had no further interest for him, and picked up a plate from the dish rack.

"Come, Mr. Lung," LeDoux said genially, "let us show Mr. West the recipe. He is a difficult man to convince, *parbleu!*"

The bouillabaisse, Westborough learned, contained a great many ingredients, in addition to the seafoods: olive oil, white wine, chopped onions, hearts of leeks, tomatoes, parsley, two cloves of garlic, salt, white pepper, paprika and saffron. It did not, however, contain almond extract: not even a soupçon. Chamaron's three thousand taste buds had united in a deplorable error.

But Chamaron, the historian recalled, was something of an epicure. He liked good food; he appreciated the nuances of seasoning. Though possible, it was not reasonable that his palate should perceive a nonexistent almond flavoring. Ergo …

Westborough sighed, reproaching himself bitterly. Had he reasoned in this manner earlier, a warning could have been issued. But the thought had never once crossed his mind of an attempt on the advertising agent's life. It had not been Chamaron whom he had been employed to safeguard.

They walked from the kitchen into the hall. "Are you satisfied, *mon ami?*" LeDoux asked.

"I am satisfied," Westborough rejoined. "Satisfied that the poison was in Mr. Chamaron's bouillabaisse."

"*Je crois que non.* How could it be placed there?"

"The green light of the candle," Westborough returned thoughtfully, "was not a mere practical joke."

IX

"Nitrobenzene is a liquid," LeDoux argued. They were in the patio waiting for the doctor's arrival. "A lemon-colored liquid. A liquid cannot be thrown into a dish from across the table. It must be poured, poured by someone who sat very near to Mr. Chamaron. Is not this so?"

"Yes," Westborough admitted uncomfortably.

"And Mr. Chamaron's nearest neighbors were—"

"Please," Westborough interrupted. "It is not for us to say who did or did not poison Mr. Chamaron. The problem has now become a police matter."

"My house is outside the jurisdiction of the Valle de Flores police force." LeDoux seemed a little proud that such was the case. "The sheriff's office must be told, I suppose. The local official is a man named Sydney Howe. He is not very intelligent. I would prefer—"

"You can have no choice." Westborough was surprised at the sharpness which had crept into his voice. "An attempt has been made to murder one of your guests. It is no longer your personal problem, but one of the public welfare."

"Does that mean that you will not handle this case?"

"I cannot handle it," Westborough answered. "It has become an official matter."

"But unofficially?" LeDoux asked with anxiety. "You will do what you can, will you not? Paul Michael is my good friend, a friend of many years' standing. I feel responsible."

"I will do what I can," Westborough promised. "It will not be much, I fear. Dear me, why does not your doctor arrive?"

"He must come ten miles." LeDoux consulted his watch. "And it has been but ten minutes since I spoke to him on the telephone."

"Only ten minutes!" Westborough echoed. "Dear, dear, it scarcely seems possible! A great deal has happened in that brief period."

"Yes, and we have learned much. We know that Paul Michael was poisoned. We know with what he was poisoned; we know when and how. And we know who is responsible for the outrage."

"That we do not know," the little man promptly took issue.

Their eyes clashed momentarily; LeDoux's black, flashing; Westborough's mild and blue.

"I am satisfied," the perfumer said darkly. "Nitrobenzene or essence of mirbane is to be found in Esterling's laboratory. The laboratory to which he alone possesses the key."

"We do not even know for certain that the poison is nitrobenzene."

Westborough made the objection largely from principle. Personally, he had few doubts of LeDoux's highly trained nose, as sensitive an indicator as any chemical tests. But Westborough, meek, seldom assertive, and apologetic for his own shortcomings, would battle with the ardor of a Zola to prevent an injustice.

"Mr. Esterling may be guilty." He added, carefully weighing his words: "Certainly, if the poison is nitrobenzene, both method and opportunity may be proved."

"What more do you want?" LeDoux demanded.

"Motive," the historian contended. "It is rather important, I believe."

Crickets chirped melodiously, uniting their fiddles in a distant symphony; innumerable stars twinkled serenely. It was as peaceable a setting as is ever found in this world of woe and strife, but in one of the rooms upstairs a man was dying.

And eight people were playing bridge, unknowing. Westborough corrected himself. One of them must know, unless …

But *that* thought was lunacy.

"Chamaron and Esterling dislike each other," LeDoux was saying. "At every conference I feel the strain between them. Their minds are so different. As different as light from shadow."

"One does not necessarily attempt to kill a man because his mind is different."

"Yours is different from mine, my friend. I cannot understand why, when every signpost points to a certain path, you prefer to plod over an unmarked trail."

"Precisely because it *is* unmarked," the historian declared. "One who commits a crime does not leave signposts. At least not so obviously."

"Your reasoning is oversubtle for me. I fear," LeDoux added dolefully, "that it will also be oversubtle for the good Captain Howe. He understands the use of the bludgeon, that one, not the use of the rapier. I am convinced he will arrest Monsieur Derek Esterling."

"But if Esterling is merely a stalking-horse for the actual criminal?"

"*Ma foi*, but you have no proof of that!"

Their minds were far apart – farther apart than they had ever been in their brief but pleasant acquaintance. Westborough remembered a piece of statuary at the Chicago Art Institute. Lorado Taft's conception of the blind figures emerging from the rock to stretch out groping hands. Touching but never knowing one another in the terrible solitude of life!

Headlights had just turned into the drive below. The doctor must be arriving. Good!

Westborough said earnestly, "Please do not encourage Captain Howe to make this arrest. I beg it of you! Please, I pray you, do not give him any suggestion the actual evidence does not warrant. Remember, please, that Mr. Esterling is your granddaughter's future husband."

"*Jamais!*" LeDoux exclaimed vehemently. "*Jamais de ma vie!* I will not permit the horrible marriage to take place."

"Even though it is proved beyond possible doubt that Mr. Esterling is not guilty?" LeDoux did not answer.

A man young and vigorous, raced up the stairs. "Dr. Baring, Mr. West." LeDoux presented them.

The doctor grunted an unintelligible acknowledgment. "Where is he?"

"Upstairs. We will show you."

"Is anyone with him?"

"No. My other guests are in the living room playing bridge."

The doctor snorted his contempt. Westborough liked the way he walked, swinging his bag as if it were a battering ram. "A man has been poisoned! But people have to go on playing with bits of pasteboard."

"As yet no one knows that Mr. Chamaron is critically ill. A horde of anxious people can be very disturbing to a sick man, is it not so?"

There was light enough in the hall for Westborough to see Dr. Baring's face. Intelligence was written upon it and also skepticism. "You did the smart thing, Mr. LeDoux. Let them go on with their bridge game. Keep them all downstairs. For the next few minutes I'm going to be very, very busy, and it won't be a pleasant sight for anyone to witness."

They had reached the Chamaron bedroom. Dr. Baring unbuttoned the patient's shirt and applied his stethoscope.

"Is he—" Westborough ventured.

"No. The heart is still beating. We may be able to save him."

"I hope and pray that you can," Westborough said fervently. "Is there a way in which I can be of assistance?"

"Can't think of any," the doctor answered. Taking the hint, Westborough departed promptly. He was overtaken by his host at the head of the stairs.

"Dr. Baring is droll, is he not? But a good doctor, one of the best. He saved my own life not so very long ago. He will save that of Paul Michael also, but now we must tell Mrs. Chamaron. That is a task from which, I confess, I shrink."

"Allow me to do it," Westborough begged. "Ask her to meet me in your study. If you play her hand we can keep the matter secret for a little longer."

"And so I must play cards now while Paul Michael—Impossible! I am not of iron and steel."

"It is the only way in which you can help," Westborough said gently. "It is vitally important that Dr. Baring be allowed to work undisturbed."

"You have reason," LeDoux owned. "*Soit!* I will send her to you. There is brandy in the cabinet; she may need it."

"Or I may need it," Westborough reflected in trepidation. "Dear me, however does one tell a woman that her husband is dying of poison?"

X

Tawny hair shimmered under the study lights as Mrs. Chamaron made her laughing entrance. "Mystery!" she exclaimed in mock horror. "I do believe you are a conspirator, Mr. West. But the lady has come at your call."

Westborough fiddled with a small ivory elephant he had absentmindedly lifted from the little writing desk. He looked vainly for aid in the pine-paneled walls, the white bear rug on the floor.

"Gracious, how solemn we are," she twitted him. "A regular hoot owl!"

Westborough's mild blue eyes regarded her from behind gold-rimmed bifocals, admiringly as well as sympathetically. Nature had made Kay Chamaron comely; art had enhanced the charm. Though the elderly scholar's days of gallantry were over he had not yet to earth's high requiem become a sod.

The scene was going to be difficult, he perceived. Even more difficult than he had anticipated. He said, in cowardly procrastination, "I have taken the liberty of looting Mr. LeDoux's liquor cabinet. I thought that you and I might have a wee drop of cognac together."

She laughed melodiously. "It doesn't go with your silver hairs and nice sweet face. Were you very bad in your youth, Mr. West?"

"Very," he replied, endeavoring, without much success, to think of something he had done which could reasonably be called wicked. "Excellent cognac!" He gazed abstractedly at the large globe standing near the desk. "Our host keeps a fine cellar."

"I should say he does. Paul Michael has been in seventh heaven. He confided to me last night that one client like Etienne LeDoux is enough to atone for – when, when, WHEN! This woman works for a living, my dear."

His eyes lingered silently upon the golden moons tipping her tapering fingers. He should tell her now, he knew, but he could not.

"Soda?"

"Neat. I rather like the brandy burn."

"But you will have a chaser?" Upstairs, he reflected, medical science was fighting for the life of this blithe lady's husband.

"Please."

"Soda or plain water?"

"Soda." She sipped cautiously of the fiery liquid.

"I have something to say to you," he confessed at last.

"And so you have been fortifying me for the shock?" Her lips formed a bow of raspberry against the cream of her skin.

"Yes, in a way. Mr. LeDoux thought—"

"Mr. LeDoux asked *you* to tell *me!*" The cool voice had become surprisingly scornful. "It's about Paul Michael, isn't it?"

"Why, dear me!" he exclaimed, dumfounded. "Can it be you already know?"

"That Paul's going to lose the LeDoux account? We were given a very good inkling of it, Mr. West."

He experienced the bewilderment of Alice tumbling down the rabbit hole. "This hasn't anything to do with Mr. LeDoux's advertising," he managed finally.

"Oh!" The intonation of the interjection betrayed extreme chagrin. "I seem to have made a first-class fool of myself." She set her brandy glass on the green desk blotter.

Instinct forbade him to abandon the path.

"Did Mr. LeDoux threaten to remove his advertising from your husband's agency?"

"Not Mr. LeDoux." She took a sip of soda water. "Since I've blurted out so much I might as well tell the rest. It was Mr. Esterling."

Always Derek Esterling! Every trail converged upon this one man.

But converged falsely, Westborough felt sure. "Mr. Esterling," he objected, "has no control over his employer's advertising."

"Not now. However, Mr. LeDoux is" – she finished tactfully – "perhaps not so young as you are. If he retires Mr. Esterling probably would come into control of everything. And he has always tried to discredit Paul Michael. But you said the brandy was to prepare me for a shock. I'm well prepared now, thanks."

"Mrs. Chamaron, your husband is ill. Extremely ill, I regret to say."

"Paul!" She sprang up, lithe as a tawny lioness. "Why did you keep me here so long?"

"A doctor is with him."

"A doctor! You sent for one without even telling me? Oh, I must go to Paul at once."

This was dreadful! Westborough, starting to hand her the brandy she had only partially consumed, picked up the trumpeting ivory elephant instead.

"Please, my dear Mrs. Chamaron!" Discovering his mistake, he dropped the elephant hurriedly. "You will only hinder by going upstairs now. Dr. Baring specifically stated he did not want to be disturbed."

"I assure you," she said witheringly, "that I also am interested in my husband's health. Please don't try to stop me, Mr. West."

"First let me say one sentence," he pleaded. "Your husband was poisoned."

He proffered the brandy glass; she dashed it hysterically to the floor. "Pray be seated, my dear." The little scholar was very gentle. "He will pull through the ordeal, I feel sure."

She sank into a tan leather chair. "Paul's already dead!" she sobbed. "Tell me the truth, please!"

"Your husband is alive, though very weak."

She sat bolt upright. "You said he had been poisoned?"

"Yes." Uncomfortably Westborough stooped to gather the broken glass from the study floor. "I am very sorry."

"You meant food poisoning, didn't you? From that rich dinner?"

"No," he replied in a weak voice. "That wasn't what I meant."

"Some person tried to *kill* Paul!" Her eyes were burning sapphires in the crucible of her head. "How can you know that?"

The question was by no means unintelligent. "I must be very careful," he deliberated, "not to implant the slightest suggestion in her mind that was not there before."

"Mr. LeDoux recognized the odor on your husband's lips. The poison is" – he closely scrutinized the expression of her quivering mouth – "essence of mirbane."

"That means nothing to me. Is it dangerous?"

"Very. A few drops might be fatal. Perhaps not more than twenty." Feeling that this sounded too gloomy, he added, "But recovery has taken place after much larger doses."

"How much was given to Paul Michael?"

"We have no means of ascertaining." He paused gravely. "May I ask a few questions, Mrs. Chamaron? Did – does your husband have an enemy here?"

"Only Derek Esterling." Her body swayed unsteadily as she stood on her feet.

Esterling again! One more accusing finger! Westborough was conscious of age and incompetence. But the festering sore had to be probed.

"Did Mr. Esterling make threats against the life of your husband?"

"Not against his life," she returned dully. "He did threaten to use his influence to see that the LeDoux account was taken away from Paul Michael."

"When did he talk to your husband about this?"

"Last night. And again tonight, immediately after dinner. It involves someone – someone else. Paul made me promise not to tell anyone."

It would be folly to press the point, Westborough recognized. Suddenly, however, the mists cleared a trifle in his mind.

"Was the demand – whatever it was that your husband was asked to do – repeated tonight *after* dinner?"

"Yes." She toyed with a gossamer shred of handkerchief.

"Mr. Esterling, then, had allowed your husband time to consider his proposition?"

"I suppose you could call it that," she replied apathetically.

"So your husband had not refused Mr. Esterling before tonight?" he persisted.

"Not until tonight." She turned with feline quickness on her way to the hall. "Mr. West, if Paul dies someone here is going to be sorry. I promise you I'll make sure of it."

He read the threat in the sudden tension of her voice. The female of the species can be a baleful foe to the destroyer of her mate, he recognized.

"Your husband will not die, Mrs. Chamaron. I beg of you not even to think of such a contingency."

Westborough was a false and foolish prophet. Paul Michael Chamaron died at two o'clock on the morning of July fifth.

PART FIVE
ESSENCE OF MIRBANE

Captain Syd Howe, of the Valle de Flores sheriff's substation, twirled the big globe in Etienne LeDoux's study. "There couldn't be two men with a name like Theocritus Lucius Westborough. You're the very fellow who helped Cranston with those island murders about a year ago." The world rocked dizzily on its axis. "Here under an alias, huh? That's consequential."

The local head of the sheriff's department peppered his utterances liberally with such adjectives as "consequential," "momentous" (which he pronounced "momentu-ous") and "significatory." Howe was a lean, sinewy individual in his early forties, with the leathery tan of the outdoor-living Californian. He had impressed Westborough on the preceding night as a man who handled his job competently. The little scholar was not able to share his host's opinion that Syd Howe was unintelligent.

"LeDoux told me he brought you here because an earlier attempt had been made to poison him. What evidence did you find?"

"I would prefer not to say just yet."

"You mean you won't cooperate?"

"Not exactly. Dear me, I realize it is highly officious on my part to take such a stand. But the discoveries I have made involve a person whom I sincerely believe to be innocent. When I receive certain information which will verify or disprove the contention I will only be too happy to communicate with you."

"H'mmmm," Howe drawled. "Just how long do you think I'll have to wait?"

"Until tomorrow, perhaps. Certainly no later than the day after."

"It's a deal!" Captain Howe's manner was frankly that of one professional to another. "Did you ever see such a case as this? Violet perfume thrown under the table. Candles made into fireworks. Maybe those are significatory and maybe they're just plain crazy."

" 'What song the Syrens sang, or what name Achilles assumed when he hid himself among the women,' " Westborough quoted smilingly, " 'although puzzling questions are not beyond *all* conjecture.' The candles, for instance, are definitely *not* beyond conjecture. Obviously they were prepared purposely to create a diversion."

"Yes, but why was he poisoned?" Howe's thumb and little finger spanned the ocean between Africa and South America. "What kind of murder is it

89

without a motive? I talked to everyone last night. No one who sat at that dinner table had a consequential motive for killing Chamaron." His index finger thumped the globe in the middle of Spain. "Westborough, you could do me a lot of good just by staying here, as West, of course, and watching the rest of LeDoux's crowd."

"But surely," the historian objected, "Mr. LeDoux's house party cannot continue!"

"You bet it will!" Captain Howe gave the world a final spin and abandoned it to inertia. "LeDoux's promised full cooperation. I came out here this morning on purpose to tip off his guests that anyone who tries to leave without my say-so is heading for arrest." He chuckled. "Just between you and me, I can't make it stick, but I don't think I'll have to. They'll stay. Except Mrs. Chamaron, naturally. It wouldn't be decent to put the screws on her."

"I do not believe Mrs. Chamaron will leave so very promptly," Westborough opined, recalling a previous interview with the lady. "On the contrary, I think you will find her most anxious to remain."

"I don't know why you're so sure, but if you are right it's all to the good. We'll give 'em two or three days of being cooped up with each other, everyone knowing that someone is a murderer. Not only that! The most contemptible kind of murderer there is – a poisoner! Nice, huh?"

"Not very," Westborough disclaimed, ruefully contemplating the prospect. "I have a feeling that Lung Fu's excellent meals will be but scantily patronized."

"Now do you see why I want you to work with me? I could plant one of my own men here, sure, but it wouldn't be natural."

"I suppose not," Westborough acknowledged. "Dear me. I can foresee an awkward difficulty in the matter of this afternoon's inquest. If I give testimony under my assumed name I am guilty of perjury."

"I wouldn't worry over that. Technically you're right, since you'll have to testify under oath, but I think I can straighten it out with the coroner's office. If that's fixed up will you continue on the case?"

"Indeed, I should be highly honored. The problem is most fascinating. On the surface it is apparently irrational, but there is a very strong undercurrent of sanity."

Captain Howe glanced at his watch. "I've got a few minutes. Suppose you give me your slant."

"With great pleasure! The inquiry naturally divides into four separate subproblems: One, the poison; two, the candles; three, the vial of ionone; and four, the motive, or lack of motive, if you prefer."

"Number four is the really consequential one," the deputy sheriff asserted.

"Number four is also the most difficult. Let us begin with the poison, which, I believe, we may safely assume *is* essence of mirbane or nitroben-zene. This chemical is contained in Mr. Esterling's laboratory. That, how-ever, you already know."

Howe grunted. "Who else knew it, though?"

"Virtually everyone," Westborough replied. "Mr. Esterling admitted pos-session of the substance during Monday's luncheon, and we later spoke of it as a poison in the presence of everyone except Mrs. LeDoux. Theoretically, anyone in Mr. LeDoux's house is therefore able to gain the toxic agent, but there are difficulties. The laboratory is always locked in Mr. Esterling's ab-sence. Moreover, he has the only key. (I except his assistant, who is not in Valle de Flores this week and may be dismissed from our calculations.) Doors may be opened sans keys, you may argue, but there are still entanglements to unravel. Owing to the fact that the house is so crowded, Mr. Esterling now sleeps at the laboratory. Ergo, a felonious attempt to enter could not have been made during the nighttime. But there were not many minutes during the day when such an attempt could have been made. When eleven people are confined under one roof, as we were yesterday, no one enjoys the luxury of solitude for very long. Therefore, one is compelled reluctantly to reach the conclusions:

"(1) Mr. Esterling might easily have had essence of mirbane in his posses-sion. (2) Any other person would have experienced considerable difficulty in obtaining that substance. However, it does not necessarily follow from these facts that Mr. Esterling is guilty of the atrocious crime."

"Anything momentu-ous about the candles?"

"They were probably prepared during Monday night. The fireworks were kept in a closet downstairs, and it would not be difficult for a person staying in the house to abstract the green fire clandestinely, returning the pasteboard cylinder after a sufficient supply of the powder had been obtained. Please note that Mr. Esterling would have had the poorest chance of any of us to do this. The lower doors to the house are carefully locked at night."

"What about the doors to that balcony above the patio?"

"They are not locked. But there are no outside steps to the balcony from the patio. A felonious entrance to the house is not an easy matter."

"Well, could Esterling have taken the green fire before he left the house?"

"Possible, perhaps, but I confess I do not know when he would have had the opportunity. So much for the green fire. Now to consider the candles themselves. Mrs. LeDoux lighted them just before the meal was announced. All were new candles at the time they were lighted. That much I have ascer-tained, but I know nothing more. We should try to discover the time at which the candles of the previous evening were replaced by fresh ones and the place where the new candles are stored."

Captain Howe nodded agreement. "That's consequential, all right."

"Shall we pass to our third subproblem? To the chemical that imitates the odor of violets?"

"Do you think that had anything to do with the poisoning?"

"Yes," Westborough replied slowly. "I feel sure that it did. Ionone has some interesting olfactory properties. I suggest, however, that you question Mr. LeDoux, to whom I am indebted for the very little I know. The substance, incidentally, is not kept exclusively in Mr. Esterling's laboratory, although some is to be found there. It is employed in the blending of a violet perfume, *Violux* – a routine manufacture in which Mr. Esterling's talents are not required. A quantity could readily have been obtained, therefore, by anyone familiar with the perfume plant: Mr. LeDoux, Mr. Preston, Miss Morton, and I do not except the two Chamarons. As business associates of long standing, both of them had been through the factory a great many times."

"Would you leave Grayne out?"

"Not altogether. During our trip on Monday we were all conducted through the section where *Violux* was in process of manufacture. I do not recall, however, that anything significant was said concerning ionone. And now to consider the last and most difficult subproblem. The question of mo—"

"Just a minute," Howe whispered, stepping noiselessly toward the closed door. "I think someone's listening in the hall."

"A thousand pardons!" LeDoux exclaimed, entering at that instant. "I venture to interrupt because of my secretary. Poor Beatrice! She weeps over Mr. Chamaron, who was one of her dearest friends. She fears also you will suspect her of killing him. It is nonsense, I tell her. No one could deem her guilty. But I agree that it is best she makes to you the clean breast. The matter cannot be longer hidden."

"What matter?" Captain Howe asked. "What can't be hidden?"

LeDoux waved his hands with Gallic ebullience. "*Que je suis bête!* You do not know that Beatrice, some might say, had a motive for encompassing the death of my poor friend, Paul Michael."

II

"Sit down, please." Howe's voice was neither kind nor unkind. "I want to talk to you."

Beatrice Morton's hazel eyes were red and inflamed, Westborough noted. Her nose was swollen as if from recent weeping. She fingered nervously a necklace of graduated amber beads. "If you like, Mr. LeDoux can remain here," Howe added, a trifle more sympathetically.

Her eyes returned wistful thanks. "I should prefer that. If I make a mistake Mr. LeDoux will be able to correct me."

"Perhaps I had better retire," Westborough said. Though he wanted very much to remain he could think of no justifiable excuse.

"I should like that Monsieur West stay also," LeDoux declared promptly. "If *le bon capitaine* consents."

"All right," the official yielded his permission. "Go on, Miss Morton. What's this story about your father and Mr. Chamaron?"

"It began a great many years ago. My father had built up a flourishing advertising agency. First it was Morton and Company, but later it became Morton and Chamaron. My father—" The corners of her thin lips drooped pensively. "I don't want to be disloyal, but it's hard not to blame him for what happened. He was a brilliant man – I only wish I had inherited a tenth of his mental capacity. But he was also unstable: you could even say erratic. After a time the advertising business bored him. He took to leaving more and more of the details in the hands of Mr. Chamaron while he gave his attention to outside things. Speculation mostly – he had developed a theory of investments. It worked out for a year or so. Father thought he was going to be a very rich man.

"Paul Michael didn't like it at all. You can hardly blame him. Oh, I'll admit I did blame him at first. It took me almost a year to see his side of it. We were all bitter at first, Mother, and Fred and I. But we all forgave him – if there was anything to forgive – years ago. You do believe that, don't you? Oh, you must believe it!"

"What did Mr. Chamaron do to your father?"

"Father did most of it to himself. Mr. Chamaron offered to buy him out, but Father was too greedy. He wanted more than his share of the firm was worth, and so they couldn't come to terms. That was back in 1929; you remember how values were inflated. It didn't matter, anyway. If Mr. Chamaron had bought Father's interest the money would have only gone with the rest down that great black sink they called the crash. We wouldn't have been one penny the richer." Her lips tightened in pain. "The crash was the real reason, I suppose, why Father—"

"What did Mr. Chamaron do to your father?" Howe asked again.

"Haven't I told you? Early in 1930 Mr. Chamaron set up his own agency, taking all of Father's best accounts with him."

LeDoux was smiling cynically. "Advertising agencies multiply by division. Like the amoeba, *hein?*"

"Was LeDoux Perfumes one of the accounts Chamaron took away?" Howe demanded.

"*Il est vrai!* I followed Paul Michael in his new venture. Why should I not? He alone had handled my company's advertising during the past year. Others felt the same as I, and so poor Henry's business vanished."

"Then he shot himself," Miss Morton said quickly. "My father shot himself. The verdict was suicide while mentally despondent. We think – Mother and Fred and I have talked it over a great many times – that Father wasn't really responsible, that perhaps something had snapped in his head. He had been acting strange for such a long while, you see. Poor Father!"

Westborough murmured sympathetically, "My dear Miss Morton, what a tragedy! I am deeply interested in the fate of your unfortunate family."

"We had rather a difficult time," she admitted. "Father didn't leave us much; he had even cashed in most of his insurance policies to tide things over after the crash. It would have been far worse, however, without Mr. Chamaron. He steered us through the legal tangles – some of Father's creditors were very vindictive – and he sold some securities for us. Everyone else said they were worthless, but he got enough for them so Fred could finish his electrical engineering course. He's with the power bureau now. I went to business school, and when I finished there Mr. Chamaron found a job for me. No one could have had a stauncher, truer friend." She was crying unashamedly. "I remember when Mother had to have an operation. I wasn't earning much then, and I was almost frantic, but Mr. Chamaron learned about it somehow and insisted upon advancing the money. He was the kindest, most generous man I've ever known, next to Mr. LeDoux."

"I am embarrassed," LeDoux said. He blew his nose in proof of it. "Tell them the truth about me, Beatrice. I am a tyrant, a slave driver, is it not so?"

"It is *not* so," she answered warmly.

"Miss Morton, did you ever visit Chamaron's home?" Howe inquired.

"Oh yes, several times. He has – had a beautiful house in Beverly Hills."

"Will you tell me about the Chamarons' home life?"

"What is there to tell?"

"Were they happy together?"

"I think so. Yes, I'm sure that they were. She's beautiful and talented and clever. And he worshiped her. That was evident in everything he said."

"But something was wrong?" Syd Howe was proving himself a not ungifted psychologist, Westborough reflected. "What was it, Miss Morton?"

"It was just a feeling I had."

"What sort of feeling?"

"I can't quite explain it. Probably it doesn't amount to anything, but somehow I did get the idea that Paul Michael wasn't entirely happy."

"Did Mrs. Chamaron ever nag or scold her husband?"

"Oh no. She was always sweet to him. I like Kay. I like her a great deal. Don't think for one minute that I'm criticizing her. It's just that – well, sometimes I think they made a mistake in not having any children. Paul Michael would have been a splendid father."

"How long ago were they married?"

"I think it has been five years."

"It has been just five years," LeDoux confirmed. "They were married in the summer of 1934. The present Mrs. Chamaron is the second, by the way. Paul Michael was unfortunate in his earlier marital relations. He was divorced from his first wife some fifteen years ago."

"What was the cause of the divorce?" Howe inquired.

"I do not remember," LeDoux said.

Howe turned at once to Miss Morton. "Did Mr. Chamaron ever speak to you about his first wife?"

"Almost never. I received the impression that the memory was rather painful to him."

"All right, Miss Morton, that'll be all, I guess."

LeDoux lingered behind after his secretary had left the room.

"*Monsieur le Capitaine*, are you satisfied?" he challenged. "Beatrice told you no lies, I swear it. I personally can vouch for every word of that tragic story."

"Still she did have a motive," Howe said thoughtfully.

"Name of a name!" The Frenchman was furious. "It is as I feared it would be. What kind of motive, might one ask? Please be kind enough to state it in so many words."

"One word," Howe rejoined tersely. "Revenge. A life for a life."

"*C'est la démence!* One does not for nine years harbor thoughts of revenge toward a person who does one nothing but kindness. The human mind is not so built. My Beatrice is not a monster."

"Still," Howe insisted, "it's the only consequential motive I've found yet."

"Dear me, the herring is much too red," Westborough intervened smilingly. "The true motive for Mr. Chamaron's death, I am apprehensive, will be rather more deeply hidden."

III

The "Matter of the Inquisition upon the Body of Paul Michael Chamaron, Deceased," took place on the afternoon of July fifth at the funeral chapel of the leading mortuary in Valle de Flores. By order of Deputy Coroner Hansen, who had journeyed some fifty miles from the county seat to preside, a flat-topped desk replaced the customary pulpit on the platform.

The witness chair was also on the raised platform, beside the deputy coroner's desk, and the witnesses sat directly below in the first row of folding chairs. Subsequent rows of chairs were occupied by a sprinkling of curious souls who had learned in mysterious ways that the inquest was to be conducted.

Captain Howe, the first witness to be called, testified that he had received a telephone call on the evening of July fourth from Mr. Etienne LeDoux.

"Mr. LeDoux said over the phone that one of his guests was dangerously ill and was likely to die. He thought that the guest had been poisoned, deliberately and with malice aforethought, by one of the folks staying there. The house is in the country, a good ten miles from town, and I didn't get there until after midnight. The deceased was in a bedroom upstairs, being attended by Dr. Baring. He was unconscious all the time I was there. Thirteen other people were in the house, counting the two servants and Dr. Baring. Everybody wanted to talk at once, and everybody seemed to have a different slant on things, so it took me a little time to learn just what had happened. As soon as I had an idea, however, I tried to get hold of the remains of a booba – fish stew for analysis, but I was too late. Mr. LeDoux's cook had already burned his garbage in the incinerator, and he had washed up all the soup plates. That was a tough break! I'd heard enough by that time to make me think the poison had been administered to the deceased in this boobalash. Then I took a flashlight and went outside to hunt for a bottle of perfume that Mr. LeDoux had thrown away."

"How was the perfume connected with this case, Captain Howe?"

"Somebody had uncorked it during dinner, just before the boola-boola stuff was served, and caused a stink like violets under the table. That made Mr. LeDoux mad, he told me, and so he threw the bottle outdoors."

"Was your search for it successful?"

"Only partly. The bottle had hit on the walk on the terrace below the house and had smashed to smithereens, but I wrapped up the pieces in my handkerchief, and here they are now." He pointed to the heap of broken glass on the deputy coroner's desk.

"Did you test these fragments for fingerprints?"

"Yes sir. The biggest piece showed a part of a thumbprint, but that was all I could find."

"Were you able to identify that print?"

"Yes sir. It had been made by Mr. LeDoux's thumb."

Howe went on to say that the deceased had died at two A.M., of which fact he had been notified by Dr. Baring. On learning that the deceased had become the deceased, he had made a long-distance telephone call to the coroner's office at Santa Bonita, being convinced that he had to do with "a willful, deliberate and premeditated murder in the first degree."

Dr. Baring took the stand, presenting the spectacle of a man suffering from righteous indignation which has been denied an outlet. The young medico, it was evident, blamed some unknown person very bitterly for the death of his late patient, although uncertain just who it was that he should blame.

It was not precisely correct, he contended, to say that he had received a telephone call from Mr. LeDoux. He had been out at the time Mr. LeDoux had called. Yes, he had later telephoned to Mr. LeDoux. … The doctor admitted that it probably didn't make any difference who had telephoned whom. At all events, a telephonic conversation had been conducted between Dr. Baring and Mr. LeDoux on the evening of July fourth. The latter had requested the former to come immediately as a guest was suffering severely from the effects of a poison.

"Did Mr. LeDoux mention the word 'poison,' Doctor?" the deputy coroner inquired.

"He did. He also told me the name of the particular poison which he believed had been administered." The announcement caused a surge of excitement over the faces of the coroner's jury, nine local citizens who made a funereal row in the background of the platform.

"What poison did Mr. LeDoux name?"

"Essence of mirbane or, as it is usually called, nitrobenzene."

"Was the deceased living when you reached Mr. LeDoux's house?"

"Yes. He died when I had attended him a little over three hours."

"What was the condition of your patient when you first saw him, Doctor?"

"Very critical. The heart was beating faintly, and he was in a state of coma."

"Will you describe the patient's physical appearance?"

"The eyes were bright and glassy. The features were pale; the skin clammy. There was a pronounced cyanosis of lips and fingernails."

"Are the symptoms you have just mentioned those of nitrobenzene poisoning?"

"I can't answer from personal experience since I've never treated a case of nitrobenzene poisoning before. But the symptoms agree with those described in books."

"What method of treatment did you employ?"

"The prescribed treatment. I pumped out the stomach and tried stimulants and artificial respiration. Unfortunately I was too late."

"Did you save the material evacuated from the stomach of the deceased?"

"Yes, certainly."

"What disposition did you make of it?"

"I put it in a jar."

"Is that jar at present in your possession, Doctor?"

"No."

"To whom did you surrender it?"

"To Dr. Resch, the county autopsy surgeon."

Dr. Resch testified that he had received a large glass jar from Dr. Baring which bore a label, "Stomach washings, Chamaron." Upon unscrewing the cover of the said jar, he had found a strong odor of bitter almonds. This odor, he explained, is characteristic of nitrobenzene or essence of mirbane.

"Of nitrobenzene alone?" inquired the deputy coroner.

"By no means. Benzaldehyde – oil of bitter almonds without hydrocyanic acid – has a smell very similar."

"Is there a method of definitely establishing the presence of nitrobenzene?"

"Chemical tests will do this. For example, a few drops of the substance to be analyzed are placed on a plate and a drop of sulphuric acid and a crystal of potassium chlorate added. A violet coloration results if the substance contains nitrobenzene."

"Did you make such chemical tests?"

"Yes."

"Are you satisfied of the presence of nitrobenzene in the stomach washings of the deceased?"

"I am well satisfied of it."

"In your opinion, Dr. Resch, was there a sufficient quantity of nitrobenzene to be responsible for the death of the deceased?"

"Yes, in my opinion. This poison is a very deadly one. So small a quantity as twenty drops has been known to cause death."

"Suppose, Doctor, that a fatal quantity of nitrobenzene has been swallowed. In how long a time will the symptoms appear?"

"Probably not for an hour or longer. It varies with individuals."

"Would a severe headache be one of the first symptoms?"

"Very likely. There might or might not be nausea and vomiting, followed rapidly by faintness and unconsciousness."

"Have you heard the testimony given by Dr. Baring at this inquisition?"

"Yes."

"Are the symptoms which he described as having been manifested by the deceased those of nitrobenzene poisoning?"

"In my opinion, decidedly."

"What are the physical properties of nitrobenzene?"

"It's a pale lemon-colored liquid. The odor resembles that of bitter almonds, as I have already said, and the taste is burning and disagreeable."

"In your opinion, Doctor, would the odor and taste be difficult or easy to disguise?"

"In my opinion, very difficult."

"Thank you, Dr. Resch. Mr. West, will you please come to the chair?"

Westborough, his knees buckling weakly beneath him, stumbled up the steps to the platform. He was about to commit a grave crime, the crime of perjury.

"Do you solemnly swear and affirm that the testimony you are about to give before this inquisition now pending shall be the truth, the whole truth and nothing but the truth, so help you God?"

Feeling that his throat had become sandpaper, he echoed, "So help me God."

"Your full name, please."

"Theodore L. West."

There! He had done it. He had told a lie under oath, which made him a full-fledged perjurer. For the moment his conscience was not relieved by the reflection that this crime against the state was being committed in the interests of justice.

"Place of residence?"

"Chicago, Illinois."

"Occupation?"

"Retired," Westborough said after some hesitation.

"Is it or is it not true that you are at present a guest in the home of Mr. Etienne LeDoux?" the deputy coroner demanded.

"It is true," Westborough mildly acknowledged.

"Were you present at the dinner in his home last night?"

"I was present."

"Where were you seated?"

"Between Mr. LeDoux and Mr. Chamaron."

"Do you know who sat on the other side of Mr. Chamaron?"

"Yes."

"Who?"

"Mr. Esterling."

Hansen consulted some papers. "Mr. West, I am going to ask you to describe in detail the various events which transpired during that meal."

Westborough was allowed to proceed as far as the incident of the flaring candle when the deputy coroner interrupted him.

"Was there any light in the room other than that of the candles?"

"Not at that time."

"Were you able to see the movements of your neighbors clearly?"

"Quite clearly."

"At the time the candle flame became green did you detect any movement by anyone toward Mr. Chamaron's dish of bouillabaisse?"

"No, I did not." Westborough paused, feeling a little ashamed. "I must confess my attention was entirely distracted by the green flame. It was very brilliant, almost blinding."

"Do you believe that it would have been possible for anyone at the table to have put the poison in Mr. Chamaron's dish at that instant?"

Westborough weighed his answer carefully. "Not for anyone," he said finally.

"Who could have reached Mr. Chamaron's dish?" Hansen persisted.

"His nearest neighbors, myself and Mr. Esterling. Perhaps, though this is far less likely, Mrs. Chamaron. The others, I am convinced, were too far away."

"Did anyone move from the table?"

"Yes; Mr. LeDoux. He had left his place at that time."

"Did anyone else leave his or her place?"

"No."

"Are you sure of that, Mr. West?"

"Yes, quite sure."

"What took place after the candles had been extinguished?"

"Mr. LeDoux urged us to continue our meal. He stated that he saw no reason why our dinner should be interrupted."

"Had the bouillabaisse been served to everyone at that time?"

"To everyone but Mr. LeDoux."

"Was it served at the table or in the kitchen?"

"At the table."

"By Mr. LeDoux?"

"Yes."

"Did you continue eating after the candle incident?"

"Yes."

"Did everyone?"

"Mr. Todd did not."

"Did anyone comment upon the taste of the dish?"

"Yes, Mr. Chamaron remarked upon an almond flavor."

"Did you perceive such a flavor yourself, Mr. West?"

"No, I could not detect it."

"Did you discuss the matter with Mr. Chamaron?"

"I am sorry to say that I did not. At the time, I regret deeply, I did not consider the subject of sufficient importance to merit an argument."

"Who did take issue with Mr. Chamaron's almond flavor?"

"I cannot recall that anyone did."

Westborough was allowed finally to retire from the platform to the comparative oblivion of his chair among the other witnesses. LeDoux was asked to describe how the party had been seated:

"I was at the southern end of the table, the end nearest to the doors opening on the terrace. My daughter-in-law sat opposite me. On the western side of the table, on my left, proceeding from south to north, were, respectively, Mr. West, Mr. Chamaron, Mr. Esterling, Mrs. Chamaron and Mr. Grayne. On my right, proceeding from south to north, were my granddaughter, Mr. Todd, Miss Morton and Mr. Preston."

"Will you describe how the bouillabaisse was served, Mr. LeDoux?"

"Manuel, my houseboy, brought it from the kitchen in a large covered tureen. I lifted the lid and ladled the bouillabaisse into soup plates which were passed down the table."

"Do you remember how these plates were passed, Mr. LeDoux?"

"I began, I believe, with the right side. The first plate traveled to my daughter-in-law, the second to Mr. Preston, the third to Miss Morton, the fourth to Mr. Todd and the fifth to my granddaughter. Then I passed to the left. The first plate traveled to Mr. Grayne, the second to Mrs. Chamaron, the third to Mr. Esterling, the fourth to Mr. Chamaron and the fifth, and last, to Mr. West."

"So the plate which reached Mr. Chamaron could have been handled only by Mr. West and yourself. Is this true?"

"It is true, *parbleu!*"

"Is it also true, Mr. LeDoux, that you had left your place after the bouillabaisse had been served to all but yourself?"

"Yes, I went to hurl outdoors a vial which someone had tossed under the table."

"Why were you so anxious to throw that vial away, Mr. LeDoux?"

"A cheap synthetic perfume, m'sieur, does not go with a good dinner. The flavors are ruined by the smell, *hein?* I was angry that my hospitality had been so insulted by what I then considered a crude practical joke. Now I realize that it was more than that. Much, much more."

"You are an authority on perfumes, aren't you, Mr. LeDoux?"

"I am head of LeDoux Perfumes, Incorporated, m'sieur. As such it might be said that I am an authority."

"Were you able to recognize the perfume contained in the bottle you threw away?"

"Instantly. The vial contained a tincture of ionone."

"What is ionone, Mr. LeDoux?"

"A substance prepared from lemongrass oil, which has an odor suggestive of violets. But not the true fragrance, by any means. The first coarse approximation to the violet odor, shall we say?"

"Could such a tincture of ionone have been purchased on the open market, Mr. LeDoux?"

"To my everlasting sorrow, I must say that it could. I have competitors so unscrupulous that they would not hesitate to foist so vile a thing upon the public as a violet perfume."

"Was such a perfume used by any of the ladies who sat at your table last night?"

"Never! They are ladies of discernment in fragrance. Two did use violet perfume, it is true, but the perfume was LeDoux's *Violux*, which is based upon a violet pomade, ionone being added only to strengthen the natural floral odor."

"Which ladies used the violet perfume?"

"Miss Morton and my daughter-in-law. It is the favorite odor of both. My granddaughter chose a pure jasmine perfume, and Mrs. Chamaron had delicately scented herself with my *Clair de Lune*."

"May I ask, Mr. LeDoux, if you could tell all this by smell alone?"

LeDoux looked both surprised and insulted. "Naturally. Perfumes are my business, *hein?* It would be strange, indeed, if I could not recognize my own products."

"Yes, of course," Hansen hastily assented. "I beg your pardon, Mr. LeDoux. You said, I believe, that at the time you considered the ionone had been introduced into your dining room merely as a crude practical joke."

The trim-bearded Frenchman nodded prompt confirmation.

"That is correct. I did make such a remark. I added, also, that I now realize it was much more than that."

"Do you wish to amplify that last statement, Mr. LeDoux?"

"But certainly. Ionone has a very strange effect. If one sniffs too long the odor vanishes, *pouf,* like that." He snapped his fingers. "One smells and then one does not smell, and the reason is that ionone rapidly fatigues the olfactory nerves. My theory, m'sieur, is—" He directed an inquiring glance toward his interlocutor. "Or is it that theories are not permitted at this hearing?"

"We are not bound by the rules of evidence which limit court procedure, Mr. LeDoux. I believe that you may be allowed to state your theory."

"I shall be happy to do so. My theory, m'sieur, is that the abominable creature, the poisoner, released the ionone in the hope that it would have a paralyzing effect upon all of our olfactory nerves. He hoped temporarily to destroy our sense of smell, so that none would be able to perceive the sharp almond odor of his poison, the essence of mirbane. And he almost succeeded, *hein?* None did notice except Mr. Chamaron."

"Why do you say that Mr. Chamaron noticed the odor?" the deputy coroner asked.

LeDoux shrugged expressively. "That is obvious, is it not? The remark which Mr. Chamaron made concerning the almond flavoring. Essence of mirbane does not have an almond *taste* but an almond *odor*. But the senses of taste and smell are closely related. My poor friend mistook the smell for the taste."

"Could that be possible?" Hansen inquired, seemingly a little surprised.

"Easily so. When the nose is held, only sweet, sour, bitter and salty tastes can be distinguished. Flavoring extracts and spices appeal primarily to the sense of smell. Blindfold yourself and place a clothespin over your nostrils. I guarantee that you will not be able to tell the onion from the apple."

"H'm, very interesting. Did you, Mr. LeDoux, hear Mr. Chamaron mention the almond flavor?"

"To the end of my days I shall regret that I did not. I believe that I would have smelled the rat if I had heard. Paul Michael had normally a trustworthy palate."

"Dr. Baring has testified that you told him Mr. Chamaron had been poisoned by nitrobenzene."

"It is true. I did so inform Dr. Baring."

"How was the fact known to you, Mr. LeDoux?"

"By smell. The odor was on Mr. Chamaron's lips."

"But are you able to distinguish the odor of nitrobenzene from, say, that of the oil of bitter almonds?"

LeDoux drew himself haughtily erect. "M'sieur, the trained sense of smell is more sensitive than chemical analysis."

Lung Fu followed his master to the stand. Confining his responses to monosyllabic affirmations or denials, the Chinese gradually allowed to be extracted from him the information that the bouillabaisse had contained no almonds, almond extract or any other substance which might possibly have given it an almond flavoring. Mrs. Chamaron was asked to step up to the chair.

Whatever her emotions, she kept them strictly to herself. Her voice was as cool, as carefully modulated as it had ever been. At only one point did she display a perceptible agitation.

That was when Hansen had asked her if her husband had had any reason which he might have believed sufficient for taking his own life.

"None. None whatsoever. My husband was a successful businessman. He had no financial difficulties; his health was good, and he was never given to fits of melancholia."

"Mrs. Chamaron, did you overhear your husband's remark about the almond flavoring?"

"Yes, I did hear him say something about an almond taste. I'm afraid that I didn't pay much attention, as I was carrying on a conversation with Mr. Grayne at the time."

"I am now going to ask you to speak frankly. Do you know of any enemies of your husband among the people who sat down at Mr. LeDoux's dinner table?"

"Not enemies, exactly."

"Let me put the question in another way. Did your husband have a recent difference of opinion with any of that company?"

"Yes."

"With whom?"

"With Mr. Esterling."

"Were you present during their discussion?"

"No. I don't believe that any third person was present. I learned they had had an argument from Paul."

Westborough, seated next to Jacynth, noted how attentively the girl was leaning forward.

"When did that argument take place?"

"On the evening of July third."

"Did your husband tell you the subject of the controversy?"

"No, he didn't mention it to me."

Jacynth uttered a startled little gasp.

IV

"Is it true, Mrs. LeDoux, that you had scented yourself with a violet perfume?"

"Yes." In a black dress with a white jabot Margaret LeDoux looked like a large, very timid penguin.

"What brand of violet perfume did you use?"

"*Violux.*"

"Who is the manufacturer of *Violux?*"

"Mr. LeDoux."

"Will you describe the odor which you have just said saturated the room?"

"It – I'm not very good at description." She was suffering agonies of stage fright; it was readily apparent. "The odor was like violets."

"The same as *Violux* perfume?"

"No, not quite. It wasn't so – so – I just don't know how to say what the difference was."

"However, there was a difference?"

"Oh yes!"

"You knew that you were not smelling your own violet perfume?"

"Yes, of course. It wasn't the same at all."

"Why did you look under the table, Mrs. LeDoux?"

"I felt something under my foot."

"What was it?"

"A tiny glass vial."

"Had you ever seen a similar shaped vial before?"

"Oh yes. A great many of them at Mr. LeDoux's factory."

"Did you pick up the vial from the floor, Mrs. LeDoux?"

"Yes. But Mr. LeDoux took it from me right away. He was very angry."

"Do you know which person lighted the candles in the candelabra?"

"Why, I did."

"When?"

"Just before dinner was announced. That's when I always light them."

"Do you burn candles every evening?"

"Yes, always. Mr. LeDoux loves to dine by candlelight."

"Were these candles new ones, or had they been burned before?"

"They were all new ones."

"Who inserted them into the branches of the candelabra?"

"I did." Her soft voice sounded very frightened. "Yesterday afternoon."

"At what time yesterday afternoon?"

"I – I don't remember."

"Where were the candles kept?"

"In a drawer of the sideboard. In a box."

"Did all of these candles look the same as usual to you when you took them out of the box to insert into the branches of the candelabra?"

"Yes."

"Did you examine them closely?"

"No, not very."

"Do you believe, Mrs. LeDoux, that *after* you had placed the candles in the candelabra it would have been possible for a person to have entered the dining room unobserved?"

"Why, yes, I believe so."

Mrs. LeDoux had not heard Mr. Chamaron say anything about the almond flavoring of the bouillabaisse. She must have been talking to Mr. Preston at the time. It was all very horrible, she thought, that a man should be poisoned – killed at their own dinner table. She didn't know what to make of it.

Aaron Todd, a wrinkled chimpanzee in a seersucker suit, ascended the platform. He declared that his name was Aaron X. Todd. That the X stood for Xenophon, if that was anyone's concern. That he lived in Los Angeles. That his principal business was real estate. That he was treasurer and a director of LeDoux Perfumes, Incorporated. That he did own stock in the said concern. That how much stock was nobody's business but his own. That if Deputy Coroner Hansen tended to his own problems he might be able to get somewhere, which he certainly was not doing now. Laughter arose from the representatives of the general public who had found their way into the little chapel.

Hansen pounded angrily with a gavel. "Mr. Todd, I will not tolerate such rudeness. I insist that you give me civil answers."

"What say?" Todd inquired blandly.

"Are you deaf, Mr. Todd?"

Todd indicated his hearing device. "I insist on civil answers," the deputy coroner shouted.

"You needn't yell about it," Todd remonstrated. Hansen's countenance became successively pink, scarlet, crimson and purple.

"*Mis*ter Todd, did you also smell the odor of violets at this dinner?"

"Nope," Todd replied.

The deputy coroner was astonished. "I asked if you smelled the odor of violets. Mr. Todd."

"I heard you ask that," Todd said.

"Do you mean to tell me you didn't smell anything?"

Todd tapped his nose. "No smeller. Had the flu a few years back; when I came out of it I couldn't smell any more. Don't much care. Miss a lot of stinks."

Hansen interrupted a second flow of merriment.

"I should think, Mr. Todd, that a person with no sense of smell would not be interested financially in perfume manufacture."

"You don't need to smell 'em to sell 'em," Todd rejoined tartly.

The deputy coroner observed testily, "When everyone has found you sufficiently amusing, Mr. Todd, we will continue the inquest." Slowly the laughter faded away.

"Mr. Todd, how intimately were you acquainted with the deceased, Paul Michael Chamaron?"

"He was LeDoux's advertising agent. I never had much to do with him. I never monkeyed with LeDoux's advertising. That's not my business."

"What is your business, Mr. Todd?"

"It isn't your business, young man."

Hansen bit his lip. "Is it true, Mr. Todd, that you refused to eat your portion of bouillabaisse?"

"It's true."

"Why did you refuse?"

"I don't like rich food."

"Did you refuse before or after Mr. Chamaron's remark about the almond flavoring?"

"I didn't hear what Chamaron said. There was a lot of gabbling going on, and—" Todd tapped his hearing device again.

Sam Preston was a more tractable witness, although rather an unproductive one. He had, it appeared, seen nothing and heard nothing of consequence. Yes, he had smelled the violet smell. Sure, he had thought it was ionone. You don't work for a perfume plant without learning a few smells. Yes, he was very surprised when the violet odor had drifted into the room.

"Brother, you could've knocked me over with a feather," Mr. Preston solemnly declared.

What had Mr. Preston done at the time the candle had blazed? Mr. Preston had done nothing. Mr. Preston was again in a state in which a feather sufficed to destroy his equilibrium. Had Mr. Preston seen anyone make a movement toward Mr. Chamaron's bouillabaisse? Mr. Preston had not. What had Mr. Preston seen? He had seen Mr. Esterling reach for a water glass. Had Mr. Esterling thrown the contents of the glass upon the unnaturally green candle? No, he had not.

"He didn't get a chance to, brother. Stu Grayne stood up and puffed, and out went Mr. Candle quicker than you can say Jack Robinson."

"Was more than one candle extinguished?" the deputy coroner inquired.

"Three or four of 'em, brother."

The deputy coroner reminded Mr. Preston that he, Hansen, was no fraternal relation of Mr. Preston's. He inquired if Mr. Grayne's act had plunged the room in total darkness.

"No, there was still three or four candles to go."

"Were these later extinguished?"

"Yes, but by that time Mr. LeDoux had turned on the electric lights."

"Do I understand you to say, Mr. Preston, that the room was at no time in total darkness?"

"That's right, bro – Mr. Coroner."

"You may call me Mr. Hansen," the deputy coroner suggested. "Mr. Preston, were you well acquainted with the deceased, Paul Michael Chamaron?"

"Sure was. Paul was a swell fellow. He and I always got along swell."

"Do you know of a person seated at Mr. LeDoux's table last night who was not on good terms with the deceased?"

"Everyone liked good old Paul. He was a swell fellow."

"That isn't exactly what I asked you, Mr. Preston."

"I've forgotten how you put the question."

"I said, 'Do you know of a person seated at Mr. LeDoux's table last night who was not on good terms with the deceased?' "

"The answer's no. Em-*phat*-ically."

"Mr. Preston, I am going to make the question more specific. Was the deceased on good terms with Mr. Esterling?"

"Well, maybe they did have an argument now and then. So what? Any two people are likely to have a difference of opinion."

"To your knowledge, did Mr. Esterling ever make threats against the deceased?"

"I should say not." Mr. Preston looked virtuously indignant. "You're barking up the wrong tree, brother. Derek Esterling is a swell fellow."

Mr. Preston had not noticed an almond flavor in his bouillabaisse. Nor had he heard Mr. Chamaron comment on such a flavor.

Stuart Grayne seated himself nonchalantly in the witness chair. He was, he admitted, an advertising copy writer and had been in the employ of the deceased.

"How long, Mr. Grayne, have you worked for Mr. Chamaron's agency?"

"Nearly a year, suh. Befo' that I was in New Yo'k."

"Are you a Southerner, Mr. Grayne?"

"South Ca'olinah."

In response to further questioning, Mr. Grayne informed his interrogator that he had not worked on the LeDoux Perfume account until a few weeks

ago. At that time Mr. Chamaron had told his employee that his South Carolina background might be very useful in connection with the advertising
program for Mr. LeDoux's new synthetic imitation of the fragrance of the
Carolina yellow jessamine. He didn't know very much about "pu'fumes,"
Grayne owned, grinning rather sheepishly, but naturally he was "willing to
do anything Mr. Chamaron requested."

"I thought a lot of Paul Michael, suh. He was a mighty fine man."

Grayne's account of the candle incident contributed no new facts. He had
not, he said, heard Mr. Chamaron's almond-flavoring remark.

Beatrice Morton came to the stand. Mr. Chamaron, she revealed tearfully,
had been a very dear personal friend of hers. She wanted to do everything
she could to see that the one who poisoned him was brought to justice. No,
she had not heard Mr. Chamaron's mention of the almond taste, but then, she
was on the opposite side of the table and not very close to him.

Miss Morton had been present, she admitted hesitantly, when an argument
had occurred between Mr. Esterling and Mr. Chamaron. Mr. Esterling, she
believed, had said something sarcastic about advertising, which Mr. Chamaron had resented. Mr. LeDoux had smoothed them over. But that had been
several weeks ago, and it hadn't amounted to much, really.

At the time of the candle's pyrotechnic effulgence, Miss Morton confessed,
she had completely lost her head.

"I screamed, and I even tried to put it out with my napkin. Then I saw that
Mr. Esterling was reaching for his water glass."

"Were you looking at Mr. Esterling at this time, Miss Morton?"

"Yes, I was looking diagonally across the table at him."

"Did you see him make a movement toward Mr. Chamaron's bouillabaisse?"

"Oh no!" Miss Morton was horrified. "He couldn't have done that. It would
have been impossible, really."

Derek Esterling, the next witness, was the one important witness, everyone seemed to sense. The psychic tension of the little chapel augmented
noticeably as the bearded young chemist took the chair.

Yes, Esterling admitted, he had sat next to the deceased yesterday at din-
nertime. For that matter, at every meal. They had all occupied the same places
since the beginning of Mr. LeDoux's house party.

Esterling was pale but composed. His attitude, Westborough meditated,
was that of a man who realizes his danger but is determined to meet it courageously.

"Is it true, Mr. Esterling, that on the night before Mr. Chamaron's death
you had a quarrel with him?"

"A business controversy," Esterling corrected.

"What was the subject of that controversy?"

"I cannot say."

"Do you decline to answer on the grounds that you will incriminate yourself?"

"I decline to answer."

Nowise disturbed, the deputy coroner requested Mr. Esterling to relate what had occurred during the fatal dinner. Esterling's account differed in no material particular from those which had been previously given.

"Did you hear Mr. Chamaron mention the almond taste?"

"Yes. He said, as I recall it, 'A neat combination of flavors. The almond touch is very intriguing.' "

"Could you perceive such an almond flavor yourself?"

"No, I could not."

"Then why did you not contradict Mr. Chamaron?"

"The remark didn't strike me as having any importance. I dislike arguments over trivial questions."

With the air of one about to light a fuse to a powder magazine, the deputy coroner whisked a bottle from a desk drawer.

"Can you identify this, Mr. Esterling?"

"I can."

"Please do."

"It's the bottle which Captain Howe took from my laboratory this morning."

"Do you know what it contains?"

"At the time when it passed into Captain Howe's possession it contained nitrobenzene."

"Are you basing that statement, Mr. Esterling, solely upon the label of the bottle?"

"No, I was asked to smell the contents before Howe removed the bottle."

"Are you able to distinguish the odor of nitrobenzene from similar odors, such as the oil of bitter almonds?"

"I'd be a poor perfume chemist if I couldn't. The odor of nitrobenzene is suggestive only in a coarse way of that of almond oil."

"Do you make frequent use of nitrobenzene in your experiments?"

"No. I use it rarely."

"Mr. Esterling, has any liquid been taken from this bottle since the last time you used it?"

"I can't say for certain."

"Where was this bottle kept?"

"In a cupboard."

"A locked cupboard?"

"No. But the laboratory is locked when no one's there."

"Who has a key to your laboratory, Mr. Esterling?"

"Myself and my assistant, Bernard Kelton."

"Does any other person have a key?"

"No."

"Not even Mr. LeDoux?"

"No one."

"Is the laboratory always locked when you or Mr. Kelton are not present?"

"It's supposed to be."

"Do you know of any occasion when it was not locked?"

"No–o." Esterling seemed aware that he was being driven into a trap.

"Where is your assistant at the present time?"

"On his vacation. Taking a motor trip through Oregon."

"Did he take his laboratory key with him?"

"I don't know."

"Can you find out?"

"I'm unable to get in touch with him before next Monday."

"Has your own key ever been out of your hands?"

"No–o." Esterling hesitated. "I did leave it at home once when I was out of town."

"How long ago?"

"The last three days of April. I'd gone to San Francisco to attend a state chemist's association meeting."

"Did you tell anyone that you were leaving the key at your home?"

"No one. I didn't decide to take the key from the ring until just before I left the house."

"When you returned did you find the key where you had put it?"

"Yes, exactly."

"To your knowledge, has Mr. Kelton's key ever been out of his possession?"

"I wouldn't know," Esterling answered.

The next witness bore the classical and very common name of John Smith. His profession was that of locksmith, and he was, he asserted, the only locksmith in Valle de Flores. He was requested to examine the key to Mr. Esterling's laboratory.

"Have you ever seen this key before, Mr. Smith?"

"Sure, I seen her. This morning Cap Howe comes in and drives me out to the LeDoux plant where he asks me to take apart a lock and—"

"We'll come to that later, Mr. Smith. Did Mr. Esterling – or somebody else – bring in a key of this shape and ask you to make a duplicate?"

"Mr. Esterling did come in to my shop once, but it weren't this key he wanted. 'Twere another key to his house."

The deputy coroner looked a little exasperated. "That isn't relative to this inquiry, Mr. Smith. I asked if you had ever seen this key prior to this morning."

"Today's the first time I ever seen her."

"Now, Mr. Smith, will you tell us about the lock you examined this morning?"

"She was a good strong Miles lock with a row of five pin tumblers in the cylinder."

"Where was the lock, Mr. Smith?"

"Oh, didn't I say? On the door to Mr. Esterling's lab. My, the smells there were out at that plant. Made a fellow sick to sniff 'em all. Perfume's agin' nature, I said to Mr. LeDoux. If the good Lord had wanted a woman to smell like a flower he'd-a made her that way."

"Please, Mr. Smith. We want to know about the lock."

"Oh, the lock. Well, I takes her off the door and has a look at her insides. Cap here, he has a theory that if someone's picked the lock there'd be scratches on the tumblers caused by the pick forcing 'em into line. Well, maybe so, but anyways, we couldn't find none, not even under a strong glass."

"Do you conclude that the lock had never been picked?"

"She'd be a right hard lock to open that way, I'm a-thinking."

"Did you also examine the locks of the laboratory windows, Mr. Smith?"

"No one could break in through them windows. There's iron bars over every one of 'em."

Jacynth LeDoux was the final witness.

The girl was not self-conscious. She took her oath with the poise of a cinema luminary. Yet there was nothing brazen, nothing self-assertive in her quiet demeanor.

"Miss LeDoux, were you present last night at your grandfather's dinner table?"

"Yes, I was there."

Nineteen years old! Westborough thought. This child, a witness to murder!

"Where were you seated, Miss LeDoux?"

"Next to Gran'-père and directly across the table from Mr. West."

"By Gran'-père do you mean your grandfather?"

"Yes. I'm sorry. That's what I always call him."

"Miss LeDoux, I want you to tell us everything that occurred during that dinner."

"But that's been told so many times!" she objected.

"Please don't think of what anyone else has said, Miss LeDoux. Describe what occurred just as you remember it happening."

Hansen interrupted after a time. "You stated that Mr. Esterling had picked up a water glass. Do you say that because you heard another witness say it or because you actually saw Mr. Esterling at the time?"

"I saw him. I had been watching him very closely."

"In which hand did Mr. Esterling hold the water glass?"

"In his right hand."

"Are you guessing, Miss LeDoux?"

"No, I am not. It was his right hand, the hand nearest to Mr. Chamaron."

"You are sure of that, Miss LeDoux?"

"I know what you're thinking," she retorted hotly. "But you're wrong. Derek didn't put anything into Mr. Chamaron's bouillabaisse."

"Miss LeDoux, please."

"I watched him from the time the candle blazed up until the lights were turned on. He wasn't out of my sight for a second. Not a single second."

"Is it true," the deputy coroner asked, "that you are engaged to Mr. Esterling?"

Jacynth raised her small face defiantly. "I'm proud to say I am."

The foreman of the coroner's jury finished his reading " '… and having made such inquisition and hearing the testimony adduced, upon our oaths, each and all do say that we find that the deceased was named Paul Michael Chamaron, a male, married, a native of California, aged forty-two years, and that he came to his death on the fifth of July, A.D., 1939, at the home of Etienne LeDoux near Valle de Flores in Santa Bonita County, California, and that this death was caused by a poison, nitrobenzene, otherwise known as essence of mirbane, and that the said poison was administered to the deceased either by his own hand or by the hand of a person or persons unknown.

" 'All of which we duly certify by this inquisition in writing, by us signed this fifth day of July, 1939. …' "

PART SIX
AFFAIR OF HONOR

Seeing his hostess laden with a tray, Stuart Grayne volunteered at once to carry it upstairs to Mrs. Chamaron. When he knocked on the bedroom door Kay listlessly bade him enter. She was wearing the same long-sleeved black dress she had worn that afternoon at the inquest. He set the tray on the dressing table and lifted the cover from a plate, disclosing a pair of appetizingly browned lamb chops.

"Just have a bite or two," he coaxed.

"Thank you, no." Her gaze flicked apathetically from the tray to his face. "Eating would seem to be rather dangerous in this house."

His mouth crinkled indulgently. "The sheriff's man dropped a hint it would be right advisable fo' me to stay around heah a day or so. But he didn't say anything like that to you, as I recall it." He patted her shoulder with good-natured concern. "This is no place fo' you, honey."

"Oh, but it is," she differed. "It's exactly where I should be. Suppose you were married."

"That takes a lot of supposing."

"And somebody killed your wife. If you knew who it was wouldn't you—"

"I don't like fo' you to talk this way. Nobody knows who—"

"I do!" Her voice was dramatically intense. "The testimony given at the inquest told me there could be only one person. That's the man who quarreled with Paul on Monday night. He hated my husband."

"Now sit down and try a morsel of chop," he pleaded. "They're just out of the broiler."

"Don't you agree?" she shrilled.

"To tell the truth," he returned placidly, "I don't take much stock in the idea. I've known Derek Esterling fo' a long, long time. He's no killah."

"Do you know why Esterling quarreled with Paul Michael?" she demanded bellicosely.

Grayne shook his head. "Didn't even know you knew, honey. You said you didn't at the inquest, remember?"

"I lied. I did know, but I kept silent on your account."

"On my account?"

"It wouldn't look so well, would it," she jeered, "if they knew my husband

113

had talked of firing you before he was poisoned?"

He stared blankly. "Did Paul Michael tell you that, Kay?"

"His hand was being forced. I made him take a stand. Not that he needed urging, I'll admit. He always liked you, Stuart. He gave you a good job. You owe Paul Michael Chamaron something, don't you?"

"I owe him a lot," Grayne said soberly.

"How are you going to pay that debt? By allowing his murderer to escape scot free? The authorities won't do anything. I learned that this afternoon. They let him off because a girl lied."

Grayne said at length, "I don't think Miss LeDoux lied." He could control his intonation, but not the sudden flush of blood to his cheeks.

"You're the last man in the world who ought to stand up for Derek Esterling," she declared scornfully. "He hates you. He's the one who tried to get you fired. Paul Michael protected you, and that's why he was killed."

"If I thought that—" With an effort he mastered his fiery temper.

"I could prove it," she said wearily, "but it would be a waste of time. There's no strength, no real character in you. Paul Michael was worth thirty of you, Stuart. And I" – her voice rose hysterically – "I've been the world's prize damn fool."

II

Though there could be no further pretense of business conferences, the wretched house party dragged on without even a shadow of excuse for being. LeDoux, Miss Morton, Esterling and Preston returned to their desks on Thursday, and the perfumer's other guests were left to amuse themselves. At ten o'clock in the morning Westborough was with Jacynth, admiring the profusion of petunias, geraniums, lantanas and zinnias blooming in the terraced garden, when LeDoux's office boy brought him a letter.

The epistle had been directed to Mr. T. L. West, in care of LeDoux Perfumes, Incorporated, in a plain envelope, as the correspondent had been instructed. Apologizing to his companion, "Mr. West" tore open the envelope. There was a brief note from Captain Cranston to explain the presence of a photostatic print. "Dear me," the historian sighed, putting note and enclosure into his pocket. " 'To side with Truth,' says Lowell, 'is noble when we share her wretched crust.' A pitifully wretched crust, in this instance, however."

"Bad news?" Jacynth inquired sympathetically.

"It is not precisely good." Westborough noted that Stuart Grayne had emerged from the house and was strolling toward the garden stairs. "May I inquire how long Mr. Esterling has worn his present hirsute adornment?"

"Oh, a long, long time. At least a year."

"Indeed? 'He that hath a beard is more than a youth.' 'Tarry at Jericho until your beards be grown.' I might quote other sayings on the subject, but I see that more interesting company than my own approaches. You will excuse me, will you not?"

He hurried to the telephone in the upstairs sitting room, speaking guardedly after the connection had been completed. The number he had given to the operator was that of Captain Sydney Howe, and it was well within the realm of probability that someone might choose to listen in from the downstairs telephone.

"Word has been received from the Corinthians. Do I make myself clear? The earlier near tragedy was caused by a certain fluidextract which, I have just learned, was ordered by a person having access to mine host's business letterheads. The letter was typewritten and signed by a palpably false name. The purchase, however, was neither billed nor delivered to LeDoux Perfumes. Someone called for the package and paid cash. Description of that someone, I regret, has so far eluded the investigators."

"Then," Howe broke in, "I'll have to go ahead with what I've got."

"Pray wait another day," Westborough pleaded. "There is one man who might know, a clerk, who, most unluckily, chose to celebrate the Fourth alcoholically and was in consequence severely injured in a traffic accident. Yesterday he lay unconscious at the hospital, 'a wretched soul, bruised with adversity,' but a fresh effort will be made today to communicate with him. I beseech you, wait. The verdict of the coroner's jury makes it possible for you to do so with a clear official conscience." He paused for a minute or so in which Howe expressed himself volubly. "My dear sir, I do indeed see your point of view. I sympathize with it most heartily. But surely you do not wish to ruin an innocent man's life by haste too precipitate? The harm can never be entirely undone. One more day, I beg of you."

"Well, one day," Howe yielded. "But if I don't do something soon my scalp may answer for it. The sheriff himself phoned this morning to tell me it stands out like a sore thumb who's guilty."

Westborough replaced the receiver with a sigh. "Dear me," he pondered aloud. "The law, in the memorable words of Sir Edward Coke, 'is perfection of reason,' but it does not necessarily follow that the law can be reasonable."

He decided upon action he had hitherto refrained from taking; to wit, a private consultation with Derek Esterling. The chief chemist was alone in his laboratory, seated on the stool before the long table. Glancing at a small bottle on the table, Westborough received one of the biggest surprises of his life. If his theory were right Esterling could not know of the existence of this bottle. But, very obviously, he did know. The historian did his best to act the part of a casual visitor.

"Do you mind if I disturb you for a few minutes, Mr. Esterling? An imposition upon your time, I confess, but I am rather at loose ends for an occupation."

Esterling courteously offered the older man his seat, giving Westborough an opportunity to comment upon the bottle. "Fluidextractum gelsemii," he read from the label. "Isn't that a remedy for nervous headaches?" He watched the chemist's face.

"Among other things," Esterling replied shortly.

"I did not know that it was employed in perfume manufacture." Westborough's tone was that of one determined to keep a conversation going, even on a very dull topic.

"It isn't."

"You do not yourself use it medicinally, I hope?"

"Why do you hope that?" Esterling demanded.

"Why – er" – Westborough found himself in something of a quandary – "why, I receive the impression from this label that gelsemium is rather a dangerous medicine to take. I dare say, however, I am wrong."

"You're right," Esterling acknowledged. "I wouldn't advise anyone who wants to keep on living to swallow even a teaspoonful of this."

The historian acted properly impressed. As if in afterthought, he inquired, "What is such a drug doing in your laboratory, Mr. Esterling?"

"I can't tell you."

Westborough blinked. "I am sorry that my question was offensive. Doubtless you have an excellent reason for wishing to conceal—"

"I'm not trying to conceal anything," Esterling declared splenetically. "When I said that I couldn't tell you, I meant that literally. I don't know myself."

"How can it be possible?" Westborough murmured.

"This morning I decided to take a careful look around to see if anything else had been disturbed here, and I found this bottle hidden at the back of a shelf. I don't have even a glimmer as to who put it there."

"Most astounding! Tsk, tsk! It is a pity that you ever handled it. The evidence in your disfavor is sufficiently strong without fingerprints."

"Fingerprints!" Esterling echoed. "This stuff has nothing to do with the nitrobenzene that killed Chamaron. I could handle this bottle from now until doomsday, and nobody could say a thing."

"I am not so sure," Westborough demurred gravely. "Mr. Esterling, will you please telephone to Captain Howe immediately? Notify him that you have discovered this bottle and explain fully all the circumstances, just as you have related them to me. But do not, I pray you, mention my name."

"Good lord!" The chemist's face reflected a genuine bewilderment. "What do you have to do with Howe? Who are you anyway, Mr. West?"

"Not quite what I seem," the historian owned. "But I beg you observe that which the Buddha referred to as 'the noble silence of the truly wise.' "

"Are you a detective?"

"I may truthfully answer that I am not. But concern yourself no more with me, I beg of you. I am merely one who wishes to be your friend, and who believes, incidentally, in your entire innocence."

"Thanks." Esterling's lips twisted into a cheerless smile. "I don't mind saying that I appreciate that, sir. The general atmosphere toward me is still – well, rather on the frigid side."

"Surely, however, you cannot complain of the behavior of your fiancée."

"No. Jacynth has been splendid." Esterling's long fingers absently drummed a tattoo on the laboratory table.

"Will you cooperate in my endeavors?" Westborough asked.

"Gladly. What can I do?"

"First I wish you to examine this document."

The "document" was a photostatic reproduction, full size, of a letter on the stationery of LeDoux Perfumes, Incorporated.

June 8, 1939

Davis Wholesale Drug Company,
Los Angeles, Calif.

Gentlemen:

Please prepare for us two fluid ounces of fluidextract of gelsemium; for your information the drug is wanted in connection with our experiments in the extraction of the aromatic principle of the yellow jasmine, *gelsemium sempervirens*.

You need not trouble to ship it to us, as I expect to be in Los Angeles on Saturday morning and will call personally for the package.

Very truly yours,
LeDoux Perfume Laboratories

By D. E. Cor

"What the devil!" Esterling exclaimed as he read. "Where did you get this?"

"If you don't mind," Westborough said gently, "I should prefer to ask the questions for the time being. First, is the name D. E. Cor known to you?"

"I never heard it before in my life."

"The signature is probably in a disguised hand," Westborough opined. "The name seems to have been written with a most painstaking care. Are your own letters, Mr. Esterling, customarily signed, 'LeDoux Perfume Laboratories'?"

"No. Always 'LeDoux Perfumes, Incorporated, by Derek Esterling, Chief Chemist.' "

"To whom are your letters dictated?"

"Whichever of the girls is free at the time. I don't have any regular stenographer. Sometimes I ask the office boy to move in a dictaphone, but that's rare. I don't have a very extensive correspondence, Mr. West. My work is mainly research."

"Yes, of course. Isn't that a typewriter?" The historian gestured toward the small flat desk at one end of the crowded table.

"You can call it that." Esterling laughed a trifle uneasily. "It's an old wreck, retired from regular office service, which Kelton and I inherited. We use it for notes on our experiments. I haven't been able yet to find a girl who is any good at transcribing chemical formulas."

"A most difficult type of work, I should imagine. Dear me, I perceive your machine has been fitted with a special key next to the semicolon. Instead of the customary '¢-@' combination there are plus and equal signs."

"Right. That one little key saves us a lot of labor in typing equations."

"Is any other machine in the factory so equipped?"

"I don't think so. Those signs aren't included on the standard typewriter keyboard."

"No, they are not," Westborough agreed. "Pray examine the photostat again. Do you notice anything peculiar?"

Esterling shook his head. "Can't say I do."

"Focus your attention upon the semicolon following the word 'gelsemium' in the second line of the message," Westborough suggested.

"There's a blur," Esterling said.

"Does it not appear to you as if the typist had inadvertently struck the wrong key and had corrected the error without troubling to make an erasure?"

"You're right. The semicolon was typed over something else."

"And that something else," Westborough asserted, "is unmistakably a plus sign."

"Do you mean to say the letter was written on this machine?"

"It might appear so." Inserting a blank sheet of paper behind the platen, Westborough wrote: "Please prepare for us two fluid ounces of fluidextract of gelsemium," and compared the clause letter by letter with the photostatic print. "Yes, it looks very much as if such were the case."

"Well, I didn't write it!" Esterling's voice was audibly shaken. "I don't have the slightest idea who did."

"The letter is dated June eighth," Westborough mused. "Exactly one week before the first conference to discuss the marketing of your new perfume. Mr. Esterling, may I ask your whereabouts on the afternoon of Saturday, June tenth?"

"Let me see. Why, right here, of course. Working like the very devil because Kelton had left me with two men's jobs that day."

"Your assistant was not present?"

"No. He had to have a tooth yanked. It had been giving him a great deal of trouble. He didn't show up at all on Saturday."

"Dear me, that is rather unfortunate. Surely, however, someone else can testify that you were here?"

Esterling shook his head. "I can't remember anyone coming into the lab that morning," he said.

"Calamitous! One might almost conclude that malign planets were exerting their baleful influence upon your horoscope."

"Why is it so important to prove where I was that morning?" Esterling demanded. But Westborough's faculties were, in the words of Henry Carey, "immersed in cogibundity of cogitation."

"On second thought, perhaps it is not the stars. Perhaps it is someone – all too human – who had in some manner learned of Mr. Kelton's dental appointment. Mr. Esterling, you have a deadly enemy. Or rather, it would appear, you and Mr. Chamaron and Mr. LeDoux had a common enemy."

"LeDoux!" Esterling repeated. "Why do you include him in the list?"

Westborough did not reply. Carefully holding the bottle of gelsemium with his handkerchief, he untwisted the screw cover. He poured a drop of the liquid on his finger tip and cautiously touched the finger to his lips.

"The taste is bitter," he declared. "Could one swallow the substance unwittingly? Perhaps, if one were expecting a bitter taste. But the smell? Mr. Esterling, your nose is far, far more sensitive than my own. Will you, please—"

The chemist took a long and careful sniff. "It's almost odorless," he pronounced.

"Ah!" Westborough exclaimed. "A very pretty theory founders from that torpedo."

III

Stuart stooped to pick up a clod of dirt. His wavy black hair was uncovered to the sun. His russet-brown sport shirt was rolled above his forearms and was open, displaying the sinewy cords of his tanned neck.

" 'Dear earth, I do salute thee with my hand.' " He crumbled the clod, allowing the pulverized loam to trickle slowly through his broad square fingers. "King Richard was right. Shakespeare knew how good it is for a man to touch earth now and then."

"I didn't know you could be so serious," Jacynth exclaimed. They had been walking for a long while among the fragrant fields, and the sun's rays slanted from the west in an acute angle to inform her it was time they returned home. Her companion wiped the soil from his hand with a handkerchief.

"Basically, Miss Jacynth, I'm a serious puhson."

"Person," she corrected.

"That's what I said," he insisted. "Puhson."

She laughed, oddly lighthearted. Two lines from something or other popped teasingly into her mind:

> *She cast her eyes upon him, and he looked so good and true,*
> *That she thought, "I could be happy with a gentleman like you!"*

"I could be happy with a gentleman like you!" A gentleman tall and dark … She shouted a warning as a wasp poised viciously above a cluster of jasmine near his groping hand.

Annoyed by the tumult of sound, the wasp flickered into nothingness. Stuart plucked the blossom – a white star, faintly pink tinged. "I've a fancy to see how one of these would look in yo' hair," he said.

She wove it obediently into the curls above her left ear. "The women of India do this with the jasmine given to them by their – " Just in time she remembered that Stuart could scarcely be called a lover. "The Arabian name is *yas min*," she substituted, dipping hastily into Gran'-père's flower lore. "That means despair-is-folly." He repeated the phrase, murdering the terminal *r* with cruel neglect. "Will you ever learn to talk like everyone else?" she laughed.

He inspected her gravely. "That's mighty pretty."

His eyes boldly said what his lips did not. His eyes said, "You're mighty pretty, honey. I like your little tilted nose. I like the color of your hair. I even like the little way your forehead bulges."

"You're like a flowah yo'self."

There, he *had* said it. He had paid her a compliment, and she was glad, glad! She thought of how strong his arms were. She thought of his body, so big, so powerful. He could scoop her up with ridiculous ease. He could swing her to the ceiling and catch her lightly before she fell.

But his strength was only a part; he was gentle and courteous. And he wasn't stupid. Gran'-père had made all stupid men forever insipid to her.

Derek was more intellectual, she acknowledged. Derek had genius. But Derek wasn't very often playful. Talking to Stuart was like a hard fast game of tennis, their minds whipping the ball of banter furiously across the net.

He liked the same things she did – many of them. "I could be happy with a gentleman like you!" But she was engaged to Derek. Derek needed her now, in a way he had never needed her before. "It's infatuation," she thought quickly. "Infatuation is not love. Love is what I feel for Derek. I love Derek."

"It's time we went to the house," she said aloud.

The landscape she had known all her life had become strangely unfamiliar. The sprawling red-roofed building, the rich crimson splash of bougainvillaea against the white stucco, the wide green lawn, the cypress by the gate like a bushy sentinel, the high wire fence, the eucalyptus windbreak, the silver-gray olive trees lining the drive from highway to the front entrance – she recognized them as through a haze, the unreal background for a dream into which she had wakingly stumbled.

She was Jacynth LeDoux. A voice more compelling than reason whispered that she was no longer the same person. A baby, a child, a girl in the teens, a young matron, a middle-aged woman and a wrinkled grandmother may bear the same name, but are not the same, despite what people term continuity of being. So something akin to time had touched her with a mystic wand, causing her to pass suddenly into a different estate.

And she did not welcome the change. The former Jacynth LeDoux had been happy. She had not been troubled by these vague, wistful yearnings. Yearnings for what, for whom?

The factory gate had been shut, they found. The workers' cars had departed from the lot behind the building, every one. There wasn't even a night watchman's car, for Gran'-père employed no such person. Perhaps a little reckless of him, since perfumes are so valuable, but robbery among these quiet flower fields seemed an almost incredible thing to contemplate. It must be long past five-thirty. ... The thoughts flashed through her mind in the fraction of a minute it took Stuart to discover that the gate had been padlocked.

People had keys to the padlock, of course: Gran'-père and Derek and Mr. Preston, to say nothing of the janitor who opened and closed the premises, and probably others, none of which were of any consequence. She didn't have one. Nor did Stuart, naturally.

The gate was much higher than even his tall head. Like the fence, it was topped by three toothed strands of barbed wire, slanted at an impossibly nasty angle for climbing. She didn't blame the janitor. No one could see them in the fields behind the jasmine bushes, which grew tall as dwarf trees. The fault was distinctly her own for losing track of the time, but fixing the blame didn't help their situation in the slightest. Stuart was appraising the fence, coolly and critically. He had the air of a man about to do something. She caught him by the arm before he could make the attempt.

"You'll tear your trousers."

He roared with laughter. "They'll be sacrificed in a good cause, honey."

"But it isn't necessary. We can yell until someone up at the house hears us."

"I don't aim to have you strain yo' vocal cords."

She acknowledged that the house was a rather long distance away.

"But we don't have to do anything. Mother knows we went for a walk through the fields, and somebody will be along before long to see what's happened to us."

"Too much like forcing yo' luck," he objected. "We can telephone from the plant."

"We might," she deliberated. "Only I don't know how to work the switchboard."

He found that provocative of further mirth. "When you've slaved as many nights in an advertising agency as I have, all kinds of switchboards come easy."

For some reason it had occurred to neither of them that they wouldn't be able to get inside the building. But Gran'-père's janitor was nothing if not conscientious. All doors and windows were securely bolted. They sat down to hold a council of war.

After all, there was nothing really to worry about. He agreed with her that someone from the house would be down before long to discover what had become of them. In the meantime – well, why not continue to sit on the factory steps?

He said nothing more about climbing the fence. She knew, though, he would hurl himself at that awful barbed wire in a minute if she asked him to. But she wouldn't let him; he would just tear his hands.

And it was nice where they were. The olive trees of the curving drive hid the gate from view. It was rather like being on a desert island. But a tame, comfortable sort of desert island, she mused, where no hardships were to be expected and from which they were sure to be rescued. It was nice being there with him.

The jasmine in her hair assailed her nose with fragrance old as the Orient, scent witchery from the ancient empires of China, Kashmir, Persia, Arabia. Jasmine, "the Isis of flowers," would always from henceforth conjure the vision of a man for her. She realized it now. This man, dark and tall, as he sat with her in the hour before sunset. She thought, a little shyly, she would not object if he kissed her.

"Yo' funny, pretty name," he was saying. "What does Jacynth mean?"

"Purple. The same as hyacinth."

" 'That every Hyacinth the garden wears ...' " As if he had been reading her secret wishes, his face bent toward hers. She closed her eyes, trembling with longing.

"Purple hyacinth," he whispered, just before he kissed her. "I love you. I'm in love with you, honey dahlin'."

She kissed him blindly. Because her eyes were closed, she failed to see Derek, standing white-faced under an olive tree.

IV

Esterling, silent as a ghost, watched from a bend of the drive. Even as his hopes crumbled he formulated a new plan. One of desperation, of futility. Retracing his steps until the trees hid him from their view, he began to whistle with purposeful shrillness.

For some reason he had been whistling that waltz rather frequently during the past few days. He was not conscious at first of the melody.

When he reached the bend again, they had separated. "Your mother was worried," he said in an ordinary tone. "She thought you must have been locked in."

"We were, Derek." Only a good observer could have detected the strain in Jacynth's manner. "Thank you for rescuing us." She took his arm, chatting naturally as she walked between the two men. Their three pairs of feet whipped tiny clouds of dust from the unpaved driveway.

"There's still time to get ready before dinner." (It was necessary, he knew, to sponsor some sort of conversation.) "But if you don't hurry you may miss the vermouth."

"I don't like it very well, anyway."

"I prefer sherry myself," Esterling owned. They walked through the gate; he swung it shut and closed the jaws of the heavy padlock. While they were crossing the highway, he resumed his nervous whistling.

"I've heard that tune befo'," Grayne declared.

"Chopin," Jacynth informed him. "But Derek is murdering it."

"I heard a phonograph record of it once," Esterling said.

His mind dwelt on live oaks draped with Spanish moss; on jessamine like clusters of yellow butterflies. He thought of two men – boys rather – who had faced each other's cocked pistols in the woods.

They turned into the drive leading up to the house.

For nine years he had been running from the humiliation of that moment. Nine years in which the contempt for this tall Carolinian had sneeringly followed him. Nine years, but he would run no longer.

They traversed the patio. Grayne, waiting politely until Jacynth had gone through the south door to the house, felt Esterling's hand falling heavily on his shoulder.

"I want to talk to you in private."

Grayne nodded immediately, and they walked back to the edge of the swimming pool. "It's time we had an understanding," the copywriter said.

"Exactly," Esterling agreed curtly. "Do you still have your great-great-grandfather's dueling pistols?"

V

There were only eight at the dinner table Thursday evening. Mrs. Chamaron remained in her room, and Stuart Grayne was unaccountably absent. Westborough corrected himself. "Unaccountably" was not precisely the word. The Southerner had presented his excuses by proxy.

"He told me he had been called to Los Angeles on urgent business," Esterling informed them for the second time. "He wanted to borrow my car, and I gave him the keys. He said he'd be back early in the morning and asked me to explain why he couldn't be here for dinner. That's all I know."

"I'm sorry to hear it." LeDoux's waxen face was eloquently articulate. "Lung Fu went to a great deal of trouble to prepare a special dish for him. Ratifia cream – a genuine Charleston dessert. I dare say, however, that the rest of us will enjoy it."

Etienne LeDoux was not often so coldly formal. Plainly he was hurt that the Carolinian had not been sufficiently courteous to present his excuses in person. Jacynth, too, was oddly downcast. The little historian was frankly puzzled.

The Chinese cook was almost the only one in the house who could not be suspected of the Chamaron poisoning. Following a procedure tacitly established after his death, all food was served in the kitchen, the various dishes being carried directly to each person by Lung Fu. Despite precautions, however, meals still seemed to be generally considered a risky enterprise.

This one was no exception. Aaron Todd was even more waspish than usual, and Sam Preston's jocularity patently false. All sniffed warily at the food, took small samples and waited with varying expressions of discomfort for the ill effects to be manifested, or, like Jacynth and her mother, ate sparingly.

LeDoux alone scorned all safeguards and behaved in a normal manner. Was the perfume manufacturer setting an example for his timorous guests? If so, one must admire his quiet courage. It had already been demonstrated that even his trained nose and sensitive palate did not afford adequate protection.

Lung Fu brought in the dessert, a rich custard of egg yolks, powdered sugar and thick cream. It was delicious. "ALMONDS!" Todd shouted after a tentative spoonful. "Poison!"

Eight men and women stared at one another in a suspicious, hostile silence. Then LeDoux directed an inquiring frown toward his cook. "Will you please explain?"

"Recipe say bitter almonds," the Chinese replied laconically.

"Won't eat it!" Todd screeched.

"It is very good," Westborough hazarded as a stopgap. "Mr. Todd, I am sure you are missing a great treat." He continued eating as if nothing had been said, but only LeDoux and Jacynth followed this reckless example.

"In the future," LeDoux said gently to Lung Fu, "I would prefer that no almond-flavored dishes be served at my table."

Westborough contrived to whisper to his host as they crowded from the dining room at the conclusion of the woeful dinner. LeDoux nodded, and Westborough slipped inobtrusively into the pine-paneled study. He took a book from the shelves – *La Rotisserie de la Reine Pédauque* – and amused himself with Anatole France until LeDoux could conveniently arrange to leave his other guests.

"I tell you I do not like it, my friend," the perfumer began without preamble. "Stuart Grayne is a gentleman, or I have never known such. But a gentleman does not thus run away without even a word of apology to his host. *Hein?*"

"Westborough could think of no suitable explanation. He did not like Grayne's absence either – any better than LeDoux did.

The Frenchman nervously twisted the jade ring on his left hand. "I am old," he sighed. "My cheeks are withered and my beard white. How can I cope with these unseen evils?"

"I am old also," Westborough said timidly. "Dear me! It is true that I have no beard."

"My friend, you must release me from the promise I so rashly made. You must allow me to tell the good Captain Howe everything you have found against Derek Esterling."

"Do you wish to break your granddaughter's heart?" Westborough asked softly.

LeDoux slapped the flat of his hand against the study desk. "But he is guilty, that one!"

"His name," Westborough interposed, "did not appear on the Davis letter."

"*Mais naturellement*. He is not a total fool. The initials are his; and the typewriter also. It is enough, more than enough."

"My dear sir," Westborough protested, "you have just proved his innocence."

"I? How could I prove a thing impossible?"

"Mr. Esterling, you said, is not a total fool. I agree with you; he is far from it. A man of no more than a moderate degree of intelligence would hesitate to employ his own typewriter for such a letter. But only a total fool would fail to correct a blunder so stupid as the printing of the most characteristic sign on that machine. Ergo, another person used the laboratory typewriter, a person, obviously, who does not mind leaving an incriminating trail in Mr. Esterling's direction. Hence it follows logically that Mr. Esterling is innocent." The little man's eyes twinkled behind his gold-rimmed bifocals. "*Quod erat demonstrandum.*"

"I cannot agree," LeDoux rejoined tartly.

"Dear, dear," Westborough said mildly. "Let us take up the matter of the fictitious name. Did a man or woman named Cor ever work for you?"

"Never," LeDoux replied firmly. "I have never known a person so named."

"The 'D. E.' portion is probably an attempt to direct further suspicion toward your unlucky chemist, but the 'Cor' is most unusual. Yet it seems tantalizingly familiar. I am positive that I have heard it mentioned since I have been engaged upon this case. Dear me! There is a clue, here, I am convinced, had I but the wit to grasp it. I remain, however, regrettably stupid."

"You cannot have heard the name," LeDoux asserted with conviction. "It is purely a fabrication of Mr. Esterling's. Of that I am certain. The truth will become known when that poor clerk in the hospital is able to talk. Derek Esterling, as you have yourself suggested, cannot disguise his distinctive appearance."

"He could," Westborough speculated, "procure the package by the simple expedient of sending a messenger for it. But in that case – well, I suppose the messenger could be found. But let us refrain from crossing any more hypothetical bridges over uncertain rivers. Frankly, I am far more worried over Mr. Todd."

"Todd!" LeDoux echoed. "He cannot have poisoned me. He would not. He is too sly to work against his own interests."

Westborough slowly filled his favorite pipe, the pipe with a death's-head bowl. A breech had been made, he perceived, in the wall of silence which had rebuffed all of his previous inquiries concerning that particular gentleman.

"Has he succeeded as yet in gaining the controlling interest in LeDoux Perfumes, Incorporated?"

"Did he tell you that?" LeDoux exclaimed, starting from his chair.

"Indirectly." Westborough tamped the tobacco with his forefinger. "Mr. Todd cautioned me vehemently against investing money in your business. He said harsh things against you personally and against the financial structure of LeDoux Perfumes. Upon examination of his physiognomy, I concluded he was not motivated by altruism toward a stranger. But no matter. 'It is not reasonings that are wanted now,' to translate a thought of Epictetus. What I do not understand is why Mr. Todd is so anxious to take over the active direction of your concern. Lacking a sense of smell, he can scarcely consider himself competent to supervise the manufacture of your fine perfumes."

"Todd is deep!" LeDoux chuckled. "Not so deep as he thinks, perhaps, but sufficiently so to be highly entertaining. I would have told you all this before, my friend, but I did not consider that it had any bearing on the occurrence I requested you to investigate."

Westborough found a paper packet of matches in his coat pocket. "It involves money, I presume?"

"Naturally. Todd enjoys an intrigue of this nature for its own sake, but he would not engage upon it unless he considered that his efforts would be suitably rewarded. It began when he came into possession of a mortgage on a portion of my land. He called, offering to accept shares of stock in payment. I was surprised. The stock of my corporation is held mainly by myself and by personal friends; it has no value on the open market. But one should not look a horse gift in the mouth, *hein?* I was relieved not to be forced to part with cash assets, which have not of recent years been any too plentiful. It was not until after Mr. Todd and I had completed our transaction that the great light dawned. Allied Cosmetics Corporation, a giant manufacturing company, is anxious to acquire the name and good will of LeDoux Perfumes. In some way the terms of the first offer had reached the ears of our astute Mr. Todd; he reasoned that he could someday make his stock of great value. He offered to buy more of my personal holdings, and I accepted. *Parbleu*, why not? I needed ready capital."

"*Lucri bonus est odor ex re quâlibet,*" Westborough murmured.

LeDoux laughed heartily. "The source was definitely an unsavory one. Mr. Todd is not overly scrupulous. In this instance, however, the biter was bitten. I never have had and never shall have the slightest intention of selling my business to Allied Cosmetics. That Mr. Todd could not comprehend. He thought at first that I was merely dickering for a higher price. *Mais que voulez-vous?* To me independence is of greater worth than any number of dollars. Gradually Mr. Todd began to realize the fly in his ointment. He saw that he was, what you might call, stuck."

"I am very much interested," the historian said.

"He could not make good his previous investments unless he induced me to change my mind, or unless he could wrest the controlling interest from my hands. He has tried both courses. The latter I encouraged by suggesting he become treasurer – a purely nominal office, since he can do nothing without my consent. He has been very useful to me. Money is needed, for instance, to market the new Southern Belle perfume. It is Mr. Todd who provides, like the good and generous father. He acquires from me more stock, yes, but not enough stock. And so you see why it is not he who attempted to poison me."

Westborough puffed thoughtfully upon his pipe. "May I offer a few conjectures? Suppose that Mr. Todd had come to learn of the game that you are playing with him. It is possible. And suppose that in lieu of unobtainable profits, he seeks a very tangible revenge. Has the thought occurred to you?"

"*Non, mon Dieu!*" LeDoux exclaimed. "He might kill, *peut-être;* I do not know."

VI

Mother, a distrait wraith in gray, poured the after-dinner coffee. She was frightened, poor dear; it always troubled her to take over the full responsibilities of hostess. She was far happier playing second fiddle to Gran'-père, but he had excused himself from his guests. Only six were in the living room, Jacynth counted; mild-mannered little Mr. West was also mysteriously absent.

Bee Morton, determinedly tranquil under the trying conditions, assisted in passing the tiny eggshell cups. Bee's forced cheerfulness was not contagious. Mr. Preston accepted his demitasse as if it held a scorpion instead of black coffee, and Mr. Todd refused with a snarl.

"Which of you poisoned him?"

The question was unpardonable. Mr. Todd had surpassed even his previous rudeness at dinner when he had made such a horrible fuss over Lung Fu's nice dessert. He should have spelled his name T-O-A-D, Jacynth reflected. He looked rather like a toad then, with the folds of skin hanging about his shriveled neck and his repulsively scaly eyelids. Derek set his cup and saucer on the lacquer coffee table and jumped to his feet, his face white. This was a new Derek. Striding across the room, he jerked the ugly toad from its cushioned chair.

"You've insulted three ladies, to say nothing of Mr. Preston and myself. I demand an immediate apology."

A new Derek, indeed! Even his voice was different.

"Young man," the toad quavered. "Young man, I'll – " The ugly old face quailed before Derek's wrathful brown eyes.

"I'm waiting for you to apologize."

This was not the man who had once run away from an affair of honor. Despite the numbing anxiety which had enveloped her since dinner began, Jacynth could not help being proud of Derek then. The toad squeaked, "I apologize," but because of its reptilian nature, it could not leave the matter there. "To the ladies and to Mr. Preston."

"I insist that you include the full party in your apology." Derek's hands were clenched, the fingernails biting into his palms.

"I won't!" the toad shrilled. "Don't you hit me, young man! I won't apologize to a murderer."

Somehow Jacynth found herself on the other side of the room. She smiled into Derek's stormy face – the artificial, frozen smile of a Japanese.

"Don't, please! Don't pay any attention to him. He's just a senile old man."

Now she knew for certain that Mr. Todd could hear as well as anybody. He had heard distinctly her low-pitched whisper. His gimlet eyes glared at them in ineffectual hatred.

"Let's go outside. Please."

Derek nodded without speaking. No one spoke as they went through the door to the terrace. The toad's venom remained in the room, fouling the air. She knew what they thought, of course. No one could help knowing what they thought, everyone but dear Mother, who remained unswervingly loyal. *Derek was the poisoner!* There! For the first time she had said it to herself.

And it wasn't true! She pressed his arm in a quick gesture of remorse. He did not return the pressure. Nor did he say anything. They walked to the far end of the upper terrace. There wasn't any moon to dim the stars, which were sparkling like corpuscles of radium in a pitchblende sky. She read the hurt in his silence. A part of her longed to comfort him.

But only a part. She remembered a woodcut illustration of a woman tied between two horses which were plunging in opposite directions. She had been fascinated by that sadistic picture when she had first found it in one of Gran'-père's old, old books. She had wondered, shudderingly, how the woman had felt in that single excruciating instant. Now she knew.

She must be loyal to Derek who needed her. That was one of the plunging steeds. But the other – her throat had become strangely choked. What had become of him? Why had he gone? Was Derek telling the truth? The three questions pricked like the stinging hairs of nettles.

"Derek," she said finally, unable to endure more of his silence, "will you talk to me?"

"What shall we talk about?" he retorted. "The moon? It hasn't risen yet."

"You can trust me."

"Can I?"

"Haven't I given proof of it?"

"Have you?"

She flushed, remembering. He couldn't possibly know what had happened that afternoon, but he talked as if he did. Oh, why had Stuart come here, unsettling her life? She would have been happy, engaged to Derek, loving Derek without knowing that there was another kind of love, a love that was at once a joy and an agony. But Stuart had come, and he had taken her in his arms, and his kisses had rained on her lips to melt her heart, and now – one horse or the other or to be torn to pieces.

It had to be Stuart, of course. He was the blazing sun to Derek's pale-bright moon. She belonged to Stuart.

But Derek had a claim that could not be callously dismissed. He stood alone, surrounded by a pack of snarling enemies. She could, if she would, keep them from his throat. While she remained loyal, no one would harm him, not even Gran'-père who, instinct whispered, was the leader of the pack. But if she turned away and let him perish? Oh no, she couldn't! Better to lose Stuart, better anything than ... Distantly she became aware of what Derek was saying.

"Yes, Jacynth, you have given me startling proofs of your loyalty."

He was hateful this way. Cold and hateful!

"Derek, where is Stuart Grayne?"

"He was called to town on business. I thought I explained all that at dinner. Probably something in connection with Chamaron's agency."

It infuriated her to hear him lie so glibly. But it frightened her a little, too.

"Do you mean he had a phone call?"

"Yes, of course."

"He was with me all afternoon. He didn't say anything to me about having to go."

"Perhaps the call came while you were dressing for dinner."

"But it didn't," she objected. "You stopped him from following me into the house; you were with him in the patio for a long while. I know that. When I was upstairs I looked out from the balcony, and you were still talking to him."

"So I'm a liar!"

They were both angry now, both shouting. It must be stopped, she realized. Someone might come from the house to see why they were quarreling. Then she wouldn't be able to learn what had become of Stuart.

"Will he really be back tomorrow, Derek?"

"I said he would. He took my car, didn't he? I wouldn't have let him have it, would I, if he hadn't told me he would come back? If you don't believe my car is gone, come to the garage and see."

He was too anxious! "Why did you lend him your car?" she demanded.

"He asked me to." Derek snapped open his cigarette case. "I didn't force him to take it. Cigarette?"

"No, thank you. Derek, will you give me your word of honor that nothing has happened to Stuart?"

"Honor!" he said scornfully. The match shook in his hand. "Word of honor – it's tautology. What's honor but another word? And how can I tell you nothing's happened to him? He may have hit someone on the road, smashed up the car and himself, how do I know?"

"You hate him so." She shivered. "And—"

She couldn't finish the thought, but his rage had no scruples. "So you've joined the croaking chorus, Jacynth? That makes it practically unanimous, doesn't it? But you're wrong, all of you. I didn't kill Chamaron. And I haven't killed Grayne – yet."

He strode away, leaving her bewildered on the terrace.

VII

The dashboard clock indicated three twenty-seven. Grayne drove into his host's garage, switched off the lights and ignition and snatched up the varnished wooden case from the seat. The moon was a plump crescent not far from its zenith. While he was pulling down the garage door, the thought came to him that it was probably the last moon he would ever see.

His limbs were cramped from eight hours of nearly continuous driving; his eyes still ached from the glare of opposing headlights. Esterling, unjaded from the strain of holding a car in the road for something over three hundred miles, would have a considerable advantage. The cunning devil was probably aware of this, but it didn't much matter. Grayne had made up his mind from the first. He had to give Esterling the same break the other had once given him. The Graynes of Charleston paid their debts of honor.

Esterling probably realized this, too. Grayne remembered their terse argument in the patio, the cold-blooded objectivity with which the scientist had taken his mind to pieces. "I cheated. You can't. You come from a family in which honor—"

"Honor!" Grayne ejaculated. *"What is honor? a word. What is in that word honor; what is that honor? air. A trim reckoning!"* Falstaff had answered the question unanswerably.

"Who hath it? he that died o' Wednesday. Doth he feel it? no. Doth he hear it? no. 'Tis insensible, then? Yea, to the dead."

Hell, stop thinking about it! He had been over this ground countless times during the past eight hours, and he couldn't come to any reasonable decision. That was understandable. A few things in humanity's experience are beyond the realm of reason. Religion, certainly, and probably honor belong in the same category.

"Can honor set to a leg? no: or an arm? no: or take away the grief of a wound?" Paunchy Sir John kept creeping back in his thoughts to tell him he was a damn fool. But Sir John needn't bother to point out the obvious. A cloud drifted over the crescent of the moon.

It was dark when he entered the patio, but not so dark that he failed to perceive the shadow running from the shadows near the south door. The dim figure was much too small for Esterling. He had barely time to set his box on a bench before she was rushing into his arms.

"Mr. Grayne of Charleston!" she sighed. "Darling, I've been so anxious! I didn't sleep a wink."

The cloud lifted from the moon, and he saw her, boyishly slim in a gold slack suit. Her hair, he found as he pressed his lips to it, was still scented with jasmine.

"I love you so!" she whispered, resting her cheek against his face. "Not Derek, you! Stuart, I can't marry Derek now. It's you or nobody."

"Jacynth-hyacinth," he said. "Little honey dahlin'."

His hands were under her armpits, the base of his palms just touching her virginal breasts. He held her gently. Passion was strangely buried. He was conscious only of gratitude, tenderness. This Jacynth – this sweet child! He loved her. She was his.

She was his, but unless Esterling's bullet chose to spare him, he would never have her. The stern code of his ancestors prevented it. *The Graynes paid their debts of honor.* The ridiculous anachronism had somehow become a part of his own blood – his inescapable heritage.

"You or nobody," she repeated. "Is that how you feel, too?"

She wouldn't understand; how could she? He scarcely understood himself. With a shock he realized that Esterling was due at any instant. He had to get her out of the court.

"I tried to go to sleep," she was saying. "I lay in bed, but it wasn't any good. So I got up and put on my slacks. And I sat in a chair by the window and tried to read. But that wasn't any good either. I couldn't keep my mind on anything but you, thinking about you, worrying about you. So I turned off the lamp, finally, and just rested there in the chair. I couldn't leave the window, you see, because – don't call me a silly fool! – I felt closer to you there. And when a pair of headlights turned into our drive I—"

He couldn't halt her flow of confidences. He couldn't hurt her by interrupting, but he had to get her away from the patio.

"Suppose, honey, you—"

"Was Derek right?" she broke in. "Did you drive all the way to Los Angeles?"

"Yes, I'll tell you – "

"Why?" she demanded at once. "What business could be that important?"

"In the morning we'll—"

"It's morning now," she sighed. "Did Derek send you?"

"How many questions can one girl think of?" he laughed.

She fondled one of his hands with her two small ones. "I've got to know all about you, Mr. Grayne of Charleston. You can't have any secrets from the girl you're going to marry. You are going to marry me, aren't you, Stuart? Come to think of it, you never did ask me – formally, that is."

"I won't ask you at all," he declared sternly, "unless you run right upstairs to bed."

"Then I suppose I'll have to. Bully! Just one more question. What's in that box?"

He hadn't known that she'd even seen the damn thing! He tried to stop her, but she was too quick. Before he could reach her she was touching the mahogany case. Before he was able to catch her hand she had raised the lid. Pandora's box had never held more grief than that reflected on her winsome little face.

"Oh, Stuart!" The reproachful exclamation told him that she guessed. "So that's why – you and Derek – that's what he meant when he said—"

"No!" He racked his brain in the effort to improvise a lie that would satisfy her. "Derek's buying them from me to present to a museum!"

"Very likely!" she observed sarcastically. "I think, Mr. Grayne, that you'll do better to confide in your future wife. Derek challenged you, of course. He's hated you for nine years, hated you because you saw him run away, so he challenged you, finally. And you! Oh, you're such a fool! I could shoot you myself."

She was gloriously angry, and he loved her for it. Loved her even more, if it were possible to add anything to infinity. But she had placed him in a devil of a predicament.

"Honey," he pleaded, "if you'll only go to bed. In the morning I'll—"

"In the morning," she flashed, "they'll be digging a bullet out of you. Derek intends to kill you. He as good as told me so. And you – you'll stand up there and let him do it. You ridiculous, quixotic fool!"

"Derek won't kill me," he returned. "He isn't that good." (But, he remembered, Esterling was very good with almost any kind of firearm.) "And I certainly don't intend to hit him. The most that can possibly happen is a pair of harmless shots. Both up in the air, probably. But if you try to prevent them—"

"I will."

"You can, honey, of course. But if you do, what happens?"

"I stop a man from murdering you."

"You stop a man from rehabilitating himself. If Derek can get up and face me courageously he'll feel—"

"I don't care how Derek thinks or feels. I hate him. Yes, that's true. I do hate him now."

"Then consider my side of it."

"Do you have one?"

"I think I do. If you stop it Derek will believe—"

"Does it matter so much to you what Derek believes?"

"On that subject, yes."

"Honor!" she said scornfully. "Your white plume trailing in the dust! Stuart, I never will understand you."

"Don't try," he requested. "Trust me instead. It's nonsense, I'll grant you, but necessary to—"

He saw that she had turned away and was gazing across to the far end of the swimming pool.

"Look!" she gasped breathlessly. "What's that white thing?"

VIII

A man was floating, face buried, the small of the back protruding from the water. A man in a white linen suit! There wasn't light enough to tell more than that.

Grayne's first thought was of artificial respiration, and then he glanced at his watch (much was to be made of this simple act afterward). It was now ten minutes to four. *There hadn't been a flicker of life from the pool for at least twenty minutes.* If there was one certain thing in this uncertain world, it was that the fellow was already hopelessly dead.

Who was he? Esterling had a white linen suit. So did everyone else – LeDoux, Preston, Todd, West. You couldn't prove anything by that. What color was the hair? How could you tell in this dim moonlight, with the head under water? Esterling was nearly six feet; the four other men were from three to six inches shorter, Grayne remembered. This man seemed to be tall, but you couldn't be certain of inches. You couldn't be certain of anything except that the poor devil was dead. Poor, poor devil!

"Can we do anything for him, Stuart?"

Grayne became aware of Jacynth's wan face, peering over his shoulder as he knelt at the edge of the pool. She had kept her head. Most women would have screamed, gone into hysterics, but she asked only the one quiet question.

"No." He straightened up from the pool. "I'd try prone pressure if it would do any good, but you can't resuscitate even a sponge diver after four or five minutes under water. It's a matter for the sheriff's men. You've got to go up to your room immediately. And stay there."

"Oh no, I—"

"Listen to me, Jacynth Hyacinth LeDoux. You're marching upstairs. You're going to take off that pretty gold suit and crawl in between the sheets until it's time to get up, unless someone should come to wake you earlier. And when they ask you what happened in the night, you are going to answer you slept like a log and don't know a thing. Not one single thing, you understand?"

"I can't do it."

"Orders, honey. You've got to carry them out."

"Suppose they say that – that you – oh, you know what I mean. I've got to tell them that – that *you* couldn't. I saw your car come in; I'll have to tell them. Derek's car, but you were driving it. And then I ran right down to the court to meet you, so you couldn't have had time to – to—"

"Jacynth LeDoux! If you dare tell one word – to anybody – of that preposterous and unbelievable story, I'll confess that I threw that man into the pool. And held him there," he added grimly.

"Stuart! You wouldn't! When you didn't, when you know that you—" She looked searchingly into his face. "Yes, you would. A man who will allow himself to be shot just to keep a person he detests from thinking that he's a coward – a man like that will do anything, won't he?"

"If you want to find out," Grayne warned, "just try disobeying orders."

As they passed the bench she caught up the case of dueling pistols, hugging it to her breast. "I'll hide this in my room," she proposed. "No one will ever think of looking—" He twisted loose her fingers.

"You'll leave it right where it was."

"Then they'll know that—"

"Yes, they'll know," he said. "I couldn't keep it hidden. The night clerk at my hotel in Los Angeles saw this box under my arm."

He walked back with her to the south door. "Was this open when you came down?" he asked.

"No, closed."

"Locked?"

"Bolted from inside." She clung to him with desperate abandon. "Stuart, if anything happens to you!"

"Nothing's going to happen to me," he assured her. "I've overlooked one thing, though."

"Have you?" she asked feebly. "What?"

"A formal proposal. We'll remedy it now. Mr. Stuart Grayne extends his compliments, and will Miss Jacynth LeDoux do him the honor of becoming his wife?"

"Idiot!" she sobbed. "Yes, yes, *yes!*"

"Now run upstairs, dear. Quietly and *pronto*." He kissed her forehead, then her lips. "That's to say good night," he declared gravely.

"Good night, my darling." Her trig little figure melted into the darkness.

Her sandaled feet were silent on the hall carpeting, he perceived thankfully. Propping the door open, he returned immediately to the patio. With his handkerchief he polished vigorously every square inch of the wooden case. When he was satisfied that no trace of her fingerprints could possibly remain anywhere on the box, he pressed the tips of his own fingers in several places on the varnished surface. Everything must appear natural to them. Just as it should be. He walked to the far end of the swimming pool.

Kneeling by the edge, he could just manage to touch the submerged head. He pulled it toward him, rather gingerly, until he could grasp the coat collar. Drawing it to the wall, he lifted it momentarily from the water. The face was dank and horrible. But it had a beard – a tiny dab of chestnut beard.

Exit Derek Esterling!

PART SEVEN
NOISE OF WATERS

Steve Rawson, chief deputy of the sheriff's office, was in LeDoux's study having a glorious time at the expense of the unlucky Captain Howe.

"The Esterling case, Syd, is going to be handled by me personally." Rawson was never happier than when an opportunity occurred to dress down an underling. "The sheriff agrees with me that you've grossly mismanaged the Chamaron thing."

Howe's leathery cheeks reddened under their tan. "In what way, Steve?"

Rawson brandished a newly lighted cigar within a few inches of his subordinate's unflinching face. "If you'd performed your duty and jailed Esterling, I wouldn't have had to drive here from Santa Bonita to investigate another murder. Would I?"

Howe ventured a defense. "It don't look now so much like Esterling did the poisoning."

The bulky chief deputy snorted, planting colossal shoes on the fluffy white bearskin rug. "Gawdalmighty, do you always need a signed confession before making an arrest? The poison is a liquid – like water; do you understand? Who else could have poured a liquid into Chamaron's soup dish?"

"Just about everyone at the table." Howe grinned at the discomposure of his superior. "With only—But you've guessed it by now, haven't you, Steve?"

"With only what?" Rawson growled. "I've got no time to waste in damn riddles."

"A rubber band to snap a gelatin capsule across the room. The gelatin would melt when it hit the hot broth."

Rawson's thick lips made an unpleasant noise. "Like a kid shooting a spitball, huh?" he jeered.

"It could be done," Howe insisted. "We tried it out yesterday afternoon."

"Who's we?"

"Westborough thought of it."

"Westborough? That damn stool pigeon you planted here? So you weren't smart enough to think up even a half-baked capsule idea by yourself?"

"I didn't plant Westborough," Howe said, ignoring the gibe. "He was already in the house, and his services aren't costing the county a red cent."

"And aren't worth a red cent," Rawson added. He rustled the notes which the Valle de Flores official had just turned over to him. "But it's the Esterling, not the Chamaron case, I came here to handle. Send me your Westborough."

"He's known here as West."

"Well, send him here," Rawson roared. "And one more thing, Syd. I know my duty if you don't. Somebody's going to sweat for murdering that fellow Esterling. And you," he shouted, "are going to be held personally responsible if any suspect gets away."

"No one's going to escape," Howe promised, thankfully leaving the room. Rawson turned immediately to bully the long-suffering aide who had accompanied him from the county seat.

Willis, wiry, bowlegged, undersized, was a veritable Pooh-Bah, serving in such varied posts as photographer, fingerprint expert, chauffeur and stenographer. Unlike Pooh-Bah, however, he drew only one salary, and that was nothing to brag about. The chief deputy said amiably, "If you miss anything I'll break your damn neck."

"Break ahead," Willis retorted, grinning. "You know how long you'd last without me."

This remark Rawson considered worthy of only a disparaging grunt. He seated himself at the writing desk, dwarfing that fragile article by his bulky presence. Westborough entered, a little tremulously. "Close the door," the chief deputy directed, without looking up from his papers. "Is your name West?"

"To be truthful, it is Westborough." The scant courtesy he was receiving did not serve to put the little man at his ease. "I presume, Mr. Rawson, that Captain Howe has explained to you the circumstances relevant to the understanding which exists between us?"

"Put it in plain English," Rawson ordered roughly. "You've been acting here as Howe's stool pigeon."

Westborough flushed. To mask his confusion, he removed his gold-rimmed bifocals and cleaned them vigorously. During the interim his nearsighted eyes saw the massive chief deputy as no more than a vaguely unpleasant blur.

"I should not state it quite so bluntly," he ventured to remonstrate.

The blur answered, "Errumph! LeDoux brought you here to find the fellow he thought was trying to poison him. Right under your nose another guy is poisoned. You tell Howe you'll be his undercover man. While you're asleep the main suspect is drowned. In my opinion, West, you're a total washout."

"A most interesting term." Westborough replaced his glasses, and the blur immediately became a choleric fat man with broad shoulders and a beet-red face. "I must make a note of it for future use."

"Are you trying to be funny?"

"Dear me, no," the historian exclaimed, aghast. "Nothing could be further from my thoughts."

Rawson sniffed suspiciously. "Start talking," he commanded. "Begin with the first thing you remember this morning."

"A knock on the door. Dear me, the account will be rather a long one, I fear, and to one as old as I standing is apt to become tiresome."

Rawson said nothing except, "What time was the knock?"

"About four o'clock, I think." With some trepidation the little scholar seated himself on the edge of a large tan leather chair.

"You think? Don't you know?"

"Three fifty-eight, to be precise." Westborough, unaccustomed to such cavalier treatment, was a trifle irritated. "The knock had been made by Mr. Grayne, who, I may say, was dressed in the same costume in which I had last seen him yesterday."

"What costume?"

"Gray slacks and a russet sport shirt."

"You're sure of that, West?"

"Indeed, yes. Did I make clear to you that my true name is Westborough? Theocritus Lucius Westborough, a humble scribe of Roman history."

"Your name here is West," the chief deputy maintained. "That's how it's going into the record. I don't give a damn what you call yourself or what you are. You haven't any privileged status, regardless of what Howe told you. You're just one more suspect to me."

"My dear sir!" Westborough exclaimed, warmly indignant. " 'Life is not so short but that there is always time for courtesy.' I commend Emerson's observation to your conscience."

"Ha, ha, ha!" Willis guffawed. "Smack in the eye, Steve!"

"Go on, West," Rawson directed gruffly.

"Mr. Grayne told me he had been sent by Mr. LeDoux to wake me up as Mr. Esterling's body had just been found floating in the swimming pool. I put on my dressing gown and went into the hall, meeting Mr. LeDoux, who carried a flashlight."

"What was he wearing, Professor?" Willis interrupted.

"Like myself, he had covered the garments of slumber with a dressing gown. We accompanied Mr. Grayne to the pool, where a horrifying sight awaited us. 'Methought, what pain it was to drown! what dreadful noise of waters in my ears!' Noting some splashes at the east edge of the pool, I suggested to my companions that it would perhaps be advisable not to walk on that side. We accordingly retraced our steps to the house in the same manner in which we had come. Mr. LeDoux, I might say, spoke very sharply to Mr. Grayne and demanded he account for his presence in the house at such an hour when he had left word that he was spending the night in Los Angeles. Mr. Grayne furnished a most surprising explanation. He declared that he had driven to Los Angeles for the express purpose of procuring a set of antique dueling pistols."

"We know all about that," Rawson broke in impatiently.

"I personally, I must confess, was a trifle shocked to learn that the code *duello* persisted in twentieth-century America, but Mr. LeDoux, a Continental, was more sympathetic, though he could not, of course, approve of an irregular meeting sans seconds. Mr. Grayne excused himself on the grounds that it had become necessary to remove the hirsute growth from his face – in other words, to shave."

"And you let him go!" the chief deputy exclaimed sarcastically.

"My dear sir, neither Mr. LeDoux nor myself nor both of us together could successfully cope with a man so physically powerful. Moreover, he had given his word that he would make no attempt to leave the house."

"The word of a—"

"A gentleman's word," Westborough said mildly, "is legal tender among gentlemen, but perhaps, sir, you are not familiar with such currency?"

Behind the chief deputy's broad bulk, Willis ventured an unmistakable wink. "Go on," Rawson ordered curtly.

"Mr. LeDoux and I talked for a few minutes in the patio. A theory occurred to me: namely, that Mr. Esterling might have been drowned by a person who went into the swimming pool with him and forcibly held his head under water. A somewhat stupid hypothesis, I realize, since Mr. Esterling had a very excellent physique. Of our entire party, probably only Mr. Grayne was capable of so overpowering him."

"Were Grayne's clothes wet or dry when he came into your room?" Rawson interrogated.

"Dry."

"Did you feel them or just look at them?"

"Both, I might say. Shall I continue?"

The chief deputy muttered an affirmative.

"I suggested the theory to Mr. LeDoux, who agreed with me that, if the surmise were correct, the evidence was vanishing more and more with each minute that passed. Under the circumstances we felt justified in undertaking an inquiry. Our investigation, like Gallia, *est omnis divisa in partes tres;* to wit, item one, a search for damp clothing other than bathing costumes; item two, a search for damp bathing costumes; item three, a search for damp towels. Though willing to put such questions to the male members of our party, I did not relish the task of waking the ladies at such an hour for such an unconventional purpose. Mr. LeDoux suggested that we entrust this part of the task to his secretary, Miss Morton; when we had aroused her from the arms of Morpheus—"

"Do you mean you found her with some guy?" Rawson demanded incredulously.

"The god of dreams." Westborough repressed a smile. "Miss Morton, I might state at this time, satisfied us that there was no damp clothing in her room; that her bathing dress was dry; that her towel rack contained no damp towels. I mention this merely to assure you that we overlooked nothing. Would you like to know the final results in our informal survey?"

Rawson grunted indifferently.

"*O tempora! O mores!*" Westborough declaimed. "I am sorry that my conversation is so boring. Nevertheless, having introduced the subject, I presume it would be advisable to bring it to a conclusion." He took a paper from his breast pocket and read: "Damp clothing other than bathing suits: none. Bathing suits: Mr. Todd, doesn't own one; Mr. LeDoux, dry in his room; Mrs. Chamaron, dry in room. Miss LeDoux, dry on line; Mr. Grayne, dry on line (both Miss LeDoux and Mr. Grayne were in the pool at the same time yesterday morning, I might mention); Mr. Preston, dry in room; Mr. West, owns no suit; Mrs. LeDoux, mislaid suit some time ago, vague about its whereabouts. Towels: investigation completely negative except for one thing: a damp bath towel on top of the soiled clothing at the bottom of the clothes chute in the laundry room." Westborough lowered the paper. "It was quite damp," he said perplexedly. "I do not know how to explain its presence; I really do not."

"Well, forget about it," Rawson ordered brusquely. "The murderer didn't go into the swimming pool. Doc Resch says there's a big bruise – contusion, he calls it – on the corpse's head. Whoever did the thing laid Esterling out with a blunt instrument before shoving the body into the pool. Your line of inquiry is as wet as your towel, West. Wetter, ha, ha!"

II

To Etienne LeDoux, Rawson displayed more civility than he had shown toward Westborough; the perfume maker had in the past made generous contributions to the county machine.

"When I turned on the patio lights," LeDoux declared, "one of the first things I saw was that case – a dark red wooden box, approximately eighteen by nine by three inches – on a bench near the swimming pool. But there are two benches, *hein?* The one to which I refer was at the shallow end of the pool, diagonally opposite the spot where the body of Mr. Esterling was floating. I demanded an explanation of its presence from Mr. Grayne. Do you wish to know what he said to me? He had accepted my late chemist's challenge to an irregular encounter without seconds. *Le diable s'en mêle!* Such little affairs are much better managed in France."

"You're sure it was Esterling who challenged Grayne? Not the other way around?"

LeDoux answered, a trifle stiffly, "A gentleman does not lie concerning an affair of honor."

"Anyone will lie concerning anything," Rawson differed cynically. "Did Grayne tell you what they were going to fight about?"

"He said merely that it was a continuation of a quarrel they had had nine years ago which had never been satisfactorily adjusted."

"Nuts!" the chief deputy ejaculated. "Did you fall for that hanky-panky?"

"Sir!" LeDoux said haughtily.

"Well, skip it. Is it true that West made a hunt for wet bathing suits?"

"*Mr.* West conducted such a search," the perfume maker replied, significantly stressing the title.

"He didn't find anything worth shouting about," Rawson said, "but just to get the thing cleared up, I'd like to know how many bathrooms you have upstairs."

"Three large bathrooms. Every guest bedroom has also a lavatory and a shower stall."

"Your place could be turned into a neat little hotel just the way it stands." LeDoux shuddered, but made no audible comment. "What about towels?" the chief deputy continued. "Do your guests keep their individual towels in their rooms?"

"But naturally. Where else would individual towels be kept?"

"How many do you furnish to each guest?"

"I cannot say. You must ask my daughter-in-law, who is good enough to keep house for me. Or inquire of Manuel, my houseboy."

"The Jap who let us into the house?"

"Manuel is from the Philippines." The perfumer's courtesy had become noticeably strained.

"Japs and Filipinos look just the same to me. Damn brown-faced squirts! Every time I see one of them I want to give him a kick in the pants. Well, how did Esterling get along with your other guests?"

LeDoux shrugged expressively.

"Did he quarrel with anyone just before his death?"

"I do not know of such a quarrel."

"After what had happened to Chamaron" – Rawson's tone was incisive – "were you still willing for your granddaughter to be engaged to Esterling?"

"My granddaughter's marriage," LeDoux returned blandly, "is not a matter to be decided solely by myself."

"Wouldn't you have tried to stop it if you thought that Esterling had poisoned Chamaron?"

"What I thought or did not think can scarcely be of pertinence to your investigation, m'sieur."

Rawson changed the subject. "When did you last see Esterling alive?"

"Shortly after midnight. Since the servants had retired, I escorted him to the south door."

"Thought he was staying at your house?" Rawson rumbled.

"Didn't Captain Howe explain to you? Mr. Esterling has been spending the past few nights in his laboratory."

"Why did he do that?"

"Because, m'sieur, in planning my house, I was so thoughtless as to provide only five guest bedrooms."

"He had a residence in Valle de Flores, I understand." Rawson verified this by his notes. "Howe's got it down here that Esterling occupied a four-room house on K Street. If you couldn't put him up why didn't he go there to sleep?"

"Valle de Flores," LeDoux declared rather stiffly, "is a distance of ten miles away. Mr. Esterling's laboratory, *au contraire*, is conveniently near to us."

"So you said good night to him at the south door, huh? Is that the one Grayne is supposed to have found open?"

"*Précisément!*"

"Did you lock the door after Esterling left?"

"I rebolted it, *mais oui.*"

"Whose duty is it to see that the house doors are locked at night?"

"Manuel's."

"Well, I want to talk to him. Will you send him in here?"

"But certainly," LeDoux promised. In a few minutes the chief deputy was surveying a small brown-skinned, black-haired Filipino with an expression of marked distaste.

"You, me havee talk-talk, man in pool."

"I presume," Manuel answered, hissing the *s* slightly, "that you are referring to Mr. Esterling?"

"Gawdalmighty!" Rawson roared. "Where'd you learn to talk?"

Manuel mentioned the name of a well-known Pacific Coast university. "I hold the degree of Bachelor of Arts," he added.

"Then why the hell are you making beds?"

"The Caucasian race is prejudiced against Malay blood." Manuel's smile conveyed amused contempt.

"Errumph!" Rawson growled. "How many towels do you distribute to each person?"

"Two bath towels and two hand towels daily."

"Where are the towels kept?"

"In the linen closet on the second floor."

"Well, I want you to run upstairs and pretend to be bringing the clean towels. Take a quick look around and tell me if anyone has less than his or her quota now."

"That has already been done," Manuel replied. "Captain Howe made the same request. No towels were missing from any room."

"Everybody had two bath towels and two hand towels, huh?"

"That is correct."

"Did you hear a splash in the pool last night?"

"I am sorry I cannot be of service to you. My bedroom is downstairs, but it doesn't open on the patio."

"Does anybody else sleep downstairs?"

"My fellow servant, Mr. Lung."

"Does his bedroom open on the patio?"

Manuel shook his head. "No bedroom in the house opens on the patio."

"None of the upper rooms? How's that?"

"I perceive you have not yet visited the second floor. The rooms are separated by a corridor from the balcony which overlooks the patio."

"H'm." Rawson didn't seem entirely convinced. "What time did you go to bed last night?"

"Eleven o'clock."

"Did you go straight to sleep?"

"I did."

"Ever take a night dip in the pool, Manuel?"

"Occasionally. Mr. LeDoux permits me to use it."

"The hell he does! You mean to say he lets *you* swim right with his—"

"Not with his family or guests," Manuel finished quickly. "The Caucasian race is prejudiced against the color of my skin. I do not mind. Personally, I am prejudiced against the Caucasian race. We Tagalogs of Luzon are a proud people."

Rawson glared suspiciously at the impassive brown face. "Were you in the pool last night?"

"No."

"Was the Chinaman? What's his name? Wun Lung?" Rawson chuckled, apparently finding this brand of humor much to his liking. Manuel, however, displayed no amusement.

"Mr. Lung is not a swimmer."

"How do you get along here with Old Man LeDoux?"

"I consider Mr. LeDoux a highly satisfactory employer," the Filipino replied chillily. "You neglected to ask me if I had locked the doors last night. I presume that the question interests you. The answer is that I did – all of the downstairs doors and windows. And now may I be excused?"

"Don't stand there smirking like an ape!" Rawson roared. "Go tell Miss LeDoux I want to talk to her. Get out!"

"With pleasure," Manuel returned, closing the door.

"That squirt!" Rawson shouted, as soon as the houseboy had gone. "Did you hear how that chocolate drop talked to me?"

Grinning broadly, Willis read from his shorthand notes, "You, me havee talk-talk, man in pool." The chief deputy glowered.

"That brown shrimp thinks he's as good as a white man."

Willis drawled, "Considering some white men I've met professionally, that isn't handing him much of a compliment. Hell's bells, chief, let's get on with this thing. Your little friend, West, incidentally, has scored a damn good point about his towel."

"What's good about it?" Rawson demanded. "No towels were missing."

"That's the point," Willis retorted. "There should have been – hell, what's the use?"

Rawson said huffily, "I can't see that a damp towel has anything to do with the murder."

"I can see that you can't see," Willis announced. The arrival of Jacynth LeDoux prevented further friction.

III

Jacynth hoped that she was concealing her nervousness. There were only two of them in the room, and that was something, but the biggest man was not a sympathetic person. She could tell it at once from his eyes, which were the cold color of sea water on a foggy day. The little one with the notebook didn't seem so bad. From the way he grinned at her she was sure he had a sense of humor. It was the big one, however, who did the bulk of the talking.

He began, in the manner of a true-or-false quiz, "Were you or were you not engaged to Derek Esterling at the time of his death?"

"True," Jacynth answered.

"Did your grandfather approve of that engagement?"

"He did at first. Later—" She left the sentence suspended.

"By later do you mean since Chamaron's death?"

"I mean during the last few days."

"Did your grandfather ask you to break your engagement to Esterling?"

"Not in so many words." She paused, wondering if these men could possibly understand. Perhaps the little one might. "But, you see, I know Gran'-père so well! It isn't necessary to put in words how he feels about things."

"If he had asked you to break your engagement to Esterling, would you have done so?"

"Gran'-père would never have asked me such a thing," Jacynth declared with a confident toss of her head. The big man made a noise like a crashing breaker.

"Errumph! Was Esterling a good swimmer?"

"No," Jacynth said.

"Could he swim at all?"

"Yes, but not very well. He hated the water."

"Can Grayne swim?"

"Oh yes. Mr. Grayne is a beautiful swimmer."

"Willis," the big man ordered, "be sure to get that in your notes. Now, Miss LeDoux, I want you to tell me everything you did last night."

"When last night?"

"Begin with after dinner."

"Well, we had coffee in the living room."

"Who had coffee?" the big man interrupted.

"Let me see. Mother, Miss Morton, Mr. Preston, Mr. Todd, Der – Mr. Esterling and myself. I believe that's all."

"Wasn't your grandfather there?"

"He and Mr. West didn't join us until later."

"Where was Grayne?"

Jacynth hesitated, wondering how much would be safe to admit. "Mr. Esterling told us he had gone to Los Angeles," she achieved finally.

"Did Grayne and Esterling ever have any trouble – quarrels, arguments, that kind of thing?"

"Oh no!" She shook her head emphatically. "They were always very polite to each other. But Mr. Esterling did have an argument last night with Mr. Todd."

She didn't mind in the least directing suspicion toward the toad, who deserved everything that could be done to him.

"What kind of an argument?"

"Mr. Todd refused his coffee. He was very rude about it. Mr. Esterling forced him to apologize."

"Is that all that happened?"

"Not quite. The to – Mr. Todd refused to apologize to Mr. Esterling. He called Mr. Esterling a murderer."

"Make a note of it, Willis," the big man called gleefully. "What did Esterling say to that?"

"Nothing. I made him take me for a walk along the terrace."

"Did you and Esterling return to the living room later?"

"In a few minutes. But Gran'-père and Mr. West had joined the others then, and Mr. Esterling didn't have to speak to Mr. Todd."

"When did you go to bed, Miss LeDoux?"

"About midnight."

"Sleep soundly or not?"

"Not so well," she confessed. "That's something I must tell you. I heard a splash from the swimming pool, a big one."

"The dev—" the large man started to say, but his small companion interrupted with a question of his own.

"Was your bedroom door open or closed at that time, Miss LeDoux?"

"Closed."

"Thank you," he said, with unexpected courtesy. The big man scowled, looking highly disagreeable.

"What time was this?"

"A little after two o'clock."

"How do you know?" he growled.

"By the clock, of course."

"What made you get up to look at the clock?" he demanded fiercely.

"Wouldn't you?" He was just a bully, she told herself, and she didn't mean to let him frighten her. "If you heard a noise like that in the dead of night, wouldn't you be a little curious? As a matter of fact, I walked across the hall and onto the balcony, where I could see into the patio. Only I couldn't see because it was too dark."

"Wasn't there any moonlight?"

"None."

"Didn't you turn on the lights?"

"I couldn't. The switch for the patio lights is downstairs. I – well, I just didn't feel like going down there just then."

"Did you think someone was in the court?"

"Oh yes. I heard more noises from the pool."

"What kind of noises?"

"As if someone were splashing around. I called out, 'Who's there?' but no one answered, so I went back to my room."

"Why didn't you wake up your grandfather or somebody and find out what was going on?"

"I thought I knew what it was. Manuel uses the pool sometimes – at night after everybody else has gone to bed – and Manuel once admitted to me that he doesn't own any bathing trunks. Putting two and two together – well, you can see why I thought it was just as well not to disturb him."

The little one looked like he wanted to laugh, but the big one became more grumpy than ever. "Hear anything else after that?"

"A car going up the drive to the garage. But that was later. Much, much later."

"How do you know it was?"

She considered the question carefully, mindful of her promise to Stuart.

"The car didn't come until nearly three-thirty."

"So you got up again to look at the clock, huh? Why was it so important to know the time that car came in?"

Well, why was it? She couldn't tell them the truth, that she had been worried over Stuart's strange absence. If she as much as hinted that she had been anxious because of him, he would – do something rash and reckless. The South Carolina gentleman protecting his lady's honor, the dear stubborn fool! But why had she gotten up? It must be a trivial, casual sort of excuse – intuition told her that. In a flash the inspiration had seized her.

"I don't have to get out of bed to see the time. The clock on my dresser has an illuminated dial."

The clock on Mother's dresser had such a dial. With any luck, Jacynth conjectured, she could make the substitution before they thought to look in her room. Mother wouldn't mind.

IV

Willis thoughtfully inserted a fresh lead into his mechanical pencil. "Ever hear of Darwin, chief?"

"Darwin? Wasn't he the guy mixed up in that embezzlement case a few years back?"

"I'm talking about another Darwin, an Englishman. He wrote a couple of books once upon a time."

"What have books got to do with it?"

"More than you might think. This Darwin was a pretty wise old cookie. He said that whenever a new observation or thought came along, a new fact which was *opposed* to the particular line he was working on, he made a written note of it right away. Facts like that, Darwin said, are damned hard to remember."

Rawson vented an annoyed grunt. "What are you driving at?"

"I'm telling you now I'm not going to be much surprised when you forget what the LeDoux girl told you. Since Grayne wasn't back here until just before three-thirty, he couldn't have been responsible for the splash in the pool at two. What that kid handed you was a bomb. It blows your line of inquiry to kingdom come."

"The hell it does," Rawson differed. "Grayne could have made the round trip to L.A. and back by two."

"Saying he could, why should he? His date wasn't until three-thirty. Howe told us."

"Grayne might have been lying to Howe."

"Yeah? You don't fight duels in the dark, chief. Three-thirty sounds more like the right time to me."

"So what?"

"So plenty. Why should Grayne bust a leg trying to get back by two just to cool his fanny waiting an hour and a half? How did he know Esterling was going to be in the patio at two? He didn't; he couldn't."

"Well, how do *you* know Esterling was there then?"

"Figure it out for yourself. The LeDoux kid – keen looker, isn't she? – heard a splash at two – one making enough noise for her to hear it through a closed door in a room not opening off the patio. Did she hear any splash near three-thirty, when Grayne came back? She did not. But she was awake then, too; she'd just heard his car – Esterling's car, rather – grinding up the drive. Why didn't she hear a splash? Simple. Esterling had gone into the pool at two; q.e.d. and p.d.q."

"The hell with that moonshine," Rawson growled. "I've got six more people to talk to: Preston, Morton, Todd, Mrs. LeDoux, Mrs. Chamaron and Grayne."

Willis grinned in the manner of a malicious gnome. "Saving Grayne for the dessert?"

"Shut up!" Rawson snapped. "And go find out what's keeping this guy Preston."

"Nothing's keeping me." Sam Preston pushed the study door open before the aide was able to move. "So you're Steve Rawson, huh? Jacynth told me I was the next hombre on your list."

The "taxeaters" – Mr. Preston's name for all and sundry representatives of city, county, state and national governments – asked a number of preliminary questions.

"Well, it was this way, Steve." (Five minutes after introduction to two archangels, Mr. Preston would be hailing them familiarly as Gabe and Mike.) "Stu and I share the double bedroom in the west wing, but Stu wasn't there last night. I had the room all to myself."

Rawson asserted, rather irritably, that the last sentence contained no information which could not be inferred from previous data. Mr. Preston was immediately aggrieved.

"If you don't want to listen, okay by me. I'm not selling any LeDoux products, am I, sitting here talking to you? Not on your life. I'm doing you taxeaters a favor." Mr. Preston smirked self-righteously.

Willis intervened before his chief could bring the heavy artillery into action. "Sure you're doing us a favor, buddy. No argument. Did you hear a splash in the swimming pool last night?"

"I didn't hear anything until Stu came in the room. I looked and saw a guy standing by the washbasin, shaving his mug. 'What the hell!' I said. He had the light on over the mirror, so I could see it was Stu. 'What's the idea of whisker scraping at this time of night?' And he said, sorta shortish, 'Esterling fell in the pool and drowned himself.' So I jumped out of bed in a hurry. 'Did you do the job, Stu?' I asked, knowing that those two felt about each other just like a mamma cat feels toward Mr. Dog when he pokes down the basement stairs to say hello to the kittens. Nothing against either of 'em, see? They just didn't like each other, and that was a fact. And Stu said, mad-like, 'I'll be damned if I did. But these damn nitwit taxeaters' " – Mr. Preston laughed with gusto as he edited Grayne's actual words – " 'these damn nit-wit taxeaters are going to think so.' Then he started to change his clothes."

"What clothes?" Rawson returned to the fray. "What clothes was Grayne wearing, Preston?"

"A pair of slacks and a sorta brown-colored sport shirt. So I said to him, 'Stu, you'd better have a drink.' I had a bottle of bourbon in the room, see? You don't get any hard liquor here except a thimbleful of cognac after dinner, so I'd come prepared for emergencies. Chamaron tipped me off to that one. Let's see, where was I?"

"Rambling all around what-you-call-it's barn," Willis answered dryly. "Maybe it'd be a good idea to let Grayne change his clothes."

Preston grinned. "Stu puts on his Palm Beach that he'd tipped the full-o'-peanuts four bits to press for him that afternoon. And I said, 'What's the idea of dressing up now, Stu?' And he said, 'I gotta date to see the sheriff, Sam, and I don't think I'll be coming back this way for a while. When I tell 'em what I know, it's the hoosegow sure as shooting.' Well, just then this little old guy Ted West stuck his nose in the room, frightened as a rabbit. 'Excuse me, gentlemen,' he said, 'but may I be permitted to look at your bathing suits?' I dug out mine for him, but Stu had left his on the line outside. Mean-time Ted was feeling our towels and poking through all the clothes hanging up in the closet. 'There's a damp hand towel here,' he said, like we'd been hiding a body. 'There ought to be,' I told him. 'Stu just finished shaving. What's it all about, anyway?' But before he could answer me, Stu got in his nickel's worth.

" 'Mr. West,' he said, 'I'd like you to look at these clothes. You know they're the clothes I just took off and so does Sam. I want you both to wit-ness that they're dry – completely dry.' And they were, too. Dry as a bone."

Mr. Preston had a great deal more to add to this – none of it very relevant.

Miss Morton, as if in deliberate contrast, had very little to impart. Like Mr. Preston, she had heard nothing from the swimming pool. She was afraid that she was much too sound a sleeper. After going to bed, she knew nothing until she was awakened some time after four by Mr. LeDoux and Mr. West, who had a request to make about bathing suits. Did Mr. Rawson already know about that search? He did? Then, she probed tentatively, he probably would not want her to go over the same ground? The chief deputy's bored silence conveyed little encouragement. Miss Morton ransacked her brain for a new note that might prove of interest.

"About Mrs. LeDoux's bathing suit," she said finally. "I told Mr. West she was vague about it, but that isn't true now. Mrs. LeDoux remembered afterward; it had shrunk so that she couldn't wear it, so she'd given it away for a church rummage sale two or three months ago. She's been intending to buy another one, but she never seems to think of it, she said. She ..." Miss Morton's voice trailed away in discouragement as the horrid truth dawned upon her. The chief deputy was not interested in Mrs. LeDoux's bathing suit.

In fact, the chief deputy was not interested in anything Miss Morton had to say. He ushered her very shortly from the study to make room for an irascible gentleman bearing the name of Aaron Xenophon Todd.

"Look here," Todd declared shrilly. "I was asleep and couldn't hear a thing." He indicated the black disk suspended from his neck. "I'm deaf without this, and I don't sleep with it." He shifted the spectacles backward on the bridge of his long square-tipped nose. "No, I don't sleep with it, so I couldn't hear any of your splashes. The first thing I knew was when that West broke into my room to ask some idiotic question about a bathing suit. I'll bathing suit him!" Todd cackled as if he considered the last remark a witticism, adding, "Haven't been near the water for twenty years."

"Not even to take a bath?" Willis asked in apparent innocence.

Todd glared. Rawson took up the thread hastily. "Todd, did you have a quarrel with Esterling last night?"

"Who said that? Someone told you a lie, a wicked lie. I didn't quarrel with him. All I said was – was—"

"That he poisoned a fellow," Willis finished soothingly. "That's nothing to get mad about. Most any man ought to enjoy being called a murderer."

"Don't be impudent, young whippersnapper. Suppose I did call him that?"

Willis returned wearily, "He could only sue you for slander."

"He couldn't have sued me, young man." Todd's quavering voice rose a shrill octave. "Everyone in the house knew he was a murderer. Every single one."

"Even the girl who was engaged to him?"

"Well, maybe she didn't," Todd conceded. "But that's no proof."

"No, and where's your proof, Scrooge?"

"Who's conducting this examination?" Rawson wanted to know. "You or me, Willis?"

"You are, chief."

"Then shut up and let me do it. There's no point in the line you've been taking. He didn't kill Esterling, we know, so what difference does it make whether he quarreled with him or not?"

"That's so," Todd chirped in concord. "What difference does it make? None, none at all. Scrooge, eh?" He frowned severely. "I'll Scrooge you, young man!"

Mrs. LeDoux was a more tractable witness. She informed them that she had not heard a splash from the pool, but she had had a dream, a terrible nightmare in which Jacynth was calling frantically for help.

"But I couldn't get to her. I couldn't reach my baby. It was as if something was standing there between us, an invisible wall. The next thing I know – well, Beatrice Morton was in the room. She told me Derek was dead."

Mrs. LeDoux uncrumpled an already damp handkerchief. "I cried a great deal, I think. Beatrice tried to comfort me. She's a sweet girl, but I didn't pay any attention to what she said. I could only think of Derek. That poor, poor boy!"

"Fond of him?" Willis asked gently.

"Yes, very. There wasn't a nicer boy anywhere than Derek. He reminded me so much of Raoul." She began to cry again. "*He* was killed, too."

"Who's Raoul?"

"Mr. LeDoux's son. My husband. We were on our honeymoon. Our little cottage on a bluff – I can see it as clearly as this room. I haven't forgotten a single detail in twenty years. Raoul had to go to town for some reason, said he would be back in an hour or two. He walked out into the fog, singing. ... We had been very happy together. The song died away; I never heard or saw him again. There wasn't any telephone. I waited all night, wondering if he had decided to stay in town, not knowing anything. ... We found him next day. They said he must have stepped from the path in the dark ... a drop of nearly a hundred feet to the rocks. Sharp, jagged rocks, with the sea dashing to spray against them! They found him there. My husband ..."

V

"I didn't hear a splash," Mrs. Chamaron declared tonelessly. "I didn't hear anything until Bee Morton came in. She asked some silly questions about my bathing suit, even insisted upon looking for it in a drawer. I don't have the least idea what she was trying to prove. Naturally, I haven't worn a bathing suit since Paul's death."

"Your husband died two days ago," Rawson stated accusingly. "Is the funeral going to be held at Valle de Flores?"

"No-o. Paul will be buried in Los Angeles."

"Why haven't you taken the body back there?"

"I intend to do that today."

"Not today, Mrs. Chamaron. If you try to leave before the inquest I'll have to put you under arrest."

"Yes," she said, "that would be very chivalrous of you." Rawson had the grace to look abashed.

"I don't want to have to do that."

She regarded her gold-tipped nails distractedly. "I shall make a model prisoner. But why am I to be arrested?"

"You'll have to give evidence at the inquest," he temporized.

"What evidence can I give? I assure you that I knew nothing of Mr. Esterling's death."

"Nothing?"

"Nothing."

"Mrs. Chamaron, for a grief-stricken widow, you've acted in a funny manner. It was your duty to take your husband's body back to Los Angeles as soon as you could. I'm sorry, but you force me to talk bluntly."

"Yes, you do talk bluntly," she murmured. "Some might even call it brutally. Well, women whose husbands get murdered shouldn't have feelings. Isn't that so?"

"We both know this yarn you've been telling about a nervous breakdown is a stall. What's the real reason you've kept on staying here?"

"To see justice done to my husband's murderer," she answered.

"Do you know who that was?"

"It's very obvious, isn't it?"

"Esterling?"

"Why are you asking me?"

"Did you kill Esterling?"

"Is this the well-known third degree?"

"It will pay you, Mrs. Chamaron, to tell me the truth."

"Indeed? Mansions in heaven, I suppose. Rather old-fashioned of you. And would you recognize the truth if it were given to you, Mr. Rawson?"

"There's no use acting like I'm your worst enemy," the chief deputy expostulated. "I'm only trying to help you."

Her laughter was a little hysterical. "I believe that I can do without your assistance, thank you. No, I didn't kill Derek Esterling, nor do I have the least idea who did."

"Did you talk to Esterling last night?"

"I haven't spoken to him in two days," she cried angrily. "I shut myself up in my room so I wouldn't have to sit at the same table with him."

"Do you admit you hated Esterling?"

"Wouldn't you hate the man who killed your wife? I think you would."

"What makes you so sure it was Esterling?"

"He sat next to Paul. The poison was from his laboratory – his locked laboratory. He quarreled bitterly with Paul Michael. What link is missing from that chain?"

"A rubber band," Willis replied.

"Right," Rawson confirmed. "Anyone at the table could have done it. You could have done it yourself. Or Grayne." He halted for a few tense seconds. "Mrs. Chamaron, did you egg Grayne on to kill Esterling?"

"No!" Her face tautened suddenly. "It isn't true."

"Did you say anything to Grayne about your husband's death?"

"Ye-es. Some very foolish things. I apologized for them afterward."

"What sort of things?"

"I don't intend to tell you. Being half out of my mind with grief, I don't consider myself responsible for what I said then."

"Did Grayne make threats against Esterling?"

"No, he did not. Never."

"Yet he challenged Esterling to a duel."

"The other way, I believe." The quickening of her eyes had faded almost instantly. "I heard it was Mr. Esterling who did the challenging."

"We've only Grayne's word for it."

"His word is reliable, however. Stuart doesn't lie."

"Stuart, eh?"

Her lips tightened. "Naturally I call him Stuart. Why not?"

"Good friend of yours?"

"He was also a good friend of Paul Michael's."

"Mrs. Chamaron, when did you first betray your husband?"

"It's not so!" Color flaunted on her cheeks like a banner guarding a dead city. "I didn't!"

"No?" Rawson's tone was as inimical as the ultimatum of a totalitarian warlord. "It's true, though; you wanted your husband out of the way so you could have Grayne. Have him legally."

"Oh, you're vile!"

"Sex," he declared roughly, "is the only possible motive for these two murders. Unlucky for Esterling, wasn't it, that he happened to learn about you two?"

VI

"I remember almost his exact words," Stuart Grayne informed them. "He said, 'The round trip should take between seven and eight hours. It's seven-fifteen now. You can be back by three-thirty. Meet me then, here in the patio, and we'll walk to a place I know to wait for the sunrise.' "

"Is that all he said?"

"Some other things. I objected that the arrangement was pretty one-sided, since I was to meet him after seven or eight hours of driving while he could be resting in bed, and he answered: 'Honor can equivocate, it seems.' " He paused, seeing again the bearded face mouthing the insult. "Then he went on to say he'd sit up till I got back. He had another appointment to keep that night, he told me."

"A convenient appointment for you."

Grayne kept his tight grip on the chair arm. "Nevertheless," he said softly, "it might be worth investigating. There is a chance, you know, I'm not lying."

"All right, then, who was Esterling going to meet besides you?"

"He didn't tell me."

"Because there wasn't anybody." The chief deputy nodded in pompous satisfaction. It wouldn't do any good, Grayne reflected, to smash his fist against those thick and sneering lips.

"Is it true that you had previously forced the deceased to engage in an assault with deadly weapons?"

"I challenged him to a duel," the Southerner corrected.

"There's no such thing. Duels aren't legal anywhere in the United States. It's murder if you kill a man in one."

"I didn't," Grayne said.

"Not then." Striding across the room, Rawson towered wrathfully above the seated man. "Why did you challenge him last night?"

"He challenged me," Grayne insisted.

"Yeah? Why?"

"He's been brooding for years over the outcome of our last meeting. He had to prove to me he wasn't a coward."

The bullnecked deputy rocked with laughter.

"I'd planned to fire in the air," Grayne continued. He knew at once that neither of them believed him. He couldn't much blame them.

The truth, however, was equally preposterous. "*I saw you with Jacynth just now. You owe me the same satisfaction you said I owed you. I cheated, I'll admit, but you ...*" The words must be buried with Derek's body, never to be resurrected.

"Is that the only reason why he wanted to fight you?"

"The only one," Grayne maintained.

"Humph! What was your first quarrel about?"

"Her name needn't concern you. We were engaged. Derek cut in on us at a dance, and they disappeared from the floor. After a while I went to look for them. They weren't on the porch."

No, they hadn't been on the piazza. He saw again the moonlight touching with silver the river's ripples. He felt the mild breeze against his face. The scent of climbing roses was in his nostrils; the strains of the orchestra sounded in his ears faintly. As in a dream, he walked to the fan of parked cars at the rear of the clubhouse. They hadn't been very clever, he mused; they might have known he would look there first.

"Where were they?"

"In the back of Derek's car."

"In a compromising position?" The chief deputy's little eyes glinted lasciviously.

"I challenged him the next day," Grayne answered simply.

Rawson's aide, hitherto a silent taker of notes, now broke into the conversation. "Shouldn't he have had the choice of weapons?"

"As the challenged person, naturally," the South Carolinian agreed. "But the only weapons available to us were these pistols."

"How'd you know how to shoot them?"

"My grandfather – they had been handed down to him from *his* grandfather – had shown us when we were small boys."

"Shown you how to load pre-Civil War pistols?"

"The past is very real to us in Charleston," Grayne tried to explain.

Rawson said irritably, "We've already established that there was bad blood between him and the deceased. Go on, Grayne. You drove to Los Angeles in Esterling's car to get your dueling pistols. Is that right?"

"Correct."

"When did you get back here?"

"At three twenty-seven. By the clock on the dashboard."

"Does that clock agree with your own watch?"

"No. The clock is two minutes faster. I went down to the garage and checked afterward."

"Why'd you do that?"

"Because I thought some damn fool 'd be asking me."

Rawson's face darkened to crimson. "Are you calling me a damn fool?" he demanded, peeling off his coat. Grayne sprang at once to his feet, but Willis separated them.

"Chief, we all know you can knock hell out of him, so why bother to prove it?"

"Something in that," Rawson agreed, replacing his coat. He glowered a few seconds and then said, "So by your watch you got back at three twenty-five."

"Correct," Grayne confirmed, settling back in his chair.

"Took you a long time on the road."

"I had a little motor trouble."

"Did you see Esterling when you walked into the patio?"

"No."

"You didn't see the body floating in the swimming pool?"

"Not then."

"Yet you saw it afterward. And you had to go right by that end of the pool. How could you miss seeing it?"

"Maybe because there was a cloud over the moon."

"Make a note of it, Willis," Rawson commanded. "He saw a cloud over the moon, but he couldn't see a dead body."

"If I choke his damn insinuations down his throat it won't help any," Grayne told himself. "I've got to go on taking it. Got to."

"How long did the cloud cover the moon?"

"A minute or two."

"No more than that?"

"I don't think so."

"While the *cloud*" – Rawson inflected the noun caustically – "was going by, what did you do?"

"I walked over to a bench and sat down."

"Which bench?"

"The one at the shallow end of the pool."

"Is that near the south wing of the house?"

"Yes."

"There's another bench, isn't there?"

"Yes, one."

"Where is it?"

"Near the northeast corner of the pool."

"Did you go over there?"

"Not then."

"You just stayed on the same bench?"

"Correct."

"How long?"

"Until I saw the body floating in the pool."

"When was that?"

"Ten minutes to four."

"How do you know?"

"I looked at my watch as soon as I—"

"You could read your watch by the moonlight?"

"Yes."

"What position was the moon in the sky?"

"Near its zenith; otherwise, it wouldn't shine into the patio at all."

"A full moon?"

"No. A good fat crescent."

"Make a note of it, Willis," the chief deputy ordered. "The moon, he says, was so bright he could read the dial of his watch. But for twenty-five minutes he couldn't see a body in the pool. A body in a white linen suit of high visibility."

Grayne held his patience with herculean effort.

"I didn't look that way, or I would have seen it. I was looking toward the south door of the house."

"During the whole twenty-five minutes?"

"Right."

"Where was the body floating?" the chief deputy demanded severely.

"Don't you know?"

"I'm asking you."

"In the northeast corner of the pool."

"Near the bench you *didn't* sit on?"

"Yes."

"Do you expect me to believe that for twenty-five minutes you never once looked toward that corner?"

"I don't expect you to believe anything. It's the truth."

"Yeah? Where did Esterling sleep, Grayne? At the house?"

"No. He'd been bunking at his laboratory."

"How would he get into the patio?"

"There's only one way, the stairs from the garage."

"Then why were you watching the house?" Rawson's voice soared triumphantly. "If you'd looked just once toward the stairs you'd have seen the body. And if you'd expected Esterling to walk up those stairs you'd have had your eyes on them. That's only natural. But you didn't. You didn't expect him because he was already there."

"Wrong! I never saw Esterling alive after seven-fifteen last evening."

"You're a lousy liar. Esterling was right there in the patio, on the bench at the northeast corner of the pool, loading one of your pistols. While he was doing that, you grabbed the other pistol by its barrel and hit him on the head with the stock. He fell into the pool, and you left him there to drown."

Rawson held out a pair of nickel-bright handcuffs.

"You're under arrest, Grayne. The charge is murder."

PART EIGHT
CAN WORDS DROWNED
BE MADE TO SPEAK?

Manuel had been ordered to open the pool's outlet, and the waters which had drowned Derek Esterling were draining slowly away. But the level, Westborough meditated regretfully, was still too deep for wading. Unless, of course, one were so indiscreet as to remove one's trousers – at high noon, however, one could not possibly be so indiscreet.

A bathing suit would placate the minions of Mother Grundy, but, unfortunately, he possessed no such garment. One might be borrowed, he cogitated, but it did not seem a fitting day to inaugurate natatory exercises. Moreover, if he left the pool unguarded, the black oblong might be seized by some other person. While he pondered, undecided, Jacynth emerged from the house.

"Good morning, Miss LeDoux." He wondered what sympathy he could offer and decided that it would be kindest to offer none. "Isn't that a billfold down there?"

Her eyes followed the direction of his index finger. "Yes, it does look like one, doesn't it?"

"I was just puzzling over the method to obtain it," he confessed. "It has probably dropped from Mr. Esterling's coat." There was a little awkward silence.

"It shouldn't be hard," she remarked finally. "Just wait a little longer."

"Yes, but by the time the pool is drained—" He faltered, experiencing a delicacy in alluding to a certain legal event to be held that afternoon. "By that time none of us may be here."

"I could get it if I had on my bathing suit." She hesitated briefly. "It won't take but a minute."

"Dear me, no!" he cried. "You must not dream of—"

But she was already gone. "Tsk, tsk," he clucked, gazing pensively at the pool's gray concrete bottom. For the thousandth time he told himself that he would never understand the younger generation. One must not, however, spurn those gifts the gods choose to offer.

Within five minutes Jacynth returned, clad in a coral bathing suit that contrasted most attractively with the golden tan of her limbs. Graceful as a youthful Polynesian, she plunged beneath the water.

"It's Derek's, all right." She stood dripping on the edge of the pool to put the salvage into his frail wrinkled hands. "I've seen it before."

"I am deeply grateful," he murmured, inspecting the contents.

The billfold contained some fifty dollars in currency, and a pasticcio of sodden papers: a driver's license, an automobile insurance identification card, a brake certificate, a social security card, a snapshot of Jacynth, a membership card in a chemical engineering society. These and other documents, as yet too soggy to be unfolded, he set to dry on the sun-warmed paving, employing as paper weights the pebbles which his companion helped him dig from the soil surrounding the spiny olive-green agaves.

Lying flat on her stomach, Jacynth rinsed her fingers in the lowered waters.

"Mr. West, I came out here on purpose to talk to you."

"To talk to me, my dear? On what subject, pray?"

"Gran'-père hinted things about Derek." She sat upright. "He said that you had the proof."

Westborough exclaimed in agitation, "Dear, dear me!" She was too young to be acquainted with such hideous intrigues, far too young! The task of informing her that her deceased fiancé had been the lowest of criminals was a most unwelcome responsibility.

"I fear," he began gently, "that the tale will be very unpleasant for you."

He informed her of the earlier attempt to poison her grandfather, of the origin of the poison from the roots of the yellow jasmine. Her face tensed with horror as he mentioned the bottle of gelsemium hidden in Esterling's laboratory.

"But why? Why would he do it?"

"The only apparent motive is a very sordid one. With your grandfather dead, the business would naturally fall into Mr. Esterling's hands after he had married you."

Her grayish-blue eyes widened incredulously. "I can't believe that of Derek."

"Nor did I for a long time. I did not see how so intelligent a man could leave such obvious signposts to point toward his guilt. I was convinced that these guideposts were false, clues deliberately – may I use the word, 'planted'?"

"Do you still think that?" she asked.

Westborough slowly shook his head. "I fear that I was oversubtle." Halting, he sorted his jumbled thoughts. "It is a fact of history that some murderers have behaved in the most stupid manner. I need cite only one instance, a highly educated scientist of a century ago, to be specific, a university professor of chemistry and mineralogy. With all facilities at his disposal, he blundered most abominably in his unsuccessful attempt to destroy the body of his victim. Perhaps, like the notorious killer of Dr. George Parkman, Mr. Esterling was blinded by self-conceit. Again, perhaps he reasoned that his crime would never be suspected, since men of your grandfather's age sometimes die suddenly from natural causes."

"When," she interrupted, "did you change your mind about Derek?"

The child was quick witted, he acknowledged.

"This morning I received a telegram. Dear me, I am not speaking very accurately. The telegram was not delivered but read to me over the telephone. The details, however, are of slight interest." He reached for his pocket notebook. "I will read you the message: 'MAN WITH REDDISH-BROWN BEARD AND SEEDY CLOTHES BOUGHT GELSEMIUM.' "

She puckered her forehead thoughtfully. "The reddish-brown beard is pretty definite."

"Yes, it is extremely difficult to doubt now."

"But who killed Derek?"

"I do not know," the historian confessed. "Nor shall I attempt to find out. Mr. Rawson made it very plain to me that Mr. Esterling's death was not my affair."

"Make it your affair," she pleaded vehemently. "Gran'-père said you had had lots of experience with – things like this. He told me how clever you are."

"Your grandfather is much too flattering," Westborough rejoined uncomfortably. "So far I have failed miserably."

"A war isn't lost until the last battle," she declared.

Odd, he reflected, that a nineteen-year-old girl, convent educated and secluded from the world, should be so clear sighted, so discerning! But no one has ever called the French a doltish race.

"Please, Mr. West! That fat bully from the sheriff's office made a horrible mistake. You must help him – Stuart. I *know* it wasn't he."

He read at once on her eager upturned face that it was not grief for Derek Esterling which motivated her now. "*Tybalt is dead, and Romeo banished; that 'banished,' that one word 'banished,' hath slain ten thousand Tybalts.*" No, it was not for Tybalt she wept. He pondered the new development carefully.

"I did hear the splash," she continued in a confusing whirlpool of words. "It was at two o'clock. I told that to Mr. Rawson. He didn't believe me, I suppose, but it *was* then, not later. I was awake both times."

"You were awake when Mr. Grayne returned?"

"I certainly was," she returned immediately. "I was with Stuart the second he came into the patio. I stayed there until – until – well, we both saw it at the same time. But I couldn't say that."

"Most astonishing!" Westborough ejaculated. "Naturally I understand your reluctance to impart such tidings."

"It isn't that!" she flashed. "I don't care two pins what people think. I only kept quiet because of Stuart's threats."

"Mr. Grayne *threatened* you?"

"He did! He said if I told anyone I was there, he'd make a confession."

Westborough was nearly as dumfounded as if Hitler were to advocate German disarmament. "Confess to Mr. Esterling's murder?" She nodded confirmation.

"And I don't dare take a chance on his not doing it."

It was true! From the mean soil of the modern world had sprung this extravagant blossom of chivalry. The peace-loving little scholar was conscious of warm admiration for the erstwhile duelist. Mr. Grayne of Charleston may have been "suckled in a creed outworn," but, by the shade of Cervantes, that creed had produced a man!

"Then we will have to find some other way."

"Does that mean you are going to help us?"

"To the full extent of my ability," he gave his pledge.

"I don't know how to thank you, of course."

"Dear me, as yet I have done nothing." Westborough, a little embarrassed, turned with relief to the rapidly drying papers. "Shall we see what we have here?"

The only thing of interest was a small slip with a few words printed in pencil:

"Dead on the field of honor. Tr."

"Honor and *Derek?*" Jacynth laughed cruelly and scornfully.

II

"The lungs were sodden with water. The tongue was congested and covered with a froth, which extended backward to the throat and into the larynx and windpipe." The inquest on the death of Derek Esterling was being held in the county courthouse, a richly ornamented building of Spanish Renaissance architecture. "The windpipe, bronchi and minute air tubes of the lungs contained bloodstained mucous froth. I found also a severe contusion on the crown of the head and several slight scratches on the face."

"Will you interpret these findings, Dr. Resch?"

"The presence of the mucous froth is evidence that the deceased had made an effort to breathe after immersion, drawing water into the air passages."

"Do you believe that the deceased met his death by drowning?"

"In my opinion, the deceased did."

The coroner's jury, which had just listened to the findings of Chief Deputy

Steve Rawson, looked somewhat confused. Westborough, no little surprised, attempted to take notes of the autopsy surgeon's testimony.

"Can you explain the scratches, Doctor?"

"I can offer the suggestion that they may have been made by the fingernails of another person. If the deceased knew how to swim I would say there exists a presumption of a struggle to hold him forcibly under water."

The little historian wrote furiously.

"How, Doctor, do you account for the contusion?"

"Either by a fall against a hard substance or by a blow with a blunt instrument. I cannot tell which from examination. However, since the crown of the head does not commonly receive injury from a fall, I incline toward the theory of a blow."

"Are you able to say whether or not such fall or blow was of sufficient violence to produce a state of insensibility in the deceased?"

"Such insensibility may have occurred."

"Is it possible, Doctor, that the deceased, stumbling accidentally into the pool, struck his head on the bottom and stunned himself before drowning?"

"If that had happened it is unlikely that there would be much water in his lungs. The water is drawn in along with air when the struggling person is near or on the surface."

"Is it possible that the deceased had been stunned by a blow on the head before his body entered the pool?"

"That theory is even more untenable. An unconscious man does not make those violent efforts at respiration which draw water into the larynx, trachea and bronchi."

"In your opinion, Doctor, was the deceased in the full possession of his senses at the moment his body entered the pool?"

"In my opinion that is the correct interpretation of the autopsy findings."

Rawson had made an important mistake – but Westborough did his best to conceal his elation.

Dr. Resch was asked to state the time at which he believed death had occurred.

"The question is difficult to answer with certainty. The body would naturally cool at a more rapid rate in water than on land."

"Could the deceased have met his death at the hour of three-thirty this morning?"

"Yes, I believe so."

"Could Mr. Esterling have met his death earlier than that?"

"It is possible."

"How much earlier would you say, Doctor?"

"It is difficult to be certain."

"Could the death of the deceased have occurred as early as two o'clock?"

"I am not able to state it could not."

The principal witness of the afternoon was, of course, the sheriff's prisoner. Studying the faces of the nine jurors, Westborough read varying degrees of shock at the tall Carolinian's frank admission of the intended pistol duel. Moreover, Grayne's statement that he had sat alone for twenty-five minutes without a single glance toward the stairs which Esterling must ascend to enter the patio was received with marked skepticism – a fact scarcely to be wondered at. In truth, Westborough acknowledged, Grayne's suppression of his meeting with Jacynth did render his tale very nearly incredible. With mounting apprehension the little historian watched the coils of circumstantial evidence continue to tighten.

"Mr. Grayne," inquired Deputy Coroner Hansen, "are you acquainted with Schäfer's method of artificial respiration?"

"Yes. I once had occasion to use that method on a friend when our canoe upset on a lake in the Adirondacks."

"Why, then, didn't you think of applying that treatment to the deceased?"

"I did think of it, but I knew it would be useless."

"Upon what grounds did you base that opinion?"

"I realized he was already dead."

"Do you hold a degree in medicine, Mr. Grayne?"

"No sir."

"Then how were you able to pronounce with certainty that the deceased was or was not dead?"

"From the time element. He had been in the pool all the while I was in the patio, probably for much longer. I don't think that anyone can be resuscitated after four or five minutes under water."

"It's claimed that some persons have been revived by artificial respiration after a submersion lasting as long as twenty minutes." Hansen paused meditatively. "An extreme limit, I'll admit."

"I was there for twenty-five minutes," Grayne said. "And he wasn't alive when I first set foot on the stairs."

"Why do you say that, Mr. Grayne?"

"If he had been, I certainly would have heard him splashing."

"What was your first act upon discovering the deceased?"

"I pulled him to the edge of the pool and lifted his head so I could see his face. The way he was floating in the water, I couldn't tell who he was."

"In other words, you altered the position of the body?"

"Yes."

"Don't you know," Hansen inquired sternly, "that a body found dead must never be touched prior to the arrival of the proper officials to examine it?"

The witness displayed irritation. "First I'm bawled out for not touching the body and then again for touching it. Maybe I made a few mistakes. Most of us make mistakes at one time or another, I reckon."

Grayne was allowed to step down from the chair.

From the statements of succeeding witnesses and his own knowledge, Westborough extracted four facts which seemed to be established beyond controversy:

(1) That Esterling, though not particularly expert, did know how to swim.

(2) That Grayne, when he aroused his host, was wearing the same clothes he had worn when last seen in the afternoon.

(3) That Grayne's clothes had been dry at four A.M.

(4) That the only noise of a splash from the swimming pool had been heard at two A.M. (After his conversation with Jacynth earlier in the day, Westborough could not doubt the girl's sincerity in this statement.)

Rawson's theory, it was evident, had many errors. On the surface, however, it appeared plausible, so plausible that to upset it more than mere pettifoggery would be required. While he pondered upon the problem, Westborough heard his assumed name being called.

The deputy coroner's opening question was considerable of a shock.

"Is West your true name?"

"No, Mr. Hansen, it is not."

"What is your true name?"

"Westborough. To be precise, Theocritus Lucius Westborough."

"Does Mr. LeDoux know that you were visiting him under a false name?"

"Yes. He invited me to do so." Gazing down, the historian saw a ripple of surprise traveling over the faces of his fellow witnesses.

"Will you explain the circumstances under which you came to be Mr. LeDoux's guest?"

Noting the perfumer's white beard bobbing downward, Westborough replied, "I shall be happy to do so. Mr. LeDoux had asked me to undertake a confidential mission."

"Are you a detective by profession, Mr. Westborough?"

"No, Mr. Hansen, I am only a student of history."

"Is it true that you were concerned last summer in the investigation of the murders of Charles Danville and Marcus Bayard in Los Angeles County?"

"My part in the investigation was comparatively a minor one."

"What was the nature of the confidential mission which Mr. LeDoux asked you to undertake?"

"Mr. LeDoux had reason to believe that an attempt had been made to poison him. He invited all who might have been concerned in that attempt to be his guests, ostensibly to participate in a business conference, but in reality that they might be kept under surveillance."

"Why did he do this?"

"He was convinced, Mr. Hansen, that the attempt would be repeated." There was an excited murmur from the spectators, and Hansen rapped for order.

"Did you discover Mr. LeDoux's poisoner?"

"I discovered circumstantial evidence implicating a certain person in that crime."

"Do you wish to state the name of the person so implicated?"

"The deceased."

Westborough was requested to divulge the nature of his evidence.

Subsequently, the deputy coroner demanded, "Is it true that Captain Howe of the Valle de Flores substation asked you to work with him unofficially on the Chamaron case?"

"It is true. But Chief Deputy Rawson made it clear to me that my services were no longer required. Not that I blame Mr. Rawson," Westborough made haste to add. A roar of laughter arose from the audience.

The coroner's jury, in returning a verdict to the effect that the deceased, Derek Esterling, came to his death by drowning, recommended that the sheriff's office take into custody the person of Stuart Grayne.

III

The black-beamed living room had become a babel of divergent voices. There seemed to be no fear of poisoning now, Westborough noted. Even Aaron Todd had accepted a postprandial liqueur, albeit somewhat grudgingly.

Mrs. Chamaron had joined the others at dinner, bringing their number to eight. For the first time they were now equally divided between the sexes, four men, four women. ... The historian's meditations were interrupted by the jovial tones of Sam Preston.

"We're all amateurs, folks. It don't matter much what any of us think about the question, but there's a professional in the house. Let's ask Ted West – Westborough, I ought to say – to tell us how he dopes it out."

"Dear me, no!" the little man cried, aghast. "I am not a professional at all; Mr. Preston has grossly exaggerated." He was not permitted to escape.

"My own idea, folks, is that Ted owes us something for the way he's fooled us. Let's have a showing of hands." LeDoux's hand alone did not raise in the air. "All right, Ted," Preston proclaimed lustily. "The verdict is you've got to give us the works."

"The works?" Westborough repeated, smiling. "That sounds ominously drastic. I will do what I can, but pray do not blame me overmuch if my efforts disappoint. There is a slang phrase, I believe, which goes, 'You asked for it.' "

"Hear, hear!" Preston interrupted, clapping his hands. Westborough waited until the noise had subsided.

"Mr. Grayne," he began, "is doing one of three things: he is lying *in toto*, truth-telling *in toto* or lying in part. Before deciding what, if any, portion of his story is acceptable, let us make an assumption. Contrary to the general tradition of English law, let us assume Mr. Grayne is guilty." He regarded momentarily the dragon-carved cabinet.

"But," he continued, "we must frame our hypothesis of guilt to accord with six known facts. Mr. Grayne's guilt becomes untenable if a hypothesis cannot be constructed to satisfy these essential conditions: (1) that the death of Mr. Esterling was due to drowning; (2) that the drowning occurred at the hour of two A.M., when Miss LeDoux heard the splash from the pool; (3) that Mr. Esterling, since he knew how to swim, must be forcibly held below the surface of the water; (4) that this could only be accomplished by a person also in the pool; (5) that when Mr. Grayne reported the discovery of the body he was wearing the same clothes he had worn prior to his departure; (6) that these clothes were not damp at the hour of four A.M.

"In order to satisfy these conditions, we must assume (1) that Mr. Grayne was able to return to this house by two o'clock; (2) that Mr. Esterling was in the patio with him at the same hour; (3) that Mr. Grayne removed his clothing before going into the pool. If one of these three assumptions can be proved invalid, Mr. Grayne's innocence has been established.

"Let us consider the first carefully. Can Mr. Grayne, leaving Mr. LeDoux's residence at seven-fifteen, drive to Los Angeles and back by two? The distance is roughly three hundred miles; to cover it in six and three quarters hours an approximate average speed of forty-five miles an hour must be made. Superficially, the feat does not appear to be overly difficult, but an allowance must be made for the traffic of Los Angeles and its suburbs. Estimating that there is a heavy traffic zone of twenty miles to be traversed both going and coming, a period of two and a half hours will not, I believe, be excessive. Subtracting, the remaining distance becomes two hundred and sixty miles, and the remaining time but four hours and fifteen minutes. Dividing, the average required for the open road is found to be sixty-one miles. Whether or not the state's efficient highway police would allow this speed to be maintained without controversy for a distance of two hundred and sixty miles is certainly a moot question.

"But if Mr. Grayne were able to reach the patio by two A.M. – a rather debatable point – would Mr. Esterling also have been there? Yes, if the appointment were at two and not, as Mr. Grayne insists, at three-thirty. But the engagement was to fight a duel, which could not possibly take place before sunrise, an event not occurring this morning until four forty-eight. These two men, hating, as Byron puts it, 'with a hate found only on the stage,' would not be likely to endure more than the necessary minimum of each other's company. An hour and eighteen minutes is certainly long enough to wait. Three-thirty is a plausible time for the appointment; two o'clock is not. Therefore, if Mr. Esterling is to be in the patio with Mr. Grayne at the earlier hour, Mr. Grayne must fetch him there.

"What does this entail? It means that Mr. Grayne must go to the laboratory or wherever Mr. Esterling is to be found, and persuade the latter to accompany him at once to the patio. Mr. Esterling, in all probability, will refuse such a strange request, but Mr. Grayne may use Hitler methods of pacification. Here, however, fresh difficulties are encountered. Our third assumption requires that Mr. Grayne remove his clothing before entering the pool. While doing this, he is scarcely in a position to hold a prisoner, and it is most unlikely that Mr. Esterling will stand placidly by to await his adversary's disrobement. The only solution for the dilemma is the assumption that Mr. Esterling is then unconscious.

"See now what the theory of Mr. Grayne's guilt necessitates. Firstly, he must drive three hundred miles at illegal and hazardous speed solely in order to return an hour and a half in advance of his appointment. Secondly, he must reduce Mr. Esterling to a state of insensibility. Thirdly, when Mr. Esterling is forced into the pool, he has – and the medical evidence will allow no other conclusion – recovered his consciousness. But if Mr. Esterling is insensible at the time Mr. Grayne disrobes – and he must be or the latter cannot undress – why was not the unconscious body thrown into the pool? The procedure would be vastly simpler.

"So ponderous has our hypothesis grown that it falls to pieces of its own weight, but – I must stress this fact – it is the only hypothesis of guilt which may be logically constructed. Ergo, Mr. Grayne's innocence becomes almost a mathematical certainty."

Westborough's eyes lingered for an instant on Jacynth's glowing, grateful face.

"Now that we know Mr. Grayne must be guiltless of murder," he resumed, "we are justified in accepting not all, perhaps, but certainly portions of his story. One such portion is Mr. Grayne's statement that Mr. Esterling had declared he had an earlier appointment to keep last night. We are justified, I believe, in accepting this as true information. Only such an appointment is able to explain Mr. Esterling's presence in the patio so far in advance of the stipulated hour.

"The name of the person who met Mr. Esterling at the earlier hour is unknown. To assume a second unknown for the murderer adds an unnecessary and unjustifiable complication. The person whom Mr. Esterling had agreed to meet is also the person who killed him. To proceed further, however, we must now consider a question of vital import:

"*Was the first appointment with a man or a woman?*"

The historian watched the seven people who silently waited for the denouement. Seven expressions of bewilderment and perplexity! Yet one should know. He observed aloud:

"To answer, we must consider two facts. The first is that Mr. Esterling did not cry out when he fell into the pool. A cry would certainly have been heard by Miss LeDoux when she heard the splash. It becomes evident, then, that Mr. Esterling was overpowered rapidly, that his head was never allowed to reach the surface long enough for him to vent a call for aid. This presupposes physical strength on the part of his assailant, probably, since Mr. Esterling was by no means a weakling, a greater degree of muscular strength than a woman would have.

"The second fact is that Mr. Esterling's assailant must enter the pool to drown the victim. The total absence of damp clothing or damp bathing suits in the rooms of the occupants of this house indicates a nude murderer. A woman would not go naked to such a rendezvous.

"But a man might." Westborough paused again to study the faces of his listeners. "A man might have already been swimming in the pool when Mr. Esterling arrived. Besides myself, there are five men in this house. Was it Lung Fu? Or Manuel?" He glanced quickly from LeDoux to Todd to Preston. "Was it you? Or you? Or you? My logic will admit no other suspects."

A voice rasped suddenly, "How do we know it wasn't you?"

IV

The dust of the Milky Way spattered a hazy trail across the sky as they walked down the garden stairs. The great red hibiscus blooms flaunted their colors to the dusk, and the oleanders were sweetly fragrant as the icing of a pink cake. A mockingbird's distant trills impinged faintly on the ear.

"Is it true," he asked, "that you wished to talk with me?"

Her hand rested lightly on his arm; she was taller than he, by a full inch. "You read faces very well, Mr. Westborough." He waited mutely. "I feel responsible for Stuart."

"In what respect, Mrs. Chamaron?"

"If I had returned to Los Angeles, as I should have done, immediately after Paul's death, he would have gone, too. Do you know why I stayed?"

"I think I do."

"The law did nothing to the man who killed my husband." Her grip tightened; he felt the strength in her slender fingers.

"The law is ponderous but sure," he said.

"Not sure enough for me."

He cried, aghast, "Do you realize what you are implying?"

Her eyes glowed darkly from a rice-white face. "You have just proved – in a very clever manner – that it is impossible for me to have killed Derek Esterling."

"Yes, that is true," he murmured.

"What is your usual fee?"

"Dear, dear! I scarcely know how to answer that."

"Paul was not a rich man, Mr. Westborough, but, on the other hand, he was not precisely a poor one. And I – I have done very well with my own work. Would a thousand dollars tempt you?"

"Tempt me to what folly, might one ask?"

Her lips parted to form a listless smile. "On the day that Stuart Grayne walks out of jail a free man I will give you my check for a thousand dollars. More if you insist."

"You set a rather high value on Mr. Grayne's freedom." There was just light enough for him to see the sudden flush of color to her cheeks.

"The check will be good. The reason why I give it need not concern you."

"I am not so sure of that," he demurred.

Her mazarine eyes focused intently on his triangular face. "You have an interesting forehead. Broad, bulging. It's the forehead of a man who reads and thinks. But—"

"But otherwise," he finished, "you find me – to use Mr. Rawson's word – a washout?"

"I didn't say that."

"No, you would not be so impolite. Are you," he added quickly, "in love with Mr. Grayne?"

The question found her guard down. "I was half in love with him."

"Was?" he repeated.

"I haven't given it much thought – lately."

She opened a gold-and-enamel cigarette case. Westborough fumbled through his pockets until he found a paper packet of matches. The flare permitted him to see the harsh lines of taut neck and throat muscles.

"I've made it sound worse than it really was. You see, I loved Paul, too. Do you believe it's possible for a woman to love two men at the same time?"

"In Tibet a woman may have four husbands if she wishes," Westborough said informatively.

"I only wanted one. Paul Michael. But – well, you know Stuart. You know what he is. That mixture of strength and chivalry! It attracts a woman, weakens her somehow. Even one who honestly loves her husband. I did love Paul Michael, I swear it."

"I am sure of it," he said, wondering.

"I think that any woman … who saw as much of Stuart as I did … would have been in love with him. At least a little."

"I am beyond my depth," Westborough confessed. "As Pope puts it, 'Woman's at best a contradiction still.' A riddle I have never learned to read with any degree of certainty. Did Mr. Grayne—"

"It wasn't a cheap intrigue," she retorted angrily. "I didn't tell him. And he – well, he treated me as he would have treated his sister. Always."

"And the *tertium quid?*"

She flushed. "Paul guessed – more than was true. Yes, I lied to him – tried to lie to him. I swore I didn't love Stuart."

"Was your husband jealous of Mr. Grayne?"

She shook her head. "Paul liked Stuart more than any man who ever worked for him. They were always the best of friends."

"Dear me!"

"I've given you the truth," she maintained, a shade sullenly. "Unfortunately, it's a truth that is not difficult to twist into some rather vile lies. Don't hesitate to say if you find my account of our three-cornered relations unbelievable."

"Accounts of three-cornered relations often do sound unbelievable, I have been informed."

"A mild manner," she proclaimed tartly, "may serve to cover a multitude of doubts."

"My dear Mrs. Chamaron! You remind me of a wounded lioness. The arrow has been withdrawn. Pray allow the healing force of time to ease the pain."

She was cold, however, to his sympathy. "You haven't said whether or not you will accept my offer."

"I cannot possibly accept it," Westborough declared.

She confronted him for a moment in hostile silence.

"It's a question of more money, I suppose."

"Not in the least," he differed. "Merely a question of a prior assignment."

"You are clever at probing," she informed him freezingly. "Few men could be so successful. I compliment you, Mr. Westborough. I hope you may live to display many more examples of your astonishing skill. I know the way back to the house, thank you."

"A whirlwind!" Westborough exclaimed, discomfited at discovering himself so abruptly alone. "I do not wonder that Mr. Chamaron sometimes found her difficult."

His pipe was in his coat pocket, luckily. A wife would have told him that pipe and tobacco pouch created an abominable bulge, but, not having a wife, Westborough was spared many minor annoyances. He filled the pipe and settled himself to contemplation.

"*Mon ami,*" a voice broke into his thoughts, "was it wise of you to say what you did a few minutes ago?"

"It was probably very foolish," Westborough replied.

"Your reasoning – a most brilliant analysis, by the way – has narrowed the field of suspects to such an extent that the murderer cannot possibly feel safe. Would it not be well to quit this case?"

"Quit at this point?"

"I wish you to, my friend. I want you to leave tonight."

The historian sucked perturbedly upon the stem of his pipe. "Do I understand you are inviting me to leave your home, Mr. LeDoux?"

"*Précisément.*" The perfumer's mustache and pointed beard were silvery in the moonlight. "It is not that I am inhospitable. It is that I fear for your life, my friend."

V

"My life, such as it is, is my own."

"You are angry, *mon ami?*"

"A trifle annoyed," Westborough confessed.

"Please believe me when I say that I make the request only because of the grave danger."

"I was not 'born in a wood to be afraid of an owl.' Jonathan Swift, I believe."

"An owl is a hunting bird," LeDoux said pointedly.

"I dislike the simile," Westborough returned. "I am not a rodent."

The Frenchman chuckled. "You do not wish to emulate the wisdom of *Monsieur le Rat* with regard to sinking ships?"

"Candidly, I would prefer to drown."

"So? One has already done that. Why is it that you are so anxious to share his fate?"

"That," the historian opined, "sounds dangerously like a threat."

"But no! Surely you do not believe that it is I who threaten you? It is merely that I cannot be responsible if you insist on spending another night here."

"I do insist."

LeDoux shrugged. "*Soit!* I shall say no more. At least you will permit me to arm you? There is an automatic pistol in the upper drawer of the study desk."

"If you please, no."

"I believe that you are making a mistake."

"Perhaps. I have made many of them, particularly on this case. So far I have only one clue, and it is of dubious value."

"What is it that you tell me? You have found a clue?"

"The message in Mr. Esterling's billfold."

"Pah!" LeDoux ejaculated contemptuously. "It is not for such *canaille* as he to talk of honor. Poisoner and coward! He did well to die."

"I should not say that too loudly in Mr. Rawson's presence," Westborough gently cautioned. " 'Dead on the field of honor' was the answer given in the roll call of La Tour d'Auvergne's regiment after his death, I believe."

"You are well informed."

The little historian meditatively polished the lenses of his bifocals. "The two letters, <u>Tr.</u>, however, are Mr. Esterling's own addition. Do you recognize a possible significance?"

"I am poor at conundrums."

"This might better be called an acrostic," Westborough deliberated. "Mr. Esterling seems to have left us a cryptic message. Unnecessarily cryptic, I must say. Why he was so vague, I cannot understand, unless, perhaps, a sense of guilt or obligation toward a certain person stopped him from leaving more than a hint."

"*Qu'est-ce que c'est?* You found a hidden meaning in those six words?"

"Seven," Westborough corrected. "You are overlooking the <u>Tr.</u>, though I admit it is not a word in precisely the same sense. I believe mathematicians would term it an 'operator.' "

"You speak in riddles!" LeDoux complained.

"Mr. Esterling, we must remember, intended the slip to be found only if he were killed in the duel. He could not know that he would be drowned and his words with him."

"Can words drowned be made to speak again?" LeDoux asked, smiling.

"To speak, yes. To speak sensibly – I do not know."

"What is this concealed message?"

"The name of a person."

"One of us?"

"The answer is very preposterous. So preposterous, in fact, that I would prefer to say nothing further. Probably I have mistaken the meaning altogether. Let us talk of other matters. Do you know that I have turned down an offer of a thousand dollars?"

"Is it that you have no use for a thousand dollars?"

"My resources so far have been ample." Westborough's eyes twinkled through the spectacles just restored to his nose. "The offer was from Mrs. Chamaron."

"That is most astonishing. For what purpose, may I inquire?"

"To clear Mr. Grayne of the charge which hangs over him."

"You refused to do that?"

"Yes, I refused."

"But I thought that you were a believer in Mr. Grayne's innocence."

"I am very much a believer. It is merely that my conscience will not permit me to accept money for doing what I have already engaged to do out of sympathy."

"You have already promised to clear Mr. Grayne?"

"To lend my best efforts in that direction."

"So? I was not aware of it. Who is the person who enlisted your services? Or is that another of your abominable secrets?"

"No, it is not a secret. Your granddaughter."

"*Ce n'est pas possible!* Jacynth barely knows the man."

"Perhaps better than you think."

"What is it that you say?" LeDoux raged.

"Unless I have misread the signs, she is greatly in love."

"With Grayne? Impossible! She was in love with Esterling. I cannot have mistaken her affection for that vile one."

"She has changed her mind," Westborough declared. Slowly the anger faded from the perfumer's waxen face. "He has strength," the historian meditated. "The strength of flexible steel."

"I am old, *mon ami*." LeDoux stood motionless, only the droop of his shoulders betraying his pain. "I must not seek to force my opinions on my sole descendant. Perhaps she has chosen wisely, perhaps not; but she has chosen. ... My poor Jacynth!" he murmured in a broken voice. "*Elle a le coeur tendre.*"

A switch clicked within Westborough's brain, turning on a flood of sudden illumination.

"Drop two vowels!" he exclaimed. "One obtains by process of elision – it is true, then. Yes, it must be true."

"*Vous parlez toujours par énigmes!*" LeDoux cried in exasperation. "What riddle is it now?"

"Are you familiar with the psychological theory that a slip of the memory is because one really wishes to forget?"

"I have heard something of the kind."

"And with the similar theory that a slip of the tongue expresses what one really wants to say?"

"Yes, yes! I do not see the connection."

Westborough's answer was: "I believe that the murderer has unwittingly confessed."

PART NINE
CLUE OF THE DEAD HEART

Miss Morton, crisply austere in a brown tailored suit, carried a stenographer's notebook and a supply of newly sharpened pencils. "Good morning," she called cheerfully. "Mr. LeDoux said you wanted to dictate a letter."

"Yes, thank you very much. Will you not sit down?" A shaft of sunlight from the east window fell on the chair before the study desk like a long golden finger. "The letter will be a long one, and, I sadly fear, a very frank one also. I trust that you are not easily shocked?"

"You don't look like a frightfully shocking person, Mr. Westborough." Her laughter held an easy, friendly note.

"Appearances are often deceptive." He was pacing the study, hands clasped behind his back like a promenading Felix. "I once wrote a book of such depravity that the Hays office forbade its production as a motion picture. My letter, I may say, is to Stephen Rawson, Chief Deputy, Sheriff's Department, Santa Bonita, California."

She took up a pencil, her manner brisk and businesslike.

"Dear Mr. Rawson: You have informed me that my assistance in connection with the Esterling case was not required, informed me in very plain terms, I might say. … Or should I say?" He paused uncertainly. "Do you believe my language is a little too abrupt, Miss Morton?"

She shook her head promptly. "Not for him. That man is a swaggering bully."

"He is something of a Tartar," the historian agreed. "Dear me, where was I?"

" 'In very plain terms, I might say.' "

"Perhaps 'in no uncertain terms' would be less blunt. Shall we continue? I am accepting my dismissal and shall leave on the afternoon train for San Francisco, in which city I expect to sojourn for a few days, sampling the delights of its incomparable restaurants and feasting my eyes upon its beautiful exposition, before I return to Chicago to resume my life of the Emperor Julian." He halted, temporarily breathless. "Am I going too fast for you?"

"Not at all. Mr. LeDoux talks a great deal more rapidly."

"Nevertheless," Westborough continued with unwonted sternness, "I cannot depart without an endeavor to correct certain erroneous impressions you have formed concerning the actions and motives of one Stuart Grayne, an advertising copy writer in the office of Paul Michael Chamaron, Inc., Los Angeles, who is at present being held a prisoner by your office. In your commendable zeal to secure a scapegoat for Mr. Esterling's death you acted in disregard of certain facts. These, I believe, conclusively establish Mr. Grayne's innocence of the crime of murder. Quote: Unreasonable haste is the direct road to error. Unquote. I trust you will not be offended by the citation from Molière. 'Censure,' as Swift phrases it, 'is the tax a man pays for being eminent.' "

"Is that the letter?" Miss Morton inquired, seeing that the little man had paused to mop his brow with a large handkerchief.

"Dear me, no; merely the prelude. I shall now endeavor to set before you the reasons for my assertion that Mr. Grayne is innocent of the grave charge you have laid upon his shoulders. ..." Westborough dictated a résumé of his arguments in the living room during the preceding evening. "A woman," he concluded, "would not go naked to such a rendezvous. That is what I confidently asserted last night, but I am now of the opinion that a qualification must be imposed. A woman would not go naked to such a rendezvous *unless she had previously been Mr. Esterling's mistress.*"

He halted apologetically. "I am sorry, Miss Morton. I warned you – did I not? – that it would be necessary to speak with candor."

"I am not shocked," she replied.

"Very well, then, let us continue: Much may be found to substantiate the hypothesis of the discarded mistress. *Primo*, the motive. Eminent literary men provide eloquent testimony. 'Heaven has no rage like love to hatred turned,' declares Congreve. 'Sweet is revenge – especially to women,' says Byron in *Don Juan*, adding in the same poem: 'Alas, the love of women! It is known to be a lovely and a fearful thing.' Most emphatic of all, however, is Colley Cibber: 'We shall find no fiend in hell can match the fury of a disappointed woman – scorned, slighted, dismissed without a parting pang.' Poets and playwrights, as you doubtless realize, have ever been astute psychologists. Though Lord Byron has been dead for over a hundred years, Cibber and Congreve for two hundred, their opinions cannot be lightly disregarded. The motive is adequate. A woman, grievously wounded in her pride and sensibilities, might resort to almost any lengths to secure vengeance.

"*Secundo*, I might mention the testimony given at the Chamaron inquest by John Smith, locksmith of Valle de Flores. Mr. Smith declared, irrelevantly, it is true, that he had once made an extra key for Mr. Esterling's house. Could not this have been given to Mr. Esterling's mistress? Could not she, entering his dwelling during her lover's trip to the San Francisco convention, have discovered the laboratory key he had left behind on that occasion? And could she not have abstracted the latter key, having it duplicated – in some other city than Valle de Flores, I must mention – and restoring the original before Mr. Esterling's return, so that its temporary absence was never suspected? Such a theory accounts for many facts hitherto inexplicable.

"*Tertio*, Mr. Esterling himself left us an important clue – a slip of paper, discovered in his wallet after his death, which bore the words: 'Dead on the field of honor. Tr.' This rodomontade, I have recently discovered, has an esoteric significance. … New paragraph, please, Miss Morton.

"Mr. Esterling was purposely cryptic. I feel certain that he recognized his responsibility toward his ex-mistress and wished to give her – shall I employ the slang term? – 'a break' in the event he met his death at the hands of Mr. Grayne – a most unlikely contingency, I may remark. Shall we proceed now to the reading of the cryptogram?

"The enigmatic Tr. might have many meanings. My own interpretation, colored perhaps by my occupation, is the verb 'translate.' Please note, however, that only the first word of the message is underlined to correspond with the underlining of the abbreviation. Ergo, only the first word is to be translated. … Another new paragraph.

"Translated into what language? A little reflection will answer this at once; the saying, you will immediately recognize, is of French origin. In the French language the word for dead and death is *mort*. Substituting this for the English equivalent, we read—"

He stopped abruptly as an automatic pistol was whisked from the upper desk drawer.

"I think I'll kill you now," Beatrice Morton said evenly.

II

Blinking, Westborough ventured a mild protest. "But the noise of the report would most certainly attract somebody to this room, in which event, you could not hope to escape legal punishment."

"You are good at reading cryptograms, Mr. Westborough, but in practical matters you are – not so good. Don't you know that the house is completely empty?"

"Is it?" he faltered. "No, I did not know."

"Mr. LeDoux and Mr. Preston are at the factory. Jacynth and her mother drove Mr. Todd and Mrs. Chamaron to the train. Lung Fu and Manuel are in town also, doing the marketing. There is nobody here but ourselves."

"Nevertheless, I do not believe you can avoid the consequences."

She held the automatic unwaveringly, the bluish barrel directly on a level with his chest. "I shall say that you made improper advances, that I was forced to shoot you to protect myself. No jury will ever convict a woman for that."

"No, I suppose not," he acknowledged uncomfortably. "So I shall be handed down to posterity as a lecherous old man! Not exactly kind of you, Miss Morton. Is it fair to slander a man who will be in no position to refute the charges?"

Her forefinger tightened slightly on the trigger. "Can't we talk a little while first?" Westborough pleaded.

"Talk? What about?"

" 'O, wilt thou leave me so unsatisfied?' *Romeo and Juliet*, I believe. Miss Morton, I have had the bad fortune to encounter a number of practitioners of the art of murder. None, however, succeeded in baffling me as you have done. Indeed, if it had not been for Mr. Esterling's message, I should never have suspected you. So it might be said I won only by a fluke."

"You haven't won," she contradicted. "You've lost – decidedly."

He winced. "I acknowledge defeat. But will you not take pity on a beaten foe? The condemned man does not ask for a hearty meal, but he would like to have his curiosity satisfied. A Scheherazade in reverse, shall we say?"

"Aren't you afraid?" she asked in wonder.

"I am very much afraid," he confessed. "You suspect, do you not, that I am endeavoring to postpone the inevitable moment in the hope that a *deus ex machina* may arrive to save me? But the instant anyone enters the hall you will be able to hear the footsteps. You can shoot me then, and your excuse will not be a whit less valid. I assure you, I have abandoned all hope. So will you not, from the kindness of your heart, grant my last request?"

"Lock the door," she ordered curtly. "Put the key in your pocket. It will make my story more believable if they break down the door and find it there."

"You think of every detail!" he exclaimed admiringly.

"Sit down. Across the room, please." She laid the automatic on the desk, informing him warningly, "I can reach that far sooner than you."

"I should not dream of putting the statement to the test."

"What do you want to know? Why and how I did it?"

"If you please," he answered.

"I've had a dull life," she began. He saw that her hazel eyes had clouded with tears. "I had to stop school when I was no older than Jacynth and go to work to support my brother and mother. I've helped support them ever since. Right now I send half of my salary to them. Beatrice doesn't mind, they say. Beatrice is self-sacrificing. Beatrice loves to do for other people. Beatrice never thinks of herself. Beatrice has no life of her own. Sweet, charitable, unselfish, homely Beatrice! It was all true. And how I hated it!"

"I think you are very nice looking," he interrupted.

"You don't think any such thing. How could you? My hair is coarse and an ugly shade of brown. My chin's too short, my mouth too big, my lips too thin and my nose is much too wide. My eyes are too little and too insipid. I haven't one decent feature. And as for figure – did you ever see me in a bathing suit? Broad hips and thick ankles! What can you do with that sort of equipment? The best thing is not to draw attention to it. So I wear tweed skirts, and tailored suits, and blouses, and low-heeled shoes and four-thread hosiery, and never any jewelry except a bead necklace. Protective coloration, you could call it. I salve my vanity by giving people the opportunity to say, 'The woman might be attractive if she only bothered to dress better.' But if I did dress better I'd only look worse, and I know it. So I'm plain by nature and a frump by choice, and I'd been more or less reconciled to being both, I think. ...

"Derek was handsome, wasn't he? Graceful as a cat, and that little chestnut beard made him look awfully distinctive. He had a nice voice and pleasant manners, too. Most of the girls were crazy about him, but he didn't even know they were alive. He didn't know I was alive, I remember. Just a piece of office furniture to be shoved out of the way sometimes when it barred his way to Mr. LeDoux. I didn't mind. No man ever had looked at me twice. Even in the university, the only dates I ever had were blind ones. And the only man who ever dated me more than once was a senior who had what he thought was a subtle approach to a job in the advertising business. All this was before the crash, you understand. My people had money then, and what might be called social position. Afterward it was worse; the only men who ever said more than 'good morning' were Mr. LeDoux and Mr. Chamaron. Mr. LeDoux because I was his secretary and Paul Michael because he felt responsible for shooing the ugly duckling into a muddy pond. Paul Michael was always very kind. I hated to kill him. But I'm getting ahead of myself."

"You do have a nice forehead, Miss Morton."

"If you think you can save yourself by flattery, Mr. Westborough, you are mistaken." Her hand wandered significantly toward the pistol.

"Pray continue your narrative," he urged hastily.

"It all began one day last winter when I ran into Derek at the Watsonia Inn. I don't eat at the inn very much; it's beyond my budget. I've told you I only keep half my salary, so dollar-and-a-half dinners are a luxury in which I don't often indulge. However, I did go there that night. I had no more than found a place when Derek came in and sat down at my table. The expression on his face said very plainly, 'She's seen me, so I can't very well get out of this. I'll have to do my best to show the poor thing a good time.'

"And he did do his best. I've never met anyone who had more charm than Derek when he cared to exert himself. Or more intelligence either, for that matter. His mind was as stimulating to me as a cold shower. I have read a lot, Mr. Westborough, and I don't think I'm exactly a dumbbell, and I do have a sense of humor. Altogether, I'm not such horribly bad company, if anybody takes the trouble to bring me out. Derek took the trouble that night, and I surprised him a great deal, I could tell. We started out formally, Mr. Esterling and Miss Morton, as we had been addressing each other for something over six years, but by dessert time we were Derek and Beatrice. 'I didn't have any idea you were like this,' he said when he reached for the check. 'We'll have to have dinner together often, Beatrice.'

"My car was parked outside, but his was laid up in the shop, so I offered to drive him home. It was raining then – a spitty, drizzling night. He asked me to come inside and insisted on showing me through his house – a tiny little doll's cottage, only four rooms and a bath. He had bought all his own furniture and was pleased when I approved his taste. He had to live there alone, he said, because no woman would marry him. 'They always open Bluebeard's closet first, and my sins pop out.' He was like that with me for a long time, gay and free. We had fun together.

"He forced me to take off my coat and sit in a big chair while he built a fire. 'You make it home for the first time,' he told me. 'The one note that's been lacking.' And after a time he said, squinting at my face through half-closed eyes, 'You look like a Madonna, Beatrice. Did anyone ever tell you that?' No one ever had, of course. And after that he said, 'It's lonely, isn't it, Beatrice? My life is Godawful lonely.'

" 'Mine is, too,' I said, and somehow found I was telling him how sick I was of being Beatrice the Good, Beatrice the Noble, Beatrice the Burden Bearer. And while I was telling him, he walked over to my side of the fireplace and picked up my hands. 'Poor kid!' he said. 'They've treated you like dirt. Let's make an alliance; how about it? Offensive and defensive. Us against the world.'

" 'Us against the world,' I repeated after him. He scooped me out of the chair and I kissed him. I kissed him, as I had never dreamed I could. After a time he broke away and stood, rather shaken, by the fireplace. 'Beatrice,' he whispered, 'do you dare to belong to me?' I answered, 'Anything.'

"He lifted me in his arms and carried me into the bedroom as if I had been a baby. He was kind and sweet and tender. I had loved him from the moment I sat down at his fireplace, I think, but after that I worshiped him. He was like a god to me. I would have gone through fire for him.

"We were careful. I never came to his house except after dark. He gave me a key, so I could let myself in if he didn't happen to be there. We were discreet about hairpins and such things; the woman who came in to clean for him wasn't given anything to gossip about. As for the dear old souls who rent me their front room, I never did have any trouble in fooling them. After I had supposedly 'retired,' I had only to lock my door and leave by the window. They wouldn't have dreamed of trying to get into my room.

"We never quarreled. I didn't ask any more from him than he wanted to give. Sometimes I used to wonder if he ever would ask me to marry him, but I didn't really care. What's marriage, anyway? I was satisfied with what I had. More than satisfied – happy. Ecstatically happy. It lasted for months, until the end of April when he went to San Francisco for that chemist's meeting. I got my first real sample of hell then.

"On Friday evening loneliness closed around me like a bleak desert. From sheer force of habit, I went over to his empty house. I wandered like a ghost through the vacant rooms, sitting in the chairs he liked, touching the things he had touched. That's how I happened to see the laboratory key.

"I recognized it right away. It has a rather peculiar shape. While I was looking at it, the truth hit me like a bomb dropped out of the sky. I knew that I'd been living in a dream world for months. I saw that sooner or later I was going to have to wake up. Derek would never marry me. We would never be any more to each other; in fact we would be less – a good deal less. It was the simple truth, and I faced it frankly. I knew I couldn't stand it when Derek left me. I'd have to kill myself. And the key told me how it could be done.

"Derek had talked to me once of a poison he kept in the laboratory – but you know all about nitrobenzene. When I drove down to see my family the next day, I carried the key with me, and I had a duplicate made in Los Angeles on Saturday afternoon. Sunday night I put Derek's key back on his dresser, exactly where I had found it. I didn't want him to have any suspicion of what I'd done. I didn't want even the slightest hint to come to him of what I had planned to do.

"Once I had a key and could pick my own time, it was easy to get into the lab. It took only two or three minutes to find the bottle of nitrobenzene and to pour out a little of it into a phial. I didn't take much. Derek had told me that a few drops were enough to kill a person. Later I thought of wiping my fingerprints from the bottle – but I had a different plan then.

"It sounds silly, doesn't it? Going to all that trouble because of a *fear*? Preparing for suicide just because of the *thought* that he might leave me? I know I was crazy to get so upset when nothing actually had happened, but I couldn't help myself. Maybe it will give you an idea of how much I cared for him. Maybe you'll have some idea of how I felt when he told me he was going to marry Jacynth. But you could never understand completely. No man could.

"He didn't waste any time at all. He proposed to her the first night she was home from school – swept her off her feet, I suppose; Derek was good at that. The next day, Sunday, the fourth of June, he told me all about it. He had loved Jacynth ever since last summer, he said. Truly loved her. Not just a physical passion. No, he didn't draw any comparisons. It wasn't necessary. Nor did he say that if he married her the entire business of LeDoux Perfumes, Incorporated, would be under his control in a few years' time. I knew, however, that entered into it. Derek was cold-bloodedly ambitious; I never had any illusions there."

"He wasn't brutal when he told me. Some men would have been, but Derek tried to be kind. It was the kindness that made me cry – more than his frankness. For he had to be frank. We had had a good time together, he said; the experience had done us both good. And no harm: nothing could happen to me because we had both been so very careful, and my reputation was equally safe. Yes, he used the word 'reputation,' I think. Nobody would ever know what we had been to each other. I could count on him to keep that secret. Of course I could; he wouldn't be likely to start any stories that might come finally to Jacynth. And what difference did it make, anyhow?

"He was terribly sorry, he said, sorry that it had to end this way. But he insisted that he had played square with me. He had never promised me anything else. ... I had to admit that he never had.

"I stopped crying when I saw how my red, swollen face disgusted him. I tried to fight him at first. I threatened to tell Mr. LeDoux everything, but Derek wasn't frightened. Do you know what he said to me? 'You would only hurt yourself, Beatrice. There never was a Frenchman yet who wasn't tolerant about a man keeping a mistress. Besides, LeDoux needs me. You could hurt Jacynth, of course; hurt her dreadfully, but would that make you a bit happier? You're not allowing for the fact that she is in love with me, and knows I really do love her. No, Beatrice. Nothing you could say would be able to keep us apart.'

"He was right. I saw it then, and I managed to smile. It was the hardest thing I've ever done, that smile. I told him that I would try to be a good sport about it. I told him that he had taught me how to be a woman of the world, so I must be one. 'Good old Beatrice!' he said, patting my shoulder as if I'd been a dog who had just brought back the ball he'd thrown. 'I knew I could count on you to take it on the chin and come up smiling.'

"But all the time I was smiling I was planning how to kill him."

III

" 'Si on juge l'amour par la plupart de ses effets, il ressemble plus à la haine qu'à l'amitié,' " Westborough quoted from the maxims of La Rochefoucauld.

"Love resembles hatred more than friendship," she translated. "I know French very well."

"I thought that you must. Mr. LeDoux must speak his native tongue a great deal."

"He thinks in French half the time." It seemed strange that they should be chatting so casually on the commonplace topic. Stranger even than her next remark: "I haven't many more minutes to give you."

"I dare say not. For favors already received I am duly grateful, but I should like to know why Mr. Esterling was not poisoned with the toxic substance you had gone to such pains to procure."

"I am disappointed in you, Mr. Westborough. How could I use nitroben-zene? Derek, with his super-keen sense of smell, would be sure to recognize the odor at once. I had to figure out some other way. I'm not much of an authority on poisons, naturally, but Derek had mentioned another one to me. He was highly interested at that time in anything pertaining to yellow jasmine, you must remember. I looked up gelsemium in a big book on drugs in the reference room of our public library. I learned it's sometimes used as a medicine, so one could probably get it at a drugstore, and I also learned it's practically odorless. The instant I read that I knew I'd found my poison. I had only to buy some gelsemium and to put it into something he ate or drank; that was all I had to do to kill him.

"The second part was going to be difficult, though. Derek was faithful now to Jacynth, or would be faithful as far as I was concerned. I wouldn't be seeing him any more in private. And I couldn't very well poison him at the office. I brooded over it all day Monday and Tuesday, particularly on Tuesday, since I'd looked up gelsemium on Monday evening. I watched Mr. LeDoux taking his bitters – he took them every noon as regularly as clock-work – and I thought how easy it would be to poison *him*. But Mr. LeDoux wasn't Derek. I couldn't reach Derek, ever. He was as safe from me as if he'd been at the South Pole. On Tuesday night, however, while I was lying in bed unable to sleep, the wonderful idea came to me. I worked it all out before I went to sleep. If I couldn't *kill* Derek I could punish him – punish him terribly. I might even send him to jail. At least I could take Jacynth away from him, make him lose all the wonderful future he had planned for himself, even lose his job. To do this I had only to poison *Mr. LeDoux instead of Derek*. Wasn't it a clever plan?"

"A bit rough on Mr. LeDoux," the historian ventured to remonstrate.

"But I didn't intend any real harm to him," she immediately defended herself. "I didn't use a drop more than half a teaspoonful of the gelsemium extract, and the book said a teaspoonful is the minimum fatal dose. I didn't want to kill Mr. LeDoux, just to make him sick for a few days. You understand, don't you?"

"I believe so."

"By Wednesday afternoon all the details were clear in my mind. I began that night, after everybody else had left the plant; I sneaked into Derek's laboratory again and wrote a letter to our biggest Los Angeles distributor, the

Davis Wholesale Drug Company, asking them to prepare two ounces of the fluidextract. Two birds with one stone! I wrote that message on Derek's old wreck of a typewriter. It had a special key on it, which made it easy to leave a distinguishing sign. I hit the plus key, backspaced, and then hit the semicolon, so it would look as if someone had done a sloppy job of correcting a mistake. I signed the letter, LEDOUX PERFUME LABORATORIES and wrote a false name under that. I changed my own handwriting all I could, naturally, but I didn't try to imitate Derek's. Forgeries are too easily detected."

"May I inquire the particular false name employed?"

"I started with Derek's initials, D. E., and finished with the first thing that came into my head. A rather funny name, Cor, C-o-r. I don't know why I picked that."

"The association rushed from your unconscious mind, not the conscious," Westborough informed her, "from the same source as the name you suggested for the new yellow jasmine perfume. Your selection, significantly, was *Affaire de Coeur*."

"Love affair – my heavens! I did give myself away!"

"The name came from the heart, if I may be allowed to pun thus atrociously. It is a little odd," he mused, "that my only real clues should have been two French words: one meaning 'dead' and the other 'heart.' The clue of the dead heart! Dear me! It is not inapplicable."

"I often spend weekends in Los Angeles with Mother and Fred," she continued her narrative. "Mr. LeDoux was awfully nice about letting me off work for that. He was grand to me, really, and I'm terribly sorry over what I had to do to him. Anyway, it was easy for me to arrange to call at the Davis Company office on Saturday. That morning turned out to be particularly good for another reason. Mr. Kelton, I learned, had made an appointment with his dentist, and so Derek would be alone in the laboratory. Unless someone happened to drop in on him – not very likely when he was hard at work on research – he wouldn't be able to prove an alibi. Once I had the main idea, it seemed like everything was working out to help me."

"Fortune favors the bold," Westborough observed tritely.

"Do you think that could be it? I don't know. Anyway, I left Valle de Flores at five o'clock on Friday evening, and I was in Los Angeles that night. I stopped at a cheap hotel in the downtown district, a horrible place, but I had to stay there. Early in the morning I visited a pawnshop on South Main Street and bought a secondhand outfit of man's clothes. They didn't fit very well, but that wasn't important. Then I went to a store where theatrical supplies are sold and bought a braid of crepe hair – as near to the shade of Derek's beard as I could find – and a bottle of spirit gum. I had learned about stage whiskers from the plays our church group in Valle de Flores puts on every now and then. I'm a very active member of the young people's society. I went back to my room and put on the secondhand clothes, hoping they wouldn't be infested with vermin. Then I put on the false beard. I made it look as much like Derek's beard as I could, and that was very close. I wasn't as tall as Derek, of course, though I am rather tall for a woman, but I was sure that the beard would be all that anyone would remember. A beard is so distinctive, particularly a little dab of a one like Derek's. It was rather dark inside the drug company's office. The man who waited on me was the only one who paid any attention to me."

"If such had not been the case," Westborough cogitated, "Mr. Esterling would today be alive – though probably unjustly in jail. A clerk in a wholesale drug company imbibes too much alcohol on his Fourth of July holiday, and a total stranger a hundred and fifty miles away meets his death. Truly, the world is an odd place!"

"He acted a little surprised," she went on, "when I told him I would pay cash, but he didn't make any fuss. I went back to my hotel – there were people coming and going all the time in the lobby, and nobody seemed to notice me – walked up to my room and changed to my own clothes. I made a bundle of the others and dropped them in a barrel with a sign over it, 'For the Poor.' Then I drove to Fred's, pretending I had just arrived in the city, and I stayed there until Sunday night, as I'd written him I would.

"On my way back to Valle de Flores I stopped and threw the crepe hair and spirit gum into the ocean. No trail at all, was there? Except the one trail I wanted to leave."

"You are amazingly farsighted."

"I had another piece of luck the next week, when Mr. LeDoux arranged for a conference to discuss marketing plans for the new perfume, but you know what happened that morning."

"I know that I have been phenomenally stupid!" Westborough exclaimed. "Mr. LeDoux, in all probability, would have drained the contents of his glass. I should have been suspicious when he told me there had been sufficient liquid in it to be analyzed. He did empty the glass, did he not?"

"Yes," she owned. "I was prepared for that. I had mixed another glass of gelsemium and water, with the usual amount of bitters, and saved enough to fill a small test tube, then threw the rest away. I lingered in the office to do that, while the others were walking over to the house for lunch. Nobody seemed to notice that I lagged behind."

"My understanding was that Mr. LeDoux kept his bitters in a locked cabinet."

"I had often had the prescription refilled for him. It was simple to buy another bottle of the gentian preparation. I really wouldn't have needed it, since Mr. LeDoux gave me the cabinet keys when he asked me to take the things to Los Angeles. But, of course, I had no way of knowing that in advance."

"And to think," Westborough reproached himself, "that I refused to suspect you on the grounds that you had the opportunity to destroy the evidence of poisoning. What so false as false logic?"

"The laboratory report was mailed to Mr. LeDoux," she resumed. "I didn't see it, so I couldn't really know for sure that they had detected the gelsemium. Chemists do make mistakes sometimes, even the best ones. I was worried more and more when Mr. LeDoux was well again, and didn't take any steps to do anything about his poisoning. Finally I was sure that I'd wasted all my time and trouble and thought to achieve nothing. The scheme had misfired somewhere. So when Mr. LeDoux told me of the house party he'd planned, I decided to start all over again from scratch."

"Miss Morton," Westborough assured her solemnly, "if you had put into some worthy object the same creative energy and initiative you have displayed in conceiving and executing these three satanically inspired plots—"

"Four plots," she interrupted. "You've forgotten your own."

"True," he owned, "I had forgotten. It is much the simplest of the four – and thus artistically the most pleasing. You learn from experience, Miss Morton, but I think you failed once. You did not intend to kill Paul Michael Chamaron."

"You're quick!" she exclaimed, not without admiration. "How did you guess?"

"It may be reasoned in this fashion: The ionone was obviously employed to mask the odor of nitrobenzene. But only Mr. LeDoux and Mr. Esterling were capable of recognizing that characteristic odor. Ergo, Mr. Chamaron had accidentally received the capsule. It was a capsule, was it not?"

"Yes. I bought a box of them in a drugstore at Santa Bonita. The nitrobenzene was in a bottle labeled almond lotion. I poured real almond lotion on top of it afterward and changed it for the bottle in Jacynth's bathroom cabinet. The one with the poison in it is in there now. It looks just the same to her."

"Good God!" the historian exclaimed.

"I don't suppose it would poison her externally, though I don't really know. Anyway, if they find it, it can never be traced to me. And I've no particular reason to love Jacynth, have I?"

"She is very pretty," Westborough observed irrelevantly.

Miss Morton smiled sweetly. "Very young, but I don't wonder that Derek found her attractive. However, my time – and yours – is running short. Do you want to hear about the dinner or not?"

"Please," Westborough said.

"You guessed why I used the ionone. The candles were a horribly fussy job. I had to time the rate of burning on the previous evening. I couldn't be entirely sure of hitting the soup course, but, by fixing two of them to go off at different times, I thought I had a good chance. I knew Mr. LeDoux would have some sort of fireworks there, so it wouldn't be necessary to bring anything like that." Her hand stretched again toward the pistol. "I really shouldn't wait any longer."

"Surely you can spare just another five minutes? You haven't told me how you introduced the capsule into the bouillabaisse."

"I thought you'd already guessed that. I brought the capsule and the vial of ionone to the table, wrapped inside my handkerchief. I reached down under the table with my left hand, pulled out the cork from the vial and hurled both of them as far away as I could. Then I folded the capsule into a corner of my napkin."

"Exceedingly clever!" he declared. "And later, I take it, you flicked the napkin in the direction of the green flame, pretending you were endeavoring to extinguish it, whereupon the capsule – I don't quite see how it was done."

"There's a way of folding a stiff napkin with one corner held down so that when you wave it, it throws a small object a short distance. I practiced for an hour and a half Monday night, trying to put another capsule I had filled with water into a hollow in a sofa pillow. I got so I could do it very nearly every time. The rest of the empty capsules, and the pieces of the box they came in, are in Jacynth's room, in the base of a bottle lamp. I think I can manage to drop a hint to the sheriff's office, after I've settled the business at hand. And a hint about the almond lotion, too."

Westborough bit his tongue.

"Your skill with the napkin trick, however, appears to have been insufficient. Is it not true that the capsule rolled into the wrong dish?"

"Yes, that's just what it did," she lamented. "Wasn't I unlucky?"

"I would say," he amended, "that Mr. Chamaron was the unlucky one."

She lowered her eyes. "I felt awfully badly about poor Paul Michael. Even worse than I'll feel when I've killed you. Though I shall feel badly about that, too, of course."

"And so shall I," he added warmly.

IV

"I wanted to warn Paul Michael," she insisted. "It was terrible to sit there, watching him eat his bouillabaisse. But what could I do to stop him? Nothing. Unless, of course, I made a full confession, but the old instinct of self-preservation seems to be very strong in me. And, in a way, Paul Michael *had* brought it on himself. I was merely the blind agent of Destiny, if you see what I mean."

Westborough did not. He failed to see how she was going to justify herself for the killing of an innocent friend and benefactor, but he knew – as well as he had ever known anything – that she *would* justify herself. He even derived a clinical satisfaction from the perversities of her twisted reasoning. The girl was so unmistakably psychopathic.

But cunning – and an amazingly clever actress.

"It's simple," she said. "I would have had money and position. I wouldn't have had to work for a living. I wouldn't have been in Mr. LeDoux's office, and I wouldn't have had an affair with Derek, if Paul Michael, years ago, hadn't stolen my father's business. I didn't blame Paul Michael; I told you the truth the other day when I said I stopped blaming him years ago. But it did seem as if fate was working out some sort of plan to punish him for what he'd done to my father. Then I felt something else," she whispered confidentially. "A tremendous sense of power! I, Beatrice Morton, was able to decide whether a man should live or die – it was like being God! I feel exactly the same way now."

"Pray continue your narrative," he urged hastily.

"Even though I poisoned Paul Michael instead of Derek, it didn't turn out too badly at first. It was almost as I'd expected the other plan to work out except for Jacynth. After she'd testified at the inquest in Derek's favor I knew she'd stand for anything. I could only keep them apart by killing him, and, besides, there was another good reason for it now. Derek suspected me."

"May one ask why?"

"My handkerchief. It slipped out of my hand when we were on the terrace watching the fireworks. Derek – of all people – had to pick it up. He and Mr. LeDoux were the only ones who could have distinguished that faint, faint trace of ionone, and even Derek wasn't entirely sure. His face was very puzzled. I snatched the handkerchief out of his hand and destroyed it at the earliest opportunity – buried it in the scrub behind the house – but I couldn't erase the suspicion from Derek's mind.

"However, all he had to go on was one whiff of ionone, which might have been imaginary. And Derek had loved me … in his fashion. He couldn't turn me over to Captain Howe unless he was sure I was a murderess. He said nothing at all at the inquest, and then I was sure I was safe. But on Thursday he found the gelsemium I'd hidden in his lab, hoping that someone else would find it. And then you told him, didn't you, that Mr. LeDoux's illness was because of poison?"

"I did hint at it," Westborough confessed.

"Derek was far from a fool," she proclaimed with rather odd pride. "He put all of those things together and had the right answer at once. He managed to catch me alone Thursday afternoon and asked me to explain. I told him I couldn't; he would have to meet me in private. He asked where and when. It was then I made my third plan. The best of them all, I think. I didn't have a knife; I didn't dare use a gun, though I knew about this one. Derek was far stronger than I am physically; he was watchful and suspicious. Yet, with only my bare hands, I killed him. I'm rather proud of myself for it."

"Tell me how you killed him," Westborough invited.

"I told him to meet me at two o'clock on the bench by the swimming pool. I came down early so I could hide a towel under the cushions of the swing. I had on a long coat and nothing else except slippers, but it was dark enough so he wasn't likely to notice. I think he was a little early, too, but I had no way of knowing. We didn't talk long. He gave me two alternatives: confess or run away. The latter was just another form of confession, of course, but it allowed him to salve his conscience. I said I'd confess. Our eyes were growing accustomed to the darkness, and I didn't like to wait any longer.

"I slipped the shoes off my feet and pushed them under the bench. Then I stood up, stepping back so he'd be between me and the pool, and threw off my coat, all of a sudden. You should have seen his face! His mouth was as wide open as it possibly could be, but he didn't get a chance to say anything. I sprang at him head first, butting him in the chest and knocking him over backward.

"I'm a pretty fair swimmer. Better than he was. I held my breath automatically as we fell, but he didn't. He came to the surface, choking and coughing, and I pushed his head down again. We threshed around for quite a while, but my naked body was too slippery for him to hold, and every time he came up I forced him under. He couldn't even cry out because of the water that had gotten into his windpipe. Finally I got a good grip and knocked his head against the side of the pool with all my strength. He stopped struggling, but I held his head under water for a long time. Until I felt sure.

"After I'd climbed out of the pool I dried myself with the towel I'd cached in the swing. I'd taken it directly from the linen closet and I dropped it into the laundry chute when I went back upstairs, so there was nothing to connect it with me. The only thing that might have given me away was my damp hair. I had to do something about that. Luckily I had a little portable electric traveling iron in my room. I used that to—" She snatched the automatic as the knob of the study door commenced to turn.

"Captain Howe and Mr. LeDoux, I believe," Westborough declared. "I thought it might be well to have witnesses to our interesting conversation."

"But the door's locked!" she whispered fiercely.

The door opened on that instant.

"I fear that I made only a pretense of locking it," Westborough apologized.

She glared at him savagely as a cornered wildcat.

"I can still—"

"*Méchante!*" LeDoux shouted, dashing furiously into the room. "Seize her, *Monsieur le Capitaine!*"

But Beatrice Morton had already whipped the muzzle to her temple and pressed the trigger. The pistol exploded with a deafening roar.

"*Mon Dieu*, she has killed herself!" LeDoux stared in fascination at the trickle of red staining the girl's brown hair. "But it is an impossibility! There were no cartridges. I swear that I removed the clip. Monsieur Westborough can so justify."

"Maybe you left a cartridge in the barrel," Howe suggested.

"I did not look!" LeDoux cried. "Idiot that I am! I gravely endangered your valuable life, *mon ami*. Is it that you can forgive my vile carelessness?"

Westborough gazed gravely on the young woman who could so easily have killed him.

"Perhaps it was more than carelessness. Perhaps, as this poor soul expressed it, you were chosen as the blind agent of Destiny."

"I would not know about such things," the perfumer said.

THE END

About the Rue Morgue Press

"Rue Morgue Press is the old-mystery lover's best friend, reprinting high quality books from the 1930s and '40s."
—*Ellery Queen's Mystery Magazine*

Since 1997, the Rue Morgue Press has reprinted scores of traditional mysteries, the kind of books that were the hallmark of the Golden Age of detective fiction. Authors reprinted or to be reprinted by the Rue Morgue include Catherine Aird, Delano Ames, H. C. Bailey, Morris Bishop, Nicholas Blake, Dorothy Bowers, Pamela Branch, Joanna Cannan, John Dickson Carr, Glyn Carr, Torrey Chanslor, Clyde B. Clason, Joan Coggin, Manning Coles, Lucy Cores, Frances Crane, Norbert Davis, Elizabeth Dean, Carter Dickson, Michael Gilbert, Constance & Gwenyth Little, Marlys Millhiser, Gladys Mitchell, James Norman, Stuart Palmer, Craig Rice, Kelley Roos, Charlotte Murray Russell, Maureen Sarsfield, Margaret Scherf, Juanita Sheridan and Colin Watson..

To suggest titles or to receive a catalog of Rue Morgue Press books write 87 Lone Tree Lane, Lyons, Colorado 80540, telephone 800-699-6214, or check out our website, www.ruemorguepress.com, which lists complete descriptions of all of our titles, along with lengthy biographies of our writer